Deal With This

Deal With This

LUCY MONROE

BRAVA

KENSINGTON PUBLISHING CORP.

BRAVA BOOKS are published by

Kensington Publishing Corp.
850 Third Avenue
New York, NY 10022

ISBN-13: 978-0-7394-8987-1

Printed in the United States of America

With special thanks to Vancouver actor Mark McConche, a truly grounded person with a generous heart, and to James McMullen, a friendly person with a lot of style. Thank you both for patiently answering my questions and for sharing your time. And to the staff at Spruce Body Lab in downtown Vancouver. You all rock!

Prologue

The elderly security guard for Frost Productions drove toward home, his thoughts in a whirl. What had that grip and the producer been doing in the studio so late together? The grip hadn't been signed in on the security log and when the guard had asked the producer about it, the man had gotten quite hostile.

What should he do about the discrepancy, if anything? He was months away from retirement and he didn't want to do anything to mess it up. He was looking forward to fulfilling his dream to travel Canada in a motor home with his wife of forty years. Making waves only weeks from his last day on the job was the last thing he needed to do.

Martha would have said the same thing.

He nodded to himself. Yes. He would simply let sleeping dogs lie. No sense in stirring up trouble when it was more likely to get him reprimanded than not. Especially considering who was involved with the breach of security protocol.

He turned on his signal to take the next off ramp and pressed the brake to slow his car. But the car didn't slow, and his thoughts shattered as his attempts remained futile and the car began to pick up momentum on the slight downgrade.

* * *

The next morning a small mention was made in the paper of a fatal automobile accident. The driver's name was not mentioned, but his job at Frost Productions as a security guard was.

Nothing was said about a break-in that happened the same night because it was not reported to the local police. One of the hard drives that stored film footage had been erased completely and the executives were furious. The discovery that only one scene would have to be reshot did not improve anyone's mood.

Two men, however, were pleased. A piece of information that should never have been transferred to the hard drive had been, and in an effort to make sure no remnant of the file remained, the entire hard drive had been wiped.

It was a pity the old man had to meet with an accident on his way home, but neither of the other men wanted to risk his relaying the fact that the grip had been on the lot the night before . . . or the producer, for that matter.

Snipping his brake line had been even easier than it looked in the movies. Fortunately, both men had enough experience with show biz to do the job right, and the one who had done the cutting had even taken the time to make it look as close to a frayed line as he could.

When no one questioned the "accidental nature" of the man's death at the wheel of his car, they knew they'd done the job right.

Chapter 1

Agent Alan Hyatt stopped in front of the door to his temporary new home and blinked.

It was purple—bright *neon* purple.

And the knocker (did people even use those anymore?) on the heavy, old-fashioned door was a huge gothic monstrosity. A lion's head easily six inches wide and eight inches high with a big brass loop hanging from its snarling fangs. The house itself was a soft buttery yellow, the scrolling Victorian trim done in white, which in some alternate reality was probably considered a nice contrast to glaring purple.

The flower beds were filled with a plethora of wildflowers that added charm, if not sophistication, to the property. It wasn't a showplace, but the large Victorian home was in good repair and it was obvious the owner had a lively, artistic bent. You could tell a lot about a person from the way they presented their home.

He, of course, knew even more, having read a file on said owner before embarking on this case.

Jillian Sinclair was an actor. From what appeared to be a typical middle-class family, she'd left home at the age of seventeen for unspecified reasons, pursued a career in acting, and actually succeeded at it. No mean feat. She wasn't currently in a long-term relationship. In fact, there was no evidence she'd ever been in one.

But she wasn't a recluse by any stretch. She liked men and dated a lot, though she managed to keep her name and face out of the tabloids for the most part. Another impressive feat. It was also borderline suspicious. The Old Man did not consider her a strong suspect, but someone working out of the Vancouver office for her television series's production company was using it as a cover for high-tech espionage.

Alan was here to find out who and nail his (or her) ass to the wall. Not exactly the Old Man's words, but close enough.

Arrangements had been made for Alan to rent a room from Jillian primarily because all of her other renters were also connected to her film company in one way or another. That, along with his cover job as a freelance reporter doing a series on the Vancouver, B.C., film industry, gave him a better place to start his investigation than he usually got.

It was almost too easy.

Which worried him.

In his experience, anything that looked easy . . . wasn't.

Sure, the Old Man probably thought the assignment was going to be a piece of cake. He'd no doubt given it to Alan as the newest agent for the Goddard Project on the principle of easing him into his job. Not that Alan was exactly a neophyte. He'd been with the FBI for almost a decade before getting recruited by TGP.

A better kept secret than Roswell, the agency had been formed after the Germans during WWII stole rocketry science from an American inventor, Robert Goddard. When the government had interrogated German prisoners, they were disgusted to discover that the technology they were trying to emulate originated with an American inventor they had basically dismissed as a crackpot.

Realizing that someone needed to oversee civilian technological development and make sure it did not end up in the wrong hands, they formed the Goddard Project. The agency had not been dismantled after the war but was still going strong and sometimes even took cases that were related to government technological secrets.

They didn't step on other agencies' toes only because no one outside of the agency itself and some top government officials realized TGP even existed.

Alan had been excited when he'd been recruited and he wanted to prove that doing so had been a good idea. And instincts honed over the last decade were telling him that no matter how it appeared, this case wasn't going to be simple.

For one thing, he didn't know what kind of technology was being stolen and brokered, only that someone at the production company was involved and that Prescott, a known information broker, had something planned for December 15, less than a month away.

The lead had come from files found on Preston's hard drive when TGP agents had busted his operation. The man had been cagey and paranoid, which meant that while they knew he'd been preparing to broker something big, they didn't know what that something was or if it came from the private or military sector.

Another issue with the case was that anything connected to the film industry made Alan jittery. He liked working in the shadows, and there wasn't anything remotely shadowy about an industry that made its money entertaining millions of people twenty-four-seven. Living in a house filled with people connected directly to a television production company was bound to be interesting, to say the least.

He was more than a little grateful his cover story had not included making *him* a member of the film community.

Comfortable with his surroundings or not, Alan had what it took to get the job done. He always had. And he was ready to prove it. He looked for a doorbell ringer, but there didn't appear to be one, so he used the door knocker. Three sure, staccato raps.

The door swung open to reveal a man of not quite average

height and petite build. There was actually *nothing* average about him. His spiky hair was the color of a flamingo, golden eyes (obviously colored contacts) were rimmed with liner and the lids covered with a glittery shadow. Wearing a lavender velvet T-shirt and low-slung hot pink jeans that couldn't be comfortable to walk in, he lounged against the doorjamb.

"Jill, sweetie, I think the new boarder is here," he called over his shoulder. "And he's hotter than the Friday night lineup during ratings week." Pursing his lips, the pink-haired man gave Alan a thorough once-over. "In fact, stations only dream of a lineup this hot."

Alan was thirty-four years old, a lifetime beyond blushing virginity. In his job with the FBI, he had seen and done things most people had never even heard about. But under the other man's frankly appreciative appraisal, the seasoned government agent felt heat surge into his cheeks.

"Down, boy." A small, definitely feminine hand patted the crushed velvet–encased chest, the rest of her body hidden behind the purple door. "You know the house rules."

"But, Jill, he's yummy," whined the man, glossy lips settling in a pout.

"You think the postman's yummy too, Gavin, and *he's* not off limits."

"But look at that jawline. Like granite. Delish. He's got a cleft in his chin, for goodness' sake." Gavin fanned himself and winked at Alan. "And his eyes . . . they're gray. You know I have a weakness for gray eyes."

"And brown, and blue, and let's not forget green . . ." The woman, no doubt Jillian Sinclair, laughed. The sound was melodious and infectious, and Alan found himself smiling in response. "Face it, sweetie, you're a pushover for rugged looks and a great bod, but you know relationships rarely work when both people are in the business."

She thought he had a hot body? She must be looking through the crack in the door. He'd used that technique himself, but for some reason the knowledge the unseen woman with the sexy voice was watching him aroused him. Crap. He liked sex as much as the next man. Maybe more. But involuntary arousal wasn't something he'd had to deal with since college, and it definitely had no place on the job. He ruthlessly tamped down the unexpected reaction until something she said registered.

Relationships. The woman had definitely said *relationships.* Jillian thought he was up for a relationship *with a man?* He knew Vancouver was known for being more open to alternate lifestyles, but wasn't this presuming a hell of a lot? Did he *look* gay? Hell no. No, he did not.

Okay. All right. Right. Barring men like the one in front of him, there wasn't a gay look, was there? And even that ... well, wasn't there the whole metrosexual thing now? But he'd had friends tell them they had "gaydar," whatever that meant. He was setting off Gavin and Jillian's gaydar, maybe? No way, not happening. So definitely *not* happening.

There had to be another explanation.

"He's not in the business. He's a reporter, you said." Gavin's tone was too damned hopeful.

That unfamiliar heat climbed up his throat again. Shit. Since when did he get embarrassed? It was time to take control of this situation.

"I'm not here for a relationship. I'm looking for a room," he growled, his sense of humor not quite up to laughing off the conversation, but not totally buried either.

There was something funny about this situation. He'd no doubt find it later. Maybe next year sometime.

Looking ecstatic, Gavin turned and grabbed Jillian's arm, the only part of her exposed to Alan's gaze. "Did you hear that? *He growled.*"

Oh, for crying out loud.

A feminine sigh filled with exasperation sounded from the other side of the door. "Yes, I heard. I also heard that he already knows one of the house rules and you'd better remember it fast, or it won't be just the empty room I'm renting."

Despite the threat, she didn't sound angry and Gavin's moue of disappointment sans even the slightest fear of real retribution reflected it. With another sigh, Jillian tugged Gavin out of the doorway. The pink-haired man moved reluctantly to the side and Jillian took his place.

Alan Hyatt was a damn good agent. So he'd read the file more than once and he'd studied pictures of the woman framed in the doorway.

Pictures that had hinted at the fire beneath the glossy exterior, but that had not prepared him for the impact Jillian Sinclair would have in person. Unlike in the publicity shots provided with her file, her burnt red hair did not fall in sleek waves around a perfectly made-up face. Instead corkscrew curls bounced past her shoulders in haphazard fire. And without the make-up, fine freckles dusted her nose and cheekbones.

Her eyes were the same jewel green as in the publicity shots, but this close he could confirm that the deep color was natural, not the result of contact lenses. She wasn't dressed as she was in the photos, either. Her current clothes were every bit as bright as the front door and as body hugging as Gavin's, but with much different impact on Alan's libido.

The woman was fine. Truly fine. And damned if that spark of mischief in her eyes didn't curl around his heart and squeeze.

"This is a bad idea." The words were out before he realized they were even in his mind, but he meant them.

He did not need to be attracted to a woman who might well prove to be key to his investigation. Sexual, yes . . . he could do the sex thing. But he shouldn't be *attracted*. And that thing with his heart. So not on his list of things to do today, tomorrow, next week, or even next year.

He'd had his fill of civilians. Non-agency women. They were not for men like him. They ended up in love with someone else . . . or just not loving him enough to accept who he was, what he was—a fifth-generation federal agent. His job was more than a career, it defined him as deeply as anything else his parents had taught him. If he was being honest, he'd have to say even more deeply than a lot of it.

Oblivious to his thoughts, Jillian laughed, the sound triggering another involuntary tilt of his lips. "Don't worry. Gavin gets over his crushes fast. He won't stalk you."

"Of course not. I'm not exactly a troll. I don't have to run after men to get a date." The velvet-clad man sniffed from his position beside Jillian. "Besides, I do know the house rules. No fraternizing with housemates."

"Right," she said firmly.

Gavin gave an exaggerated shiver. "That doesn't mean I can't appreciate beauty when I see it." Then with a last admiring glance at Alan, he flounced off.

Alan's sense of humor finally got the better of the bizarre situation and he burst out laughing.

Jillian put her hand right over his mouth and Alan's entire body went on alert while another surge of arousal shot through his groin. The scents of cinnamon and vanilla mixed with sweet femininity, teasing him.

"Shh . . . he'll hear you and think you're laughing at him."

Alan stifled his amusement but raised his brow in sardonic acknowledgment. He *had* been laughing at the little diva.

"It would hurt his feelings," Jillian said earnestly.

He pulled her hand from his mouth, involuntarily caressing her wrist before letting go. She had small bones and incredibly soft skin. He could feel her pulse speed up.

Her emerald eyes widened and she took a step back.

He followed her, leaning in close. "Maybe he needs to learn a little discretion . . . to save his feelings."

Jillian took another step backward, this one quicker than the first. Then she stopped and relaxed into a deliberately casual pose, blowing at a corkscrew curl that had fallen over one eye. "I keep telling him that, but he's just a flamboyant kind of guy."

Alan gave Jillian a friendly once-over. "It looks to me like he's not the only one."

"Wha—" Her eyes had gone wide again and she stumbled back another step and then her expression cleared. "Oh . . . uh . . . you mean the clothes."

"Yeah. So far, I haven't noticed you flirting outrageously."

"In the right element . . ." She shrugged. "But no, not here. Not with you, Mr. Johnson."

"Alan, please."

So, she adhered to her own house rules. That was a good thing, he told himself. And almost believed it.

She nodded once and then turned to lead him into the first room to the left off the entryway. When the house was built it was probably called the drawing room, but nothing so formal would work to label it now. A large sectional the color of eggplant covered most of two walls. The other chairs, if you wanted to call them that, were brightly colored beanbags. Huge throw pillows in aqua and orange were strewn over the sofa and dotted the hardwood floor as well. In the center of it all was a big square coffee table, the top a mosaic of tiny tiles in a swirling pattern the same colors found in the rest of the furniture.

Jillian sat at one end of the couch. "Believe it or not, this is my camouflage," she said, waving her hand to indicate the tiny bright orange top and skintight neon green jeans she wore. "I've always played roles where I'm this really put-together woman on screen who would never consider wearing Day-Glo orange."

Alan settled on the sofa near its junction, leaving a full cushion to separate them. "I wouldn't think you'd need camouflage for your current role." He'd watched the pilot episode of Jillian's low-budget series, in which she played an alien woman with catlike features.

Jillian reacted as if he'd sat right beside her and put his hand on her knee, jumping a little and laughing nervously.

"Are you all right?"

She sighed and laughed self-deprecatingly. "Yes, I'm fine. I'm not sure why I'm so jumpy today."

Alan leaned back and laid his arm along the sofa back. His fingertips were inches from the tantalizing woman before him.

Jillian eyed his hand and then deliberately flipped her long red curls over one shoulder. "Anyway, about the camouflage thing . . . they tame my hair for shooting, and make-up alters my features a little, but you'd be surprised at how good fans are at looking past the flash."

"And that is bad?"

"I'm a pretty private person." Then she laughed. "I know, that sounds funny for a woman who makes her living performing for others, but that's different. When I'm working, it's in front of cameras, not a live audience. And I'm not sure I can explain it for someone not in the business, but that's me being paid to act like someone else. Not really revealing myself. But the rest of the time, I'm really *me,* and that person prefers as little fan recognition as possible."

He weighed her words for fallacy, looking for anomalies and filing them away for future reference in case she was more or *less* than she appeared. The fascination he felt was entirely job related.

"Wow, you know, I can tell you're a reporter. You're so intent on me . . . what I'm saying, I mean. Maybe that explains the other . . ." She shook her head, her voice trailing off as if she'd been speaking to herself there at the last. "I'm, um . . . surprised you're not taking notes."

"It's not an official interview."

"Oh, of course." She grinned. "I'm open to doing one if you want. I figured that was part of the reason you asked Bobby to recommend you for the room."

Bobby was the contact the agency had used to secure Alan's housing arrangements. Alan didn't know much more about the man than that, but it was okay. The recommendation had come as a favor to another friend who had agency ties. "He was doing my friend a favor."

"And that friend owed you one?"

"Or I owe him one now." He smiled.

She grinned back. "I get it."

"I'm not sure I do."

She looked confused.

"Get it. You say you're a private person, but you rent rooms in your house." He pointed at himself. "To strangers."

She wrinkled her nose and laughed a little. "Amanda says that's my repressed nurturing instincts. I like taking care of people, which doesn't mean I want to pick up your stuff all over the house." She frowned at him to let him know she meant it.

"No problem. I'm not a slob."

"Good."

"It's a smart move financially too."

"Yep. I'm not exactly in Julia Roberts's pay range." She smiled self-deprecatingly. "I don't even get my own trailer on the lot."

"I guess every production company has its own way of doing things."

"Not to mention budget restraints. I don't kid myself. Our show doesn't have the perks that those with bigger production companies do. It isn't racking up the viewer points either, not enough to set the world on fire or get worldwide syndication. But it is steady work, and the series got renewed for a second season."

If one of the primary people was involved in selling technological secrets, Jillian and a lot of other people were going to be out of work.

"Who's Amanda?" he asked, not dwelling on the possible negative ramifications of doing his job.

It came with the territory.

"My best friend." Jillian's voice had softened just a bit. "She got married three years ago to this really sexy technogeek who just happens to be a multimillionaire as well. She and Simon have got a gorgeous little girl too. Their marriage . . . the whole family bit . . . for them, it's the real deal."

Jillian sounded wistful and a little disbelieving.

Interesting.

"What kind of techno-geek is Simon?"

"He's Simon Brant . . . you know, Brant Computers?"

He did know, and suddenly Jillian looked a lot more like a suspect than she had before. If Simon Brant's wife was her best friend, Jillian had access to some pretty important, not to mention cutting-edge, technological information.

"Do you visit them often?"

"Whenever I can. It's only about a four-hour drive to the ferry for their island."

Alan's gut knotted. Not because Jillian was a suspect, but because he realized how much he hadn't wanted her to be.

Chapter 2

Jillian showed Alan to his space. It wasn't huge, but it had its own bathroom and the bed was in a small alcove under the eaves, opening up the rest of the room to be used as a living area.

His eyes skimmed the closet through its open door. Big enough, if not huge. "Nice."

She smiled, looking pleased. "Thanks. I opened up the area under the eaves and drywalled it in every room to increase the space."

"You did it?"

She shrugged. "I have several weeks off between filming. Perry and Sierra helped. They've been rooming here since the beginning. You'll meet them at dinner. If you eat with us, that is. We take turns cooking."

"Sounds good."

"I'm sure you'll fill up your nightlife soon enough. The gay community in Vancouver is well developed."

"*Gay community?*" he asked faintly. "You think I'm gay?"

"Um . . . aren't you?" she asked, sounding hopeful.

Why would she want him to be gay? It was obvious she was attracted to him.

"No."

"Oh." She looked worried. "Well, het nightlife is pretty rockin' around here too."

"Het?"

"Heterosexual."

"I see."

"Three of your housemates are gay. Sierra's a het, but she's still off-limits. I really don't tolerate fraternization between my boarders. It's too messy. Is that going to be a problem for you?"

"What, exactly?"

"Well, both, actually . . . having gay housemates and not dating Sierra."

"No."

She smiled again. "That's good. Bobby's gay. I kind of assumed anyone he'd recommend would be too, or at least comfortable with those with a different sexual orientation."

Well, that explained her earlier question.

"Yeah."

"Good, so we'll see you for dinner?"

Alan didn't get a chance to respond because Jillian's cell phone rang.

She gave him an apologetic look and flipped it open, mouthing, "It's my agent. I've got to take this."

And then she left the room.

Alan rubbed his hand down his face. So, the three men living here with Jillian were gay? That hadn't been in the file. Not that it made any difference to his investigation, but it always bothered him when information was missing from a file.

It was obvious none of his housemates were in the closet, or Jillian wouldn't have been so frank about them. Which meant whoever had compiled the background check had been sloppy. And that irritated Alan . . . it concerned him too. What other information might be missing, and was it important?

He got up, closed his door, and locked it. Then he went

into the bathroom, turned on the shower, flipped open his phone, and rang the Old Man.

"Who did the background dossier and the occupants of Jillian's house?" he asked without preamble when the other man answered the phone.

"Alan?"

"Yes."

"Give me a second and I'll tell you."

Alan waited while his boss accessed computer records.

"We pulled them from another agency."

"Is that common practice?"

"Actually, for stuff like this, yes. We don't have the man-power of other agencies and our requests for routine infor-mation are always masked, so they don't know where the information is going."

"Well, whoever did it did a lousy job."

"How so?"

"Three of my housemates are gay. That wasn't in the file."

"Does it matter?"

"Of course not, but it makes me wonder what else was missed."

"Maybe the compiler was just being P.C."

"What a bunch of bullshit. There's no room for that kind of thing in a background file."

"I agree."

"They missed the fact that Jillian's best friend is married to Simon Brant as well."

"The computer genius?"

"Yes."

The Old Man swore.

"Exactly. There's no telling what else was missed, but you'd better rethink your policy of using other agencies for this kind of stuff."

"You think so, do you?"

Alan wasn't sure what he heard in his boss's voice, whether

it was irritation or amusement, but he wasn't swayed by either. "Yes. I do."

"Maybe you are right."

"Do you have someone who can double-check the dossiers?"

"Beth could do it. I'll have her contact you with her findings."

Alan's jaw clenched at the mention of his former fiancée, now married to another TGP agent. "Great," he growled. And then remembered Gavin's reaction to his doing that earlier and growled again.

That was all he needed . . . to try to investigate his case while one of his *male* housemates was flamboyantly crushing on him.

"So, I hear from Gavin the new guy is to-die-for gorgeous." Sierra tucked her straight brown hair behind her ear as she closed the fridge with a bump of her hip.

Gavin leaned against the doorway and sighed dramatically. "He could be a dead ringer for Henri Castelli."

That had to explain it.

Jillian had had a crush on the Brazilian actor since she saw a photo of him on a blog she liked to visit. She'd never met the man in person, but she'd lusted after him from afar, going so far as to get some of his work with English subtitles. Yum.

That had to be why she was so turned on by her newest housemate. While she liked men, she did not react to them this way . . . so out of control. It went against her personal code of noninvolvement. Sex was fun, it could even be intense, but it wasn't supposed to touch her deep inside.

And she felt like Alan was already touching places he wasn't supposed to go. Not that she was going to have sex with him. She was more strict with herself than with her boarders regarding the nonfraternization policy.

She didn't do long-term relationships, and that meant that if she dated a boarder, she'd end up living in the same house as an ex. So not her thing.

"The resemblance is definitely there," she agreed with a sigh. Hugely there.

Sierra was chopping bok choy for the stir-fry. "It's a real shame, then."

"What?" Jillian asked.

"That he's a boarder. You could have lived out your hottest fantasies."

"You and your rules, Jillian," Gavin groused as he donned a chartreuse chef's coat so he could help Sierra. "I'd like to live out my hottest fantasies."

Sierra rolled her eyes. "Isn't that overkill for making stir-fry?"

"I'm doing the sauce and frying," Gavin said as he pulled ingredients from the cupboard. "I'm not risking this shirt. Believe me."

"What is it, vintage velour?" Jillian asked with a laugh.

"Exactly. This bad boy set me back more than a hundred dollars. I'm not getting peanut oil on it."

"Olive oil is healthier," Sierra snarked.

"But not as appropriate for Asian cooking. The flavor's off," Gavin said, sounding like an armchair chef.

"You're such a princess," Jillian teased.

Gavin sniffed. "If I were royalty, I'd nix your rules."

"My rules protect you as much as me. Your crushes change more often than your hair color now that you've landed a role that allows you to dye it."

"For that man, I would make an exception."

"Well, tone down the admiration," Jillian said dryly. "He's straight and I don't think he's even slightly bent."

"He did seem a little stunned by my appreciation."

Sierra made a noise that sounded suspiciously like a snort. "I think most men would react that way to you in crush mode, Gavin. But especially a straight guy. You're more blatant than anyone I know."

"I just know what I like."

Jillian laughed. "You like the postman too, but I didn't see you coming on to him like a dryer sheet on a pair of polyester pants."

Gavin actually blushed.

Sierra's eyes went wide and then she winked at Jillian. "Oh, man, I think he really likes the Castelli wannabe."

Jillian shook her head decisively, for some reason feeling protective of her newest boarder. Besides, the last thing she needed was Gavin in I-think-I-may-be-falling-in-love mode. He could do more drama than any daytime television show. "They just met. It's lust, pure and simple. And may I remind you? The man is straight."

"Don't worry, Jill . . . I'm not going to make a pest of myself."

"No one thinks you are a pest, Gavin," she hastened to assure him. Gavin with offended dignity was only a marginal improvement over Gavin in love.

"I know I can kind of flame."

Jillian managed to bite back a laugh and noticed that Sierra's lips were sealed tight too.

"Babe, you flame like a beach bonfire during spring break," Perry said from the doorway. "There's no *kind of* about it."

This time? Gavin positively turned red, looking embarrassed but not hurt. Thank goodness.

But that? Was interesting.

"We can't all be Grade A studs," he said with an exaggerated flutter of his eyelashes.

Perry laughed, looking the stud part to perfection in a muscle shirt and painted-on jeans. "I'm glad you think I'm so manly."

He was gorgeous, built, and a doll in the personality department, but he'd never made her so much as tingle. Not once. Of course, Perry was gay. She and her skin therapist, not to mention dear friend, had a theory that gay men gave off this platonic vibe that was really kind of nice.

Not Alan, though . . . that man sent high-voltage current through every single one of her nerve endings.

Damn.

Too bad *he* wasn't gay.

"Oh, please. The only people who wouldn't think you are a major stud are straight men and blind women," Gavin said.

Perry ruffled Gavin's pink spiky hair. "And you? Are a sweet little twink, yeah?"

Gavin's mouth dropped open, but he recovered quickly and gave the room a coy look filled with confidence. "Well, yeah. There are none sweeter."

Everyone laughed, but even as amusement spilled out of her, Jillian felt a prickle of awareness. She turned her head, not meaning to but not able to help herself.

The new boarder stood in the doorway.

His expression was serious and fixed on her, though she got the sense that he was aware of the others in the room.

Tamping down a totally inappropriate surge of lust, she gave him her best it's-okay-we're-all-friends-here smile. "Hey, Alan."

"Hey. You said something about dinner?"

"Yeah, um . . . Gavin and Sierra are making stir-fry."

"Sounds great."

His voice was . . . it was *wow*. The kind of voice an actor wished he had because it would get him callbacks on it alone. All husky and deep. But the man wasn't an actor. He was a reporter. And her boarder. Darn.

Alan shifted in the mostly comfortable bed. He always had a hard time sleeping when he started field work on a case. This time, maybe even more than most.

He wanted Jillian.

But unless he was getting close to her for the case, it would be incredibly stupid to start something with his landlady. Not only was there her whole rule about not dating tenants, but he couldn't afford the distraction. He had less than a month to find a spy and hopefully keep whatever technology said spy was trying to sell out of the wrong hands.

He'd jacked off in the shower, but just thinking her name had him going hard as a smoking gun barrel again . . . and just as hot.

Damn.

He needed to think about something else before he had to explain the need to wash his sheets come morning.

Okay, so dinner hadn't been too bad. Gavin had flirted, but he was actually a nice guy, if a bit flamboyant, and Alan had discovered he'd liked the other man's humor. Perry's too. No way would he have guessed *that* man was gay. Apparently Alan had no gaydar.

Perry was a grip for Frost Productions, which meant he worked preparing and tearing down sets on not just Jillian's show, but several others. He wasn't someone Alan would peg for selling technological secrets, but at this point, he wasn't ruling anyone out. Perry certainly had access to more sets than some might. However, Alan wasn't sure how important that was.

He looked forward to meeting the other boarder, Hank, too. A low-level film editor on Jillian's show, he'd been absent from dinner due to work. No doubt about it, Alan needed to start playing his reporter card. He needed to understand how the production company worked in order to get an idea of who would be the most likely suspect or suspects for espionage.

He had to be careful not to focus too much on his housemates just because he lived with them. There was an entire production company full of suspects, and until he got more information on them or the type of technology being brokered, he couldn't do much to narrow down the list.

Interviewing employees in a film production company was easier said than done, for damn sure. Alan had spent the morning on the phone trying to set something up and hit one blank wall after another. Even with his cover, the best reaction he had received was a kindly worded unwillingness to help. Production staff were too busy to set up interviews right now. Actors were best approached through their agents. Film crew had better things to do than chat about their jobs over coffee.

When he asked if he could tour the studio to get a feel for the way things worked, he was told that policy was not to allow public access. Insurance reasons were cited. Issues of convenience. The lack of staff time to accompany him came up again. And again. And again.

He would have been better off establishing another cover, maybe. Like some sort of federal inspector, or a potential investor. But who knew the Vancouver film industry would be so different from Hollywood? Hell, more than half the shows produced here were for U.S.-based companies.

He called more than one studio, just to keep his cover looking legit, but the story was the same everywhere. Not that he minded the other production companies having such a policy, but man, they didn't make it easy.

Which is what his gut had told him all along, so he might as well stop whining. He'd be bored out of his mind if the job were easy. And a bored agent could mean a sloppy agent, or at least a sexually frustrated one more likely to blow his case for a taste of his too-tempting landlady.

He brought the access problem up with Jillian over dinner that night.

She nodded, her beautiful face creased in a commiserating frown, her sexy red hair swishing over her shoulder, still tamed into soft curls by the stylists from her set. "It's all about who you know in this business."

"You'd think the production company would welcome the free publicity my article will give them." And it would get written.

Just not by him. That's the way the agency worked. They'd

managed to maintain decades of secrecy because of how carefully every case was handled. They wouldn't compromise his cover, even after the fact—unless resolution of the case demanded it.

"The publicity hounds would . . . but you're calling the wrong people, and you doing the calling is another point against you. In this business, your people call their people and stuff happens."

"So, what, I should have the magazine who wants the article call the publicity department?" He could arrange something like that.

"Yep. But there's an easier way." She smiled and his pants got tight. "I can talk to some people for you, set some stuff up."

"That would be great." But he'd consider going the other route too. He needed as much access as possible to the studio and its employees. "Thank you."

"No problem. And like I said, I'm happy to do a quick interview. I'm sure everyone here in the house would."

There was a chorus of assents around the table. Alan gave them his best grateful reporter smile, ignoring the fact that the thing he most wanted to do right now was Jillian. "Thanks."

"So, who's going out tonight?" Gavin asked, striking a pose in his chair. "I'm dressed to kill."

Today's outfit was a clinging shirt the exact shade of his hair and tight leather pants that looked painted on. The man gave new meaning to the word *flamboyant*, not to mention *courageous*. Alan would never have had the guts to actually sit down wearing those pants.

"I'm in. I haven't been out in ages," Perry said.

Hank, the thin blond film editor Alan had finally met three days after taking up residence, sighed. "I'm supposed to go back to the studio tonight and go over edits."

"I'm not letting you all drag me to a gay bar again. The last time I went, I drank too much beer while watching the rest of you have fun," Sierra said.

Gavin did a twirly thing with his fingers. "You got asked to dance."

"I'm straight, doofus. Hello? I didn't want to dance with someone of my own gender."

"You could have danced the fast ones," Perry said, humor sparking in his brown eyes.

Gavin nodded. "That's what Jill does."

Sierra's frown said everything about what she thought of Perry's suggestion and Gavin's comment.

"Face it, Sierra. Despite Jillian's little weekly sessions with you and the others, you're still shy—maybe even repressed," Hank said, sounding bored with the conversation, regardless of how inflammatory his words might be.

The brunette's frown darkened while hurt flared briefly in her expression.

Gavin looked at his perfectly buffed nails. "You're not going to find the love of your life sitting at home." Then the pink-haired man winked, his eyes filled with warmth.

And Sierra's frown broke with a small gurgle of laughter. "I'm not going to find him in a gay bar either."

Everyone joined her laughter and Alan looked at Sierra. "I'll go if you will." It had to help having another straight person in the group.

He wondered how far Jillian's nonfraternization policy carried. Was he allowed to dance with Sierra . . . with Jillian?

"Oh, now you have to go." Gavin looked determined, and Alan hoped that did *not* mean the younger man was going to ask him to dance.

"Alan's in a new place . . . he needs to meet people. You wouldn't hold him back, would you?" Jillian asked, the cajolery no less effective for its obviousness.

Sierra laughed and shook her head at him. "You set me up, but I'd like to point out that Alan's not going to meet someone of *interest* at a gay bar any more than I am."

It was in Alan's nature to pull a chain when it was available, but he had it in him to feel at least a little bad for doing it. Sierra really did not sound like she wanted to get stuck watching other people dance all night. "I'll sit at the table with you."

"But, Alan, I was looking forward to dancing with you," Gavin said with a pout, confirming the fear that had Alan itching between his shoulder blades just as if he had a gun trained on him.

"You'll have to settle for me," Perry said before Alan could answer.

"I guess I could suffer it," Gavin said coyly, and that's when Alan averted his gaze. Watching two other guys flirt was weird. Not gross or bad, but definitely strange.

"I was hoping to dance with him too." Jillian's pout carried a heck of a lot more impact than Gavin's had.

And her comment answered one question, at least. He *could* dance with her.

"It's a gay bar, right? Men and women don't dance together there. Do they?"

Jillian's eyes widened. "You've never been to a gay-friendly bar, have you?"

"*Gay-friendly* is not the same as *gay* and don't let her tell you any different. Last time they said we'd go to gay-friendly, but we ended up at a meat market for alternative lifestyles only." Sierra gave everyone else at the table a glare.

"At least it wasn't fetish night," Hank said. "That can be scary, even for one of the brotherhood."

Fetish night? Alan cringed inwardly at the images that thought provoked. "So, where are we going tonight? Gay or gay-friendly?"

"Friendly," Jillian said in a tone that brooked no argument. "It's only fair."

Alan hid his relief by drinking from his water glass, but his body's tension went down about fifty notches. That wouldn't be so bad.

Chapter 3

After the third guy asked him to dance and Alan turned him down, he wasn't sure it could get much worse.

At least Sierra had been asked to dance by a man—a straight man, even—after she'd turned down the first woman. She was on the small dance floor now, along with most of the group. Hank had decided to come after all when his boss called to cancel his late-night editing session at the last minute.

Jillian was hanging back with Alan, though he was sure she could be out there if she wanted to be.

There was no way he was the only man in the bar with a boner for her. Not that he was going to let it show. Unless it was for the case, the woman was definitely off-limits.

For a lot of reasons. Jillian's rules being only a minor consideration. After all, Alan liked to break rules.

But when it came to his personal life . . . well, he didn't have much luck as an agent. Look at the fact that Beth had dumped him because of his job and then ended up married to another agent. It was enough to give a guy a complex.

And he'd had no better as a mild-mannered accountant. Ivy Kendall had chosen someone else too. Of course, he should have known better than to let feelings grow for someone on assignment.

It had been a mistake to date Ivy. She'd thought he was

dead boring because of the role he'd played for his investigation in Delicious, Ohio. That had been one role he'd used his middle name for his cover rather than his first. Edward—or rather Ed—just sounded like a mild-mannered accountant.

And that's just what she'd mistaken him for. Mild mannered. Boring. So much so that the first woman to interest him in anything more than the horizontal mambo since his failed attempt at getting married had avoided his calls and ended up with another man. Just like Beth had ultimately ended up with Ethan.

He didn't know how his dad had found a woman like his mom, or his grandfather, his grandmother, but Ethan's luck with long-term commitment was as black as it got. Beth had written him off when he'd missed their wedding because of the job. He'd had no choice, no physical way to make it home in time or even call and warn her. He'd been in a jam, and because she wasn't listed as next of kin . . . yet . . . she hadn't been apprised of his missing-in-action status.

Not that it would have made any difference. She'd known he was an agent. Known what that meant. Said she loved him. But in the end, she hadn't wanted to deal with ramifications of his job for a lifetime.

It was the one time in his life he'd questioned his decision to become a federal agent. His job had screwed him royally then and he'd known it, but it was also all he'd had left when Beth had walked away. Later, his cover had ruined any chances he might have had with Ivy.

But he no longer doubted his calling. He was meant to be a federal agent. The cost could be high, only now he was sure it was worth it. The epiphany had come a year after losing Beth, when the drug ring he'd been investigating when he'd been "detained" were indicted on numerous charges, most of which he could take full credit for.

He'd known then he couldn't stop being what he was, and if Beth had loved him for *who* he was, she wouldn't have wanted him to. The fact that she ended up married to another Goddard Project agent only proved that point. Even so, he was convinced that trying to have a lifetime commitment with a civilian was doomed to failure. His mother and grand-mother and the two generations of women before them were unique.

"What are you thinking about? You look kinda disturbed."

Alan jolted, shocked he'd let himself get lost in ruminating when he should have been digging. He shrugged. "Just frustrated by my job."

It wasn't a lie, but he knew she'd take the words to mean his inability to get interviews for his article. He'd learned a long time ago that it was easier to stick with the truth when possible. Like his grandfather had told him once, every federal agent had his own method for dealing with the job. That was one of Alan's.

To be as honest as he could be without losing sight of his goal . . . ever. It made the things he said more believable too.

"That explains it," she said, looking thoughtful. "But don't worry. We'll help you out. I may not get paid like royalty, or even treated like it, but I do have the clout to get you on the set if you want."

"I'd like that. Very much." He took a sip of his drink and then smiled. "Thanks."

"No problem."

Jillian watched him for several seconds in silence and then seemed to come to an internal decision. "So, you want to dance?"

He didn't answer right away, his brain fighting with his body for control.

"It's a slow one. All you have to do is stand there and hold me." She smiled reassuringly.

Dancing wasn't the problem, but he wasn't going to tell her that. Holding her was the problem. It was going to be sheer torture, but he knew he was going to do it. Even as his brain was telling him what a bad idea this was, his legs were shifting . . . his body coming to his feet.

Surprise and then something he couldn't quite decipher chased across Jillian's expressive features. But she stood quickly and led the way onto the subtly lit dance floor. Sierra was nearby with a guy who looked like he could play wide receiver for the Miami Dolphins. Gavin was dancing with Perry, but Alan didn't see Hank. Jillian turned to face him and put her arms out and he stopped noticing anyone else.

Damn, the woman was beautiful. It wasn't just her peaches-and-cream complexion, with the smattering of sexy freckles, or the curves that he wanted to taste and touch. Her beauty shone from the inside.

She was sweet. She was vibrant.

She was a suspect.

But right now, that little fact was the last one his mind wanted to catalog.

He pulled her into his arms with practiced ease, only realizing he should have kept his distance as her body pressed enticingly against his.

A small gasp escaped her, that strange something flickering in her eyes again. "I thought you didn't dance much."

"I didn't say that," he said as he moved their bodies to the sensual strains of the music in a rhythm that fed his craving for her with dangerous intensity.

"You hesitated about dancing with me."

"I think you know why, Jillian."

She was silent for several seconds and then sighed. "Because we're attracted to each other?"

"Yes."

"I won't break my own rule."

"I'm not asking you to." Not yet.

"Tell me something?"

"Maybe."

She smiled at that. "I've heard a lot of bad press about reporters."

"Hasn't everyone?"

"Are you one of the good guys, or do you use subterfuge to get the story when you want it bad enough?"

"Who says good guys never practice deception?" He'd long ago come to terms with the roles he had to play for his job.

Only idealists and innocents had the luxury of truly believing the ends never justified the means. Most people lived their lives the best way they knew how and sometimes had to compromise for the greater good. At least he still believed in *the greater good*, which meant he had maintained some of his early idealism. *Go him.*

"I do."

"Maybe you need to consider another perspective."

"I don't think so. I hate lies." And liars.

The words were silent, but he heard them anyway.

That wasn't exactly the attitude of a woman who was willing to sell other people's secrets or compromise the safety of her country for a big personal payoff. If she wasn't practicing a little subterfuge of her own.

When the silence stretched a little, she said, "I'm sorry if I've made you uncomfortable."

"I'm not uncomfortable. I know I'm not one of the bad guys and I'm pretty certain you'll come to that conclusion once you get to know me."

"You don't lack confidence, do you?"

"Not usually."

"I'm glad I didn't offend you. I've been accused of rushing in where angels fear to tread," she said with a self-deprecating smile.

He laughed. "No. You? Not really."

"Yes. Really."

"Someone has to be willing to ask the tough questions."

She smiled up at him, her green eyes brilliant with delight. "Exactly."

"You're just one of the movers and shakers."

"My producers have another name for it."

"Yes?"

"Pain in the neck."

He laughed again, but the sound choked off as her body brushed his. Electric desire jolted through him. It took all of his formidable control to stop him from pulling her hips into his. Either she was going to blow his mind, or he was going to blow his objectivity. Or, hell—maybe both. He wasn't sure which one would be worse in that moment of acute sexual need, though.

Gritting his teeth against desire so strong his bones ached, he pulled back enough so that she wouldn't accidentally rub against his arousal.

Swaying seductively to the beat, she didn't seem to notice. "So what's it like?"

"What?"

"Living a lie."

His body went rigid before he realized she was talking about her perception of his job as a reporter. She hadn't made his cover. He wasn't just losing control of his body, he was losing his mind.

This had to stop right now.

If anything, the stiffness in his spine increased.

"Oh, crap." She sighed. "I'm sorry. I'm doing it again, aren't I?"

"Doing what?" he asked. Talking to this woman was like getting dropped in an alternate dimension.

"Being somewhat nosy and impetuous."

Ah, the "where angels fear to tread" thing.

"Did I say I lived a lie?"

"You admitted you don't always tell the truth . . . for the sake of the job."

Is that what he'd said? He wasn't sure, but that's apparently what she'd taken his words to mean. Regardless, it was close enough to the truth, and as usual he opted for as much honesty as he could. He wondered what Jillian would think of that particular personal rule.

"It's not so different from your job."

Shaking her head, she met his gaze, her expression earnest. "I get paid to portray a role, but that's not real life. I don't pretend to be anything I'm not off the set."

"Don't you think everyone pretends . . . at least a little?"

"No. Not me, anyway."

"So you never pretend to be happy when you are sad, or calm when you are angry, or that you like someone's new outfit when you think it really looks bad on them?"

"Actually, I try really hard not to," she said earnestly, and damn, he just wanted to kiss her. "I don't have to yell when I'm angry, but I don't have to pretend to be happy either. I'm very much what-you-see-is-what-you-get."

"And that's important to you."

"Very."

"Why?"

Her sinuous movements faltered for just a second, but she was back to dancing before he could comment on it. "They say we're all shaped in some way by our childhoods."

"That's true." He'd certainly been influenced by growing up the son and grandson of federal agents, not to mention the generations that came before.

He wondered what had led Jillian Sinclair to such a staunch belief in a high level of personal transparency. Or was she transparent? Being honest did not always equate to being completely forthright. Like she said, she didn't have to pretend to be happy, but she also didn't have to express her anger overtly. Though somehow he doubted lack of expression was a problem for her.

"Sometimes the lessons we learn in childhood don't translate to life as an adult." Because of what his parents had had together, he'd believed he could have it all too. The job. The family. The full life. He'd been wrong.

"Mine did. I insist on it."

He wanted to know more than ever what had put such a fierce look on her face, what lessons she'd learned that were so important he got the sense she never intentionally compromised on them.

"Like what?"

"Like refusing to live a lie because it invariably ends up hurting someone else."

"Some lies are unavoidable."

"My mom used to say the same thing. I didn't agree. I still don't."

"What did she want you to lie about?"

Jillian's eyes widened. "I don't—"

The music changed to a blaring rock beat and whatever Jillian said got lost, but he had a feeling it wasn't an answer to his question. He'd been right, honesty for her wouldn't necessarily equate to transparency. His sexy landlady had secrets, but he had every intention of finding out what they were. It was his job.

She jerked out of his arms with unflattering speed.

He wasn't about to complain, though. He hadn't stopped reacting to her nearness throughout their conversation and he was seconds from blowing it with an inappropriate caress. He'd never been as tempted to dismiss caution and seduce at will. The reaction was so foreign to him that he stumbled backward off the dance floor with something less than his usual controlled grace.

Another man came up to ask Jillian to dance before they'd gone more than a couple of steps and she returned to the dance floor with a big smile. Alan had to fight the inexplicable urge to follow and muscle the other man out of his way.

Damn, this was freaky. Having so little control of his libido was a complete aberration for him. He'd used his sexuality as a tool to get the job done, just like he used charm and his intelligence. Never had he felt his desires were actually controlling him.

He couldn't blame it on the fact that he'd been too long without sex either, because he could go months and still not let his physical needs interfere with the job. He'd done it before. Many times. This feeling of possessiveness? So foreign he might as well be visiting the craters on Mars. Hell, no . . . *that* would probably feel more familiar.

He'd been engaged once and seriously contemplated a long-term commitment to another woman, but neither time had he felt this primitive desire to mark his territory. To let everyone else know the woman in question was *his*.

But she *wasn't,* and she wasn't going to be either. He muttered a low and deadly curse.

He didn't even have territory where Jillian was concerned. She was his landlady. A possible suspect. Nothing more.

So why did he want to grab the guy dancing with her and toss him into next week?

And the things he wanted to do with Jillian didn't bear thinking about. Not if he wanted to walk out of the club walking upright and not bent double from arousal.

Because of where he was in the case, she couldn't even be a casual liaison. He didn't know enough to determine if being sexually involved with her would help or hinder him. Although the lack of control was definitely a drawback, and even there he didn't know if having Jillian would increase it or decrease it. She was totally and completely off-limits for now.

"You might as well forget about her. She *never* breaks her own rules," Gavin said from Alan's elbow.

His head jerked around to face his housemate. "I don't plan on asking her to."

"But you want to."

"What would you know?"

"You think because I'm gay I don't recognize when another guy is jonesing on a woman? Please. Attraction is attraction and, honey, you've got it bad."

"Nah. She's a beautiful woman, and half the men here are noticing her. Doesn't mean I've got a major hard-on for her."

"Whatever you say." But Gavin looked supremely unconvinced.

Considering the fact that Alan was lying through his teeth, that was understandable. Only he was usually very good at deception. Maybe he needed to fall back on misdirection.

"What about you? See anything you like tonight?"

"Plenty." Gavin laughed. "You headed back to the table?"

Alan found himself joining him in the amusement. Yeah, he had been. Should have been. Whatever. "Yes."

"I'll go with you. I could use a drink and a sit."

"You've been dancing since we got here."

Gavin shrugged and put his hands out. "What can I say? We do what we must to not disappoint our adoring public."

Alan chuckled. "So, all those guys you were dancing with were fans?"

"In one way or another. I'm not just an actor . . . I'm sexy. Or hadn't you noticed?"

This time Alan's laughter rang out loud enough to turn heads.

"You implying you *don't* think I'm sexy?"

"No comment."

Gavin grinned, sitting down in artfully arranged relaxation. "You're a cautious man, Alan."

"It pays in my line of work."

"I can see that. Offend a potential source and lose him, right?"

"I didn't say—"

Gavin's hand came up in a stop gesture. "Hey, I know you don't play for my team. Don't sweat it."

"So Jillian's really strict about her rules?"

A sad smile flitted over Gavin's face. "Yep. She's asked

boarders to leave when they hooked up." He grinned, his whole demeanor changing. "But she can be a real pussycat about other stuff."

"That's good to know."

"Yeah. Not that any of us would let her get taken advantage of."

The warning was clear and Alan respected him for it. "You're all pretty close, then?"

"Most of us. Hank keeps to himself, mostly, but I think he's loyal to Jillian, anyway. One of the things about this business is that like usually draws to like. Actors hang with actors, staff with staff, you know?"

"So he's standoffish because he's an editor rather than an actor."

"Partly, and I think he's just a reserved kind of guy too."

"You and Perry seem to be friends, but he's not an actor, is he?"

Gavin's cheeks pinkened under the glitter highlighting his cheekbones. "I sort of ignored him when I first moved in with Jillian. He's a grip, you know? Not an actor . . . not part of my scene. And well, sometimes grips and technicians, they've got a real attitude about background actors. Which is what I was before I landed my current role." He shrugged. "Not that Perry ever called me a *meat prop* or anything, but you know, sometimes I have this tendency to push back before I've been pushed. The best defense is a good offense, right? Only that can really mess you up."

"You seem friendly enough now."

"You think?"

"Well, yeah."

"I think he's nice to me for Jillian's sake. I'm pretty sure he thinks I'm kind of a flake."

"Why?"

"That whole background actor thing, and well, Jillian's not joking entirely when she calls me a princess."

From what Alan could tell, Gavin's flamboyant ways didn't bother Perry, but he was definitely not an expert on gay culture. "Why the issue with background actors?"

"Stage crew works really hard all day. Perry's muscles aren't all from weight lifting, yeah?"

"And you didn't work hard?"

Gavin shrugged. "A lot of the time background actors will sit around for hours doing nothing but waiting to get called to work a scene. They get paid for being there whether they go on film or not. You can kind of understand the crew's frustration. After all, they're lucky to get their union-prescribed breaks."

"So you're saying Perry doesn't respect you now or didn't respect you then?"

Gavin grimaced. "I'm not sure. My attitude when I first moved in didn't help his view of me."

"But you've changed, and I'm sure Perry has noticed."

"I hope so."

"The film industry is a different world, isn't it?" The caste system was a lot more ingrained than Alan would have expected it to be.

"It can be insane, to tell you the truth, but I can't imagine doing anything else."

"So you're a regular actor now?"

Gavin nodded with a smile. "I've got a permanent gig. I play a bald alien on Jillian's show."

"Bald?"

"Yeah. I wear a skin. It's pretty cool, actually. When I was in background, I couldn't do the really fun things with my hair because I never knew what I might get called for. Now I can dye it whatever color I like. I'm thinking of going purple. What do you think?"

"That if anyone can pull off purple hair, it's you."

Gavin smiled, looking pleased. "Thanks."

"You two flirting? That's against Jillian's rules, you know." Smiling, Perry sat down next to Gavin.

"Flirting isn't against the rules. Hooking up is."

"And how far from hooking up is flirting?" Perry asked.

"A lot further than I want most of the time," Gavin muttered.

Jillian was as good as her word and arranged for Alan to meet with the lead film editor, the casting director, props director, and lead sound technician the following week.

She looked very pleased with herself when she finished listing off his appointments. "I've also got approval to take you on a personally guided tour of the studio."

"That's great, Jillian, thanks." He leaned forward and kissed her cheek.

It was a natural move. He'd seen Perry, Gavin, and even Hank do the same several times.

But he doubted very much if the sensation of silky skin against their lips gave them boners that threatened the integrity of the fly on their pants.

She inhaled and then visibly relaxed. "You're welcome."

Her voice was huskier than usual, indicating that the kiss affected her on something more than the platonic level as well. That knowledge pleased him way more than it should. And turned him on even more than the sexy glow-in-the-dark outfit she was wearing did. Not that he'd seen it in the dark, but it was that strange green, almost white of glow-in-the-dark paint, and knowing Jillian, that's exactly what it was.

She wasn't wearing make-up and had her abundant red hair pulled up atop her head in a loose ponytail of corkscrew curls. No filming today, she'd explained. She looked like she'd just climbed out of bed, and all he wanted to do was take her back to his.

"So, when's the tour?" He tugged playfully on her ponytail, the need to touch her taking on a sense of inevitability.

Just like the zing to his groin from being so close to her.

"We can do it later today, if you like."

"I'd like."

"Great. I'll just return some calls and then we can go. Say, forty-five minutes?"

"Perfect." That would give him time to check in with the Old Man.

And hopefully get his hormones back under control.

How odd would it look if he started taking cold showers several times a day? He could say it was a cleansing ritual . . . for religious purposes.

Chapter 4

Jillian drove a lime green Volkswagen Beetle convertible. With the top down and the heat on full blast. It was winter, but the sun was shining and somehow it didn't surprise Alan when Jillian pressed the button to retract the roof.

Darting in and out of traffic at speeds better suited to a Ferrari, she chattered the whole way to the studio. The woman talked with her hands and looked at him more than once to make eye contact. While she was driving.

When they reached the studio parking lot, Alan had come to the conclusion that the government was missing a prime interrogation technique. Even seasoned agents would not stand up under the threat of Jillian's driving.

He was wondering how to convince her to let him take the wheel on the return home when she got into an argument with the security guard at the entrance to the studio.

"Excuse me, but I am entitled to bring a guest on the set."

The blond guard smiled, but didn't budge. "Of course, Miss Sinclair, but you have to get prior approval."

"I got approval."

He pointed to his clipboard. "Mr. Johnson's name is not listed on my sheet."

"That is not my problem. This tour has been approved."

"I don't know what to tell you, Miss Sinclair." And the

poor guy—his name tag identified him as Ralph—looked like he meant it, but also like he wasn't about to break the rules. Even for the star of the show.

You had to admire that kind of commitment to the job.

Jillian didn't appear to share Alan's opinion. "You can tell me you're going to step aside."

"I'm sorry, Miss Sinclair."

She turned to face Alan. "Don't worry, we'll get this cleared up. The new security policies around here are ridiculous. You'd think we were trying to steal government secrets or something." She turned back to the guard. "Call Mr. Frost. Tell him I'm here with my visitor."

"You want me to call the *executive producer*?"

"Would you rather I called him and told him you refused to allow me onto the set with my guest?"

Ralph paled. "No, Miss Sinclair." He swallowed. "I'll, uh . . . I'll call him." He started fiddling with papers. "Let me just find his number."

Jillian rattled off a series of digits.

The guard started dialing and then spoke into his cell phone. His eyes widened and he nodded as if the person on the other end could see him, stuttering out apologies and agreement. "Right, right . . . sorry, I just . . . the security protocol . . . right . . . won't make the same mistake."

He hung up and assigned Alan a visitor's badge. "I'm sorry, Miss Sinclair. I'm just doing my job, you know?"

"I know, and you're good at it, Ralph. Don't worry about this. You don't make the rules, just abide by them."

The guard sighed with obvious relief and smiled. "You're good people, Miss Sinclair. Glad this didn't happen with someone else."

Alan wondered if all the guards were as conscientious and what that might mean for whoever was trying to broker proprietary technology.

Jillian just smiled before leading Alan into the studio. "Watch the cables. They're everywhere."

And they were. Thick black cables crisscrossed the floor of the cavernous room that housed three different sets as well as a couple of cubicle-type offices for Jillian's science-fiction series.

She turned to Alan as she stopped in front of one of the sets. It looked like it was supposed to be the bridge of her ship. "Security has been a bear since one of executives got some hyped-up bee in his bonnet."

"So, before . . . you could have brought a guest onto the lot without getting prior approval?"

"Not everyone could, but me? Yes. There's a real hierarchy in the film industry, you know?"

"Gavin was saying something about that last night."

She shook her head. "He was a little goofy about it when he first moved into my house. But he's relaxed."

"He mentioned that too, but he seems nice enough."

"He is, which is why I knew he'd get his head on straight eventually. This industry fosters egomania like no other."

"I don't see much of that in your boarders—or you, for that matter."

"I went through my idiocy early on. When I was still a teenager." She grinned. "I've grown up. Most people do."

"But not all."

"No, not everyone comes to the realization that contrary to what their agents are telling them, they are not the centers of their own little universes."

Alan figured he knew what Jillian meant after meeting her costar. The man made William Shatner seem shy and diffident in comparison.

"Did Jillian tell you that the multiple personality disorder thread for my character was my idea? Not every actor knows how to see the big picture in the plot too."

Alan wanted this man to be his perp, but feared he was too wrapped up in himself to even think about brokering technological secrets.

The best part of the tour by far was Jillian Sinclair.

The worst part was the effect she had on him.

He found himself standing closer to her so he could get more of her elusive scent. She didn't wear perfume. The spring-time freshness was too subtle for that. Probably her shampoo, but even knowing the fragrance was something so mundane did not diminish its addictive appeal. Of course, the fact that the unmistakable feminine musk underlying it was all Jillian did not help.

Alan wanted to nuzzle right into her neck, and various other enticing places, and just inhale. Okay, and then maybe taste and touch . . . shit . . . he wanted this woman.

"Alan?"

"Huh?"

Jillian was looking at him questioningly. "I asked if you wanted to see more of the technical behind-the-scenes stuff."

"Yeah, that would be great."

Jillian knew more about the technical workings of the sets and the show's production than he would have expected. He took copious notes on everything she said. "I feel like I'm taking Film 101."

She laughed. "Bored?"

"Not at all. Just surprised you know so much."

"I never went to college, you know? I took some classes on acting, but for the most part? Boring. Having someone else tell me how to do what I love best just didn't work for me. I found I liked knowing how everything worked more. So I took classes on set design, editing, prop design . . . you name it, I've probably taken at least one class on it."

"So, you really are a jack of all trades."

"Well, all trades related to the film industry."

"Do you have dreams of directing one day?"

"Yes. And eventually, producing. I'm supposed to direct two episodes next season. It's part of my contract."

"That's great."

"Yeah, I'm pretty excited." She led him out of the prop

room. "If this show goes enough seasons, it will be my last full-time acting gig."

"Moving to film?" he asked and promptly tripped on one of those big black cables.

He fell toward Jillian, her hands automatically coming out to steady him and his grabbing onto her. They ended up with her leaning on the wall, him leaning against her with one of his hands on her hip and the other on her shoulder.

It was the perfect position for kissing and his body perked up, hormones screaming at him to take the plunge.

Reason prevailed and he managed to apologize rather than lock lips.

"No problem. Are you okay?" she asked, both of her hands planted firmly against his chest.

She wasn't pushing him away and he wasn't quite up to the task of stepping back. Yet.

"Yes. I forgot to watch for the cords."

"It's one of the first things you learn."

"It would have to be."

"Yeah . . ." She swallowed and licked her sweet bow lips. Damn.

"Maybe you should hold my hand and guide me," he said in a low voice that he usually reserved for the bedroom.

Double damn.

"If it will make you feel safer." Her voice was huskier than normal too, and her pupils had almost swallowed the emerald green of her irises.

Triple damnation. She was turned on.

He willed himself to step back.

Nothing happened.

She stared up at him, silent but for the short little breaths she took.

His head began to lower while his libido cheered and his brain shouted at him to go to the men's room and soak his head under a cold faucet.

Her mouth opened slightly, ready for his to descend.

"Miss Sinclair?" It was Ralph, the security guard. "I just got off the phone with the prop master. He wanted to request you not tour his room."

Alan found his lagging self-control and sprang backward.

Jillian sidestepped and moved toward the security guard. "I don't know what he thought we would do."

"Probably break something. He's pretty protective of his stock."

Jillian made a little growling noise. It was cute. "Yes, I know. He's quite the *artiste*," she muttered to Alan. "We just won't tell him we already toured the room, yes?"

"Whatever you say."

"If he asks, I'll tell the truth," she said on a sigh.

"Let me know if he asks."

Her brows drew together. "Why?"

"So I keep our stories straight."

She groaned. "I hate subterfuge."

"I know."

That made her eyes widen, almost with fear. Like the idea of his knowing her worried her. The woman was a 3-D Chinese puzzle and he planned to have all the pieces put together before this case was over.

"Thanks, Ralph."

"No problem, Miz Sinclair."

She turned back to Alan, her smile almost too bright. "So, what were we talking about?"

"I had asked if you planned to do movies once this series has run its course."

"Maybe. I'd like to do a movie or two, but mostly? I want to work behind the camera, and I'm hoping I can make that happen in a full-time way."

"What's stopping you?"

"From directing? Experience. Mostly. From producing, which is my real love . . . the green stuff. It takes a lot of seed money to build a name as a producer, not to mention some killer scripts."

"Another reason to rent rooms out in your house."

She laughed. "That's mostly to cover living expenses. My friend Amanda has almost all of my acting income in an aggressive investment plan. She's helping me realize my dreams."

"She sounds like a good friend to have."

"We've always been there for each other."

"I've got a brother like that. He's my best friend."

"That's great. That you're close to your brother like that. It's the way family should be."

"Do you have any siblings?"

"Yes. A younger brother. I haven't seen him in a while."

"Why?"

"It's hard to get home. He's talking about coming to visit. He might even transfer to the University of British Columbia next year. Our parents aren't too happy, but I'd love it if he lived closer."

"I hear that. My brother and I do a lot of IM-ing, e-mails, phone calls . . . it helps. But sometimes, we just have to get together face-to-face. Even if we didn't want to, Sir would insist on it."

"Who's Sir?"

"My grandfather. He raised us since our parents died when we were teens."

"And you call him *Sir*?"

"He's got his quirks, but he did a good job with us."

"I'm sure he did."

"What about you? You're originally from Southern California, right? I bet you call your parents by their first names."

Jillian laughed, but the sound was edged with something not in the least humorous. "No way. We had a very traditional home. At least once my mom married my stepdad. I had to call him Dad even though my own father is still living."

"That must have been hard."

"It was, but not because of any feelings of disloyalty I felt toward Scorpio. The truth is, he never played much of a parental role."

"Scorpio, the painter?"

"Yes."

Well, he knew where Jillian got her red hair from. But she didn't seem to have much else in common with her famous father. Scorpio was legendary for his affairs with young, gorgeous women and his parties that rivaled the decadent depravity of ancient Roman orgies.

"I guess you were lucky to have a stepdad, then."

"You'd think so, wouldn't you?"

"You don't." He was getting tastes of Jillian's secrets, and they only made him thirstier for more.

"One thing I learned growing up is that appearances can be and are often deceptive." She sighed. "Not that I think living with Scorpio would have been better. Sometimes, life doesn't give you any good choices. But you know? I realized after moving out that it could have been a lot worse too."

Despite the temporary insanity that prompted his request she hold his hand, Alan kept his distance for the rest of the tour. If Ralph hadn't shown up, Alan would have kissed Jillian senseless. He couldn't believe his own behavior. No matter how strongly she impacted his libido, he was not some rookie agent to be derailed by a pretty face. Or even a beautiful face. And intriguing personality. And charming personality. And the same sense of humor as his own.

Practically growling with frustration at himself, Alan forced out question after question about how things worked and who did what on the set and in the studio.

True to what she'd told him earlier, Jillian had enough knowledge to give him elucidating responses to every single query.

* * *

Which is what he told the Old Man, when he called to check in. He was on his cell in the middle of Stanley Park, supposedly on a run. Not that he wouldn't get a solid jog in, but first he had to connect with his boss.

"So, you think she's a suspect?"

"She's got access to some of the most advanced computer technology before it goes public through her relationship with Simon and Amanda Brant. She wants money to pursue her dreams of becoming a producer and she knows her own industry inside and out. And she would definitely know how to use the production company as a cover for passing on high-tech secrets."

The Old Man harrumphed.

"Excuse me?"

"What does your gut tell you, Hyatt?"

"That she's too honest to get dirty that way," he said without hesitation. "But . . ."

"But?"

Bile swirled in his stomach, making it cramp. He hated admitting this. It was as bad as telling his grandfather what a monumental mistake he'd made with Beth. "My libido could be influencing my gut," he admitted.

"You're falling for this Jillian Sinclair?"

"I didn't say I was falling for her."

"But you want her?" There was an interesting note in his boss's voice . . . almost enthusiasm.

Alan dismissed the thought as incredibly unlikely. However, because of the nature of the job, he was used to discussing subjects and reactions that most employers would consider strictly off-limits, so he didn't hesitate to answer. "Any red-blooded man would."

"Is that going to be a problem with the case?"

"No." But damned if he didn't sound less certain than he meant to.

"You need a lecture on focus and getting the job done?"

"No." Frustration with himself surged through him. "I know my priorities."

"Priorities change, son."

"Mine haven't," Alan said from between gritted teeth.

"Your grandfather was a hell of an agent."

"Yes, he was, sir."

"He ever tell you how he met your grandmother?"

"No."

"Maybe you should call him and ask."

"Maybe I will someday." But not today.

Any feelings he had for Jillian were strictly sexual. Overwhelming. Distracting. Intense. But definitely sexual. That's all he would ever allow them to be too. He'd made all the mistakes he ever wanted to make in the romance department. No chance he was making another one. No matter how alluring he found his landlady.

The Old Man sighed, like something about Alan's answer disappointed him. "Any other suspects?"

"Who isn't one? We don't know what the technology is that Prescott was supposed to broker. We don't know who his accomplice wanted to sell it to. We don't know if his contact here was a man or a woman." The only thing they did know was that whatever it was, Prescott had a timetable attached to brokering the information.

A note attached to the name had indicated the deal was supposed to be brokered midmonth. After the show stopped filming, but before the entire production crew broke for the holidays.

"Well, are there any obvious conduits for the technology?"

"Depending on what it is, too many. You've got state-of-the-art computers with super-high-storage capacities. A prop room filled with gadgets that could be as real as they look, and a prop master who is very protective of them. An entire company full of people that cross the U.S.-Canadian border on a regular basis, not to mention the production materials that get shipped up from the parent company in Los Angeles."

As Alan listed off the possibilities, he had to fight the sensation of drowning under them that curled at the edges of his consciousness.

"You were assigned to this case because I knew it would be tricky but you have the experience to find our guy or gal, as the case may be, and shut him down."

So much for the Old Man assigning him an easy case. The knowledge warmed Alan even as it made him more determined than ever not to let his libido—or anything else—impede his investigation.

"The most promising leads I have so far are the prop master's reluctance to have anyone in the prop room, and that one of the studio execs recently insisted on increased security measures."

"Have you spoken to him?"

"No. I'm not sure which one it is, but I'll ask Jillian when I get back to the house."

Alan found Jillian in the living room with Sierra and several other women. They were sitting in a circle on the oversized cushions on the floor speaking in low voices. They all had something in their hands, but he couldn't tell what they were holding. Candles burned on the squat coffee table, giving off a pleasant spicy scent, and the soft strains of an eighties love song played in the background.

As he stepped into the room, the talking ceased and all eyes turned to him.

"Excuse me. I'm sorry. I didn't realize you had guests."

Jillian smiled. "No problem. I should have told you the Sex Suffragettes meet here once a week. We pretty much take over the living room for a couple of hours. Did you need something?"

"Sex Suffragettes?" He practically swallowed his tongue getting the words out.

Jillian smiled sunnily. "Yep. You know the suffragettes campaigned for women to get the vote . . . to enjoy equal political freedom and responsibility with men, right?"

"Um . . . yes." Where was this going?

"So we're each personally committed to enjoying freedom and responsibility equal to what men enjoy in regard to our sexuality. It's sort of a grassroots movement like the original suffragettes. We started with a small group of three women and grew until there are now three other groups meeting in the city," Jillian said proudly.

"That's great . . . I think." He wasn't sure what it all meant, but was sure he'd rather ask Jillian about it in a less public setting.

His gaze skimmed the women. Some looked shy, embarrassed even, by his presence. Others looked at him with confidence, a bit of mischief, or even a sultry sensuality. Jillian just looked incredibly earnest.

He cleared a suddenly dry throat as his brain registered what his eyes saw. Not just the women's differing attitudes, but what each one of them held in her hands.

Dildos.

They were all holding dildos.

No two were alike. Some were very . . . realistic, while others were plain . . . or just plain weird looking. Jillian's was big. Damn. Maybe even bigger than him. Not that he was comparing or anything.

Heat rushed through his body and he started backing up.

"We started the group after I read the book *White Tigress, Jade Dragon*. If they could have their own society, I figured we could too," Jillian offered, waving the dildo in her hand with her typical expressiveness.

She acted as if there was nothing more natural in the world than a circle of women in her living room holding phalluses.

He hadn't read the book, but he'd heard of the White Tigresses. They were women who belonged to an ancient but obscure Chinese society that believed in enhancing physical and spiritual strength through sex. Not only were the adherents supposed to be incredibly accomplished in the sexual arts, but they were supposedly formidable warriors as well.

"But . . ." The practices he'd heard about in connection with the White Tigresses could not even begin to be described as safe sex, or feminist. Could they?

Sierra gave her shy laugh. "From the look on your face, Alan, you must have heard of them. We aren't Taoists and we're living in the twenty-first century, so, um . . . we don't embrace a lot of the teachings."

Jillian said, "But I do require that all new members read the book."

"It's very enlightening," one of the other women offered.

"I'm sure it is," Alan said while trying not to picture Jillian practicing that kind of *enlightenment* on his body.

The White Tigresses were particularly known for the art of fellatio.

Jillian stood with her usual fluid grace. "The original White Tigresses were right about one thing, it's very beneficial both emotionally and physically to accept one's sexuality."

"I . . . uh . . . I'm sure it is." Oh, hell. He sounded like an adolescent faced with his first boy-girl discussion.

But the image of Jillian accepting her sexual self and all that entailed was like a living, walking wet dream.

"Was there something you needed?" she asked again.

"I was hoping we could talk some more about the Vancouver film industry. When you have time." He resumed his stopped progress of backing out of the room, managing not to look like an idiot in the process.

"We should be finished in half an hour or so. Do you want me to come find you in your room?"

He nodded and spun on his heel, leaving posthaste to the sound of soft feminine laughter.

But the last thing he needed was to dwell on just how far Jillian Sinclair embraced the tenets of the ancient White Tigresses. The idea of her on her knees in front of him, doing what the practitioners were supposed to be best at, had *his* knees close to buckling.

Chapter 5

Instead of going to his room, Alan went to the basement. Jillian had converted it into a pretty nice weight room and workout area.

Perry was working on his hamstrings on the Universal machine. He nodded at Alan and grunted as he pushed against the weights.

"Hey," Alan said as he headed straight for the free weights.

He added discs to each side and then lay down to start a set of bench presses.

"You're supposed to have a spotter for that, yeah?"

"I won't tell if you don't."

Perry chuckled. "You're a big boy. I figure you can decide what risks you want to take."

They both went through a set, silent but for the grunts of effort with each exhale.

"Did you know about the Sex Suffragettes?" Alan grimaced after asking the question. Of course Perry knew. Damn, he was rattled.

Perry's laughter was full-blown this time. "Don't worry, you're not the only man in this house disconcerted by it. I'm not sure even gay men talk about sex as openly as those women . . . and well, it's a whole different thing from a woman's point of view too."

"Do you think they really practice some of the teachings of the White Tigresses?"

"Sure." Perry winked. "The idea get you a little hot and bothered?"

"That's one word for it."

"Oh yeah, and what would you call it?"

"Mental torture," Alan answered with more candor than he'd meant to.

"You like Jillian, yeah?"

Alan made a noncommittal sound. "Any man would find the idea of her embracing her sexuality a little distracting."

"Any straight man anyway, but don't feel bad. The rest of us have our form of torture around here."

"You mean Gavin?" Alan asked, taking a stab in the dark.

He didn't see Perry lusting after the nondescript Hank, though he could be wrong, of course.

Perry grimaced. "He's got a hot little body, but at first . . . well, let's just say I'd never met such a princess before."

"Jillian said he was a little hard to live with when he first moved in here."

"The little prick gave new meaning to the term *prima donna*, but he's gotten better. Way better," he muttered under his breath.

"That's good."

"In some ways. In others . . . it just makes things harder." Perry shook his head. "Never mind. We've got a good thing here at Jillian's. I'm not doing anything to mess it up."

Perry finished his last rep and stood. "Do you want me to stay down here to spot you?"

"Not necessary."

"Okay, then. I'm off to the showers."

"Enjoy."

"Alone? Not so much."

Alan had to stiff-arm so he wouldn't drop the barbell as he tried to control his laughter.

Between sets, he stripped off his T-shirt so all he had on was his running shorts. The basement was cooler than the rest of the house, on a different heating system than the other two floors, but Alan's thoughts were heated. His body was wet with sweat from the exercise, but his arousal remained a slow burn inside him.

He had moved through his bench presses, a complete set of curls, and was working on his dead lifts when Jillian came into the basement.

Her eyes seemed to go unfocused as she looked at him. "I thought you were going to be in your room."

He grunted as he lifted the heavily weighted barbell over his head. "I decided to do some lifting before I showered from my run."

"Oh." The word was no more than a breathy sound.

"I'm sorry you had to come looking." He finished the rep, bringing the barbell all the way to the floor.

"That's, um . . . pretty impressive. Did you lift weights competitively in college or something?"

He shrugged. "Nope, but I've always enjoyed it."

"I can tell." Now, that? Was definitely sultry interest.

And she inhaled, her nostrils flaring lightly, as if she was taking in his scent. Some women couldn't stand a man's clean musk, but Jillian apparently wasn't one of them. And that turned him on all over again.

Crap.

He could not afford for this insane attraction to be *that* mutual, and from the confused look on Jillian's face, she wasn't too thrilled about it either.

"So . . . you were . . ." She sighed. "I mean, you said upstairs that you wanted to ask me some questions."

"Yeah. We covered a lot during the tour of the studio, but I've got a couple of points I wouldn't mind you clarifying."

"Sure. Did you want to take a shower first and meet me back in the living room?"

"I've got three more of these to do."

"No problem." She stood like she was going to watch him do the dead lifts.

And a deeply masculine, very primitive part of him wanted her to.

He did the lifts, and if he flexed extra muscles in the process, he wasn't mentioning it. But when he was done, Jillian Sinclair looked like she'd been good and sideswiped.

Could he seduce her despite her rules and strict adherence to them? The insidious allure of a challenge thrilled through him. And that was worse than the libido thing.

Because there was one thing Alan Hyatt had never been good at turning his back on. A true challenge was as seductive to him as Jillian's sexy body.

Feeling more antsy than she could remember being since her first audition, Jillian waited in the living room. This was not a date. Not an assignation. But, darn . . . the man was so fine. Watching him do the dead lifts had been just short of orgasmic.

His body was all hard angles and defined muscle. But it was more than that. Her newest boarder had that elusive quality so many actors strived for their whole careers—*presence*. Ultramasculine, sexy presence.

When she'd been giving him a tour of the studio, she'd thought he was going to kiss her. *And she'd wanted him to.* Bad . . . bad . . . bad. She needed to do something about this infernal attraction before she acted absolutely idiotic, broke her own rules and made a pass at him.

It did not help that she'd spent the last two hours talking about sex. Every time she'd shared her own views, she'd thought of Alan and how good he probably was at anything and everything sexual. It had only gotten worse after he'd interrupted them.

Jillian liked men. She wasn't a slut, but she wasn't a prude either. She enjoyed having a boyfriend, though she never let her feelings get too deep . . . not deep enough for it to hurt when the inevitable happened and the relationship ended.

But she'd never reacted to a man like she was reacting to her new boarder. And frankly, she would have been happy to keep it that way.

"Is this a bad time?" Alan asked from the doorway.

"Huh?" She looked up and felt that twinge deep in her womb. "What? Bad time? Oh, no."

"You looked like you were thinking about something pretty hard. Something that was maybe bothering you?"

She forced a smile, only then realizing her face was set in nothing short of a scowl. Oh. "Not bothered. Just . . . um . . . figuring something out. Hey, I've got an appointment at the spa tomorrow. I bet I could get you in at the same time. Gavin goes with me sometimes, but he's not due for a body wax yet and I have the dermabrasion done weekly. Have to keep my flawless complexion . . . at least until I'm working behind the camera instead of in front of it."

Oh, man . . . she was babbling. She never babbled. Okay, well yes, sometimes when she was really enthusiastic about something. Especially when she was with her best friend, Amanda Brant. But Jillian didn't babble in situations like this. And why the heck had she invited Alan to go with her to the day spa?

Spending more time with him was such a bad idea. And yet she heard herself saying, "You'll love the masseuse there. Absolutely top notch."

"The spa?" he asked like he'd never been to one.

"Yep. The spa. You can do some more research on the film industry around here. My skin therapist said that a good percentage of their clientele work for the studios. Most are actors, but some of the execs as well. I bet the impressions you could gain from the employees there would be really helpful. And well, only a fool turns down a chance at a professional massage."

"I can think of other types of massage that are more preferable."

Oh, crud . . . Gavin was right. It was beyond sexy when this guy talked in that low sexy growl. And he was flirting with her.

"Yes . . . well . . . um . . . I still think you'd like the masseuses at the day spa." Was that her sounding all tongue-tied? If she told Amanda, her best friend would fall off her chair laughing. "You could even get a facial. Lots of men get them."

"A facial? No way. Not my thing."

She grinned, feeling a little more in control for some reason. "Have you ever had your head, face, and neck massaged?"

"That would be no."

"Then you don't know what you are missing. It's a little piece of Heaven on earth."

"Right." He almost rolled his eyes. She could tell he wanted to, but he managed to refrain.

Instead of feeling annoyed, she laughed. "I go once a week and it's worth it just for the massage alone. I call the skin treatments a career necessity, but the truth is it's my one indulgence. And really, you shouldn't give up this opportunity to do more research for your article."

"I'm sure you're right about talking to the employees, but I'm not getting a facial." He was not exactly today's metrosexual man.

"Look, why don't you let me give you a massage and then you can decide whether you want me to try to get you worked into the schedule? I can't do anything nearly as professionally as my skin therapist, but I've had enough treatments to do a fair job, I think." Besides, she'd learned the art of massage several years ago and enjoyed using it as a form of sexual foreplay.

Not that this was going to be sexual in any way. It was strictly for Alan's edification.

A distinctly predatory glint came into Alan's steely eyes. "Sure, why not?"

And Jillian couldn't help wondering where her sanity had run off to. Had she really just offered to touch her new boarder? On purpose and for a prolonged period of time? Oh man, she had lost her mind.

She really had.

But did she try to back out? No, she did not. In fact, she heard herself ask him if he wanted to do it in the living room or the workout room so they could relax in the whirlpool afterward.

Alan opted for the workout room and offered to meet her down there after dinner.

She definitely needed to have her head read.

Alan walked into the workout room, wearing nothing but a pair of swim shorts. Jillian was already down there. She had a short toweling robe on over her swimsuit. She'd brought down a folding chair that reclined, the kind that people used outdoors. The seat cushion and back were padded, but the frame was made of metal tubing.

She'd also lit a couple of candles near the whirlpool and one bank of lights was off; only the dimmer ones in this end of the room were on.

Her eyes hotly devoured him before she veiled her gaze with a sweep of her lashes. Then she waved her arm to indicate the chair and candles and gave him an oddly shy smile. "I wanted to set the mood."

"Like the spa?"

"As close to, yes. After all, I'm trying to convert you, right?"

"I don't think it'll work, no matter how much I enjoy the massage," he felt compelled to tell her.

"That's all right. Think of it as research into the lifestyle of your subject matter, regardless."

He wasn't sure he could think of anything but the delectable woman in front of him once she started touching him, but he nodded in agreement anyway.

And he was right. Once Jillian's fingertips connected with his face, he stopped thinking about the case, research, or even pretending to be an uninterested reporter. He couldn't help moaning as she began her massage at his temples, moving to his cheekbones with fluid, sensuous strokes that sent his dick into model-rocket mode. Straight, perpendicular, and ready to shoot toward the stars.

He didn't know how long she touched his face before she moved to his head and then his neck, but when she was done, relaxation and sexual hunger vied for dominance over his confused neurons. The scent of Jillian's own arousal was not helping. Her hips were too close to his head and the fragrance of her feminine nectar teased his nostrils until they were flared like an animal in heat.

"What do you think?" she asked in a husky tone.

"If I got this kind of treatment weekly, I'd be too turned on to concentrate."

She gasped. "I'm not trying to excite you."

"I'm not actively trying to excite you either, but I'd say I'm doing a good job."

She made a choking sound and her hands fell away from his neck. "I . . . uh . . . I think I'd better skip the whirlpool. I've, um, I've got things to do."

And she whirled away from him and out of the workout room before Alan could move from his chair. It took iron will and self-control to tamp down the primal instinct to chase his prey and assert his masculine victory in the most basic way.

Damn. Why had he agreed to this in the first place?

He did soak in the bubbling waters of the hot tub, but they did nothing to assuage his growing hunger for the gorgeous redhead. He wanted her. His body cried for her and he didn't know how long he was going to be able to ignore its clamoring demands.

Alan took Jillian's advice and chatted with whoever had a minute to talk while she was getting her facial treatment the next day. She'd been right and the employees had a lot of information about the industry and its players. He deftly guided several of them to talk about Frost and anyone they knew who worked in his production company, filing away their comments with the other things he'd managed to learn thus far.

More than one of the therapists tried to convince Alan to have a facial, but he refused. When he learned they had a store in D.C., though, his face lit with an evil grin. He considered buying Ethan a gift certificate for a full facial, head massage, and eyebrow wax for Christmas.

The other agent would probably just give it to Beth to use. But if Alan got matching gift certificates . . . well, that had distinct appeal. Alan didn't really begrudge Ethan his marriage to Beth. After all, rekindling their love affair had been a long shot, but that didn't mean he had to avoid an opportunity to needle the other man.

So he bought the gift certificates as well as one for a full-body massage and wrap for Jillian. It would be a way of saying thank you when he moved on. His gut was telling him she wasn't in on the theft of the technology and he didn't have to give her the certificate if he decided against it.

Jillian came into the lobby, her skin smooth and shiny clean. "Hi."

He smiled. "Hi, yourself. You look nice and relaxed."

"I feel it."

"Great."

She smiled. "After a treatment, I always go for a smoothie at the coffee shop just up the street. The blueberry one is full of antioxidants. Want to?"

"Will you be offended if I get a coffee instead?"

She laughed, the sound going straight to his groin. "Not at all. Let's go."

The coffee shop was crowded, way more than usual. But then it was the right time for teens to be out of school and the store was filled with them. Loud and boisterous, they made Jillian grin.

Until she found herself crowded up next to Alan in the line. Then her grin faded as every bit of the relaxation she'd achieved through the spa treatment melted away under the zinging electric current generated by his nearness.

This was ridiculous. And stupid. She'd found herself having NC-17 fantasies about Alan and not her favorite unattainable crush during her spa treatment. Which was not surprising considering the way she had reacted to giving him a massage, but was hardly conducive to maintaining a friendly distance.

So why had she invited him for coffee?

She must be into self-inflicted torture. But darn it, not only was she hot for him, she *liked* being around him, no matter what her house rules were. What was that, stupid times two, maybe?

Sheesh.

A girl with Goth black hair, lipstick of almost the same shade, and a short leather skirt shrieked and fell back toward Jillian, laughter ringing around her.

Alan's arm wrapped around Jillian's waist, dragging her out of the way while his other hand steadied the girl. Then, smoother than she would have been able to do it, he maneuvered them both just enough so that she was tucked in against him while he stood between her and the rowdy group of teenagers.

"Wow, that was fast. Thanks." She tilted her head to meet his gaze.

And the air stuck in her throat. The man was just too masculine. Too **gorgeous**. Too intriguing for her own good.

He smiled, sending shivers of warmth through her. "No problem."

She sucked in air. "Um . . . you're fast on your feet."

"One of my many talents."

Another tussle had Alan tucking her into him so their bodies touched chest to thigh.

Oh . . . wow . . . just . . . *wow.*

His hands were big and the way he held her made her feel safe. Not to mention the other wow-type things. But the sensation of being protected was more disturbing even than the sexual energy thrumming through her.

No one made her feel safe. No one ever had. Not her parents. Not a boyfriend . . . certainly no one in the business. The closest she'd ever come was the times she spent with Amanda and Simon Brant, but even with them, the sense of safety was not completely pervasive.

She always held part of herself back. It was the only way to keep control of her life. She was the one who took care of others. But when it came to her life, she relied on herself and always had, even when everyone thought she lived in the perfect middle-class American household with her mother who led the PTA and her stepdad who golfed with the mayor on the weekends.

She tried pushing away, gaining a little space, but Alan's hold was firm. And that didn't make her feel trapped.

Why didn't it make her feel trapped? She abhorred being held against her will. It was against her independent spirit and brought back painful memories from her childhood, when a drunken stepfather would hold her arm in a viselike grip before hitting her in one of his irrational rages.

Amanda and Simon played light bondage games, and she remembered thinking her friend was crazy to do so. Jillian could not imagine ever trusting a man to bind her hands during sex. But here she was, in Alan's arms . . . *not feeling trapped.*

His gray eyes searched hers. "You okay?"

Was her confusion showing on her face? She quickly

schooled her features to mask it. "Fine, I just . . . don't want to crowd you."

But why wasn't she trying to push away anymore? Why had her first efforts been so feeble?

"Better that than you getting trampled." He was smiling as he said it, his good humor including the teens still joking around.

She liked that too, the way he didn't get impatient with the kids. Her stepdad would have gone through the roof, or rather cutting and snide if they were in public. But then he got annoyed easily with anyone who didn't further his ambitions.

Alan was patient with Gavin, even though the other man's flirting was obviously disconcerting for him. He hadn't snapped at the teenagers, not when she'd almost been knocked over and not now as the group took twice as long to place their drink orders as they could have.

She wasn't feeling impatient, either.

All she felt was an overwhelming desire to let her fingers explore the hard muscles pressing so enticingly against her own soft curves. She couldn't stop herself from tilting her head just the tiniest bit forward in order to take his scent in. He smelled so good, even after a workout like yesterday.

It wasn't like any person she'd ever known. Definitely not a cologne, but the man himself. Spicy. Infinitely male and just plain delicious. Just right. Like an aphrodisiac to her olfactory senses.

"How long do you think it will take you to get the information for your story?" she asked.

She didn't know how long she could deal with this inexplicable attraction . . . this weird sense of safety . . . the intense reaction to him without going insane.

"I don't know." He shrugged, caressing her body with his and making her knees weak. "A month, maybe."

"Bobby thought the renting thing was short term, but he didn't say he thought it would only be a month."

"It could be longer." But Alan's tone and posture said he didn't think it would be.

"Good." Maybe she could survive a month of this craziness.

"Good? You want to get rid of me?"

"No, I, uh . . . I'm just glad you think you can get the information you need for your feature and it won't take you too long to make it worth it."

He raised his dark eyebrows. "You sure about that?"

"Are you flirting with me?"

"Is that not allowed?"

"Um . . . the no in-house fraternization rule."

"Gavin flirts with you."

"Gavin's gay and he flirts with everybody." And even at his most outlandish, when he was threatening to go straight because of how some man had treated him, he never made Jillian *feel* anything.

But with Alan, she did nothing but feel and palpitate. She'd even found herself panting yesterday after seeing him do the dead lifts.

Alan just cocked his brow again and smiled, then turned her to face the counter, which was miraculously cleared of the teens. He stood close behind her as she contemplated her order, so close she could feel his body heat and something else. Something that told her that his reaction to her was very physical.

A shiver worked through her body, starting in her inner thighs and working up her torso and down her legs at the same time. She gasped. Then blushed.

She couldn't remember the last time she'd blushed.

Alan didn't seem fazed. He ordered her blueberry smoothie when she couldn't seem to get any words out and a specialty coffee for himself.

She noticed something later, after their drinks were done and they were sitting together on a couch in the corner, the only two seats left in the coffee shop. What was the matter with today's teenagers that none of them had copped the spot on the couch to cuddle and engage in politically incorrect public displays of affection?

So here she sat right next to Alan, their bodies touching, and she noticed that while Alan seemed to be as attracted to her as she was to him, his attention wasn't entirely on her. It was like there was this little part of him that was watching everyone else. It was weird.

"Is that a reporter thing?" she asked.

His gaze focused entirely on her and she could feel the difference. "What?"

"That thing you do. You know, while you're talking to me, even looking like your eyes are on me, you're aware of everyone else around us. Part of you is focused on them. Except right this second."

He looked startled. "No one notices that."

"I'm sure they do, I'm just the only one nosy enough to ask."

"No, trust me . . . they don't. I worked hard to perfect the skill so they wouldn't."

Those words just added to her inner turbulence. Was he implying that she was in tune with him on a deeper level than most people?

"Maybe you need to work harder," she said, in an attempt to deny such a connection.

"Maybe I do," he said as his head tipped downward and his lips barely brushed hers before he pulled away.

Everything went still inside Jillian, like peaceful still. Like this was perfect . . . this moment being close to him. The feel of his lips against hers. Like they belonged there. The way it felt to be the entire focus of his attention. As if that was exactly the way it was supposed to be.

Terrified at the direction her thoughts were taking her, Jillian surged to her feet. "I think it's time to go."

Alan just looked at her, not moving. "You're not done with your drink."

"I don't want it anymore."

"Are you sure?" But he seemed to be asking her something else entirely.

She stood frozen, unable to deny or affirm, but by sheer strength of will she forced her head to nod. "Yes . . . I'm sure."

But she wasn't. She so wasn't. Not about anything.

Chapter 6

That night Perry came home from work with a face so grim he would have made an excellent extra in a postapocalyptic epic.

Gavin beat Jillian to his side, laying his small hand against Perry's muscular bicep. "What's the matter? Did something happen on the set?"

For once, there wasn't the slightest trace of levity or flirtatiousness in Gavin's attitude. He just looked worried to death, and Jillian definitely sympathized, because Perry looked like death.

"Are you okay, Perry?" she asked.

"Oh, my gosh, Perry, you look like your dog died," Sierra said as she entered the room.

Perry just stared at them all, not saying anything. His eyes were dilated, like he was in shock. Jillian grabbed his hand. It was cold. Gavin was now rubbing the other man's arm, but Perry didn't seem to notice.

Alan walked into the living room, his gorgeous gray eyes taking in the scene with an intensity that made Jillian shiver despite her concern for Perry.

Then Hank walked in, looking even worse than Perry with noticeably red eyes.

Oh, crudlinks . . . they'd started something together and now they were going through the big breakup and she was going to have to referee it and evict them both because she couldn't play favorites. Her stomach cramped. Perry had been one of her first friends on the show. She didn't want him to leave.

"Perry, Hank . . . sit down," Alan said, his voice laced with authority. "Jillian, do you think you could make them some tea or coffee? Sweeten it good, and not with that artificial crap you use to keep your waistline pencil thin."

He didn't give any instructions to Gavin or Sierra, but he didn't have to. Both were fussing over Hank and Perry as they saw them seated close together on the big sectional couch.

"Um . . . I don't think hot tea is going take care of what ails Perry and Hank." Jillian sighed, really sad. "In fact, I think the rest of you should leave so the three of us can talk."

Gavin started to protest while Sierra just shook her head.

Alan's jaw set stubbornly, his eyes speaking a message she was not used to getting. "No. Get the tea, Jillian. They need it. They're both in shock."

"Shock, why are they in shock?" Sierra asked.

Jillian had thought that at first—with Perry, but when Hank had come in, obviously having recently cried, she'd realized something else was up.

"I don't think—"

Alan cut her off. "Jillian, get the tea. Now."

And she didn't yell at him or tell him what he could do with his orders. She went in the kitchen and made the tea, sweetening both mugs liberally as instructed.

When she came back, Gavin was crooning to Perry that everything was going to be all right and Sierra was holding a quietly crying Hank. Jillian gave then each a mug of tea, which Perry took an immediate sip of, but Hank just held his, like he wasn't sure what to do with it.

Alan sat on the coffee table in front of him and guided the tea to this mouth. "Drink it, man. You need it."

"I'd prefer whiskey," Hank said in a gravelly voice.

"That comes next," Alan replied as he helped the man take another sip of the sweet tea.

Alan waited until both men had consumed most of their tea and put the mugs down before asking, "Okay, so what happened?"

"Lonny is dead." Hank said the words and then started to sob.

"Lonny, the grip from the studio?" Jillian asked.

"Yeah," Perry said.

"He wanted to be a film editor," Hank choked out. "I was helping him with his classes, training him on unused footage from Jillian's show."

Hank's reaction said there'd been a lot more between the two men than professional mentoring. A lot more.

Perry had been one of Lonny's good friends too. They'd never dated that she knew of, but they went out to the bars together, hung out on weekends, and they liked American football, both to watch and to play.

"How did he die?" Sierra asked, looking a bit shocked herself.

Perry visibly shuddered. "He was mugged on his way to his car."

"Mugged?" Alan asked, his reporter's inquisitiveness showing in how keenly he waited for confirmation.

"Somebody . . . I mean . . . maybe more than one . . . they hit him in the back of the head and stole his wallet. I . . . I . . . found him. On the ground." Perry's words came out haltingly and then he laid his head back against the sofa and closed his eyes.

"The blow was hard enough to kill?" Alan asked and Jillian glared at him.

He could save his reporter's questions for later.

"Yes." This time it was Hank speaking, tears still running silently down his cheeks. "They said he died pretty much instantly."

Hank started to sob more loudly and Alan said a word that was both ugly and appropriate.

"You think this grip's death is related to the case?" the Old Man asked as he and Alan once again talked over Alan's cell phone while he ran in Stanley Park.

It was frigidly cold today and Alan used a Bluetooth headset and kept jogging while they talked just to stay warm. "I can't be sure, of course, but my gut is telling me yes. Muggings, especially in Vancouver, are rarely deadly."

"The mugger could have hit harder than he thought."

"I checked into it, talked the coroner into letting me see the body. Whoever hit him didn't kill him on accident. The blow was strong enough to fracture the skull and it landed exactly where it had to, to ensure death. I don't think that was a coincidence. It had the feel of a professional hit. And the crime scene was too clean. The body was stripped of all valuables, but there were no fingerprints anywhere. And they left the car alone."

"Maybe the mugger wasn't after a car."

"Lonny had hit the unlock button and had the keys in his hand. There were valuables in the glove compartment and on the passenger seat, though the laptop that he usually carried with him was missing."

"Far from conclusive facts, but I trust my agents' instincts."

Alan nodded, though his boss couldn't see him. "There was also no evidence of a scuffle, and the way the body fell indicated he was facing his car when he was hit."

"So, the perp snuck up on him."

"Lonny's car was in the middle of a gravel parking lot. He would have heard someone coming."

"You think he knew his killer, that maybe he was walking with him?"

"It makes more sense than a man allowing someone to get

close enough to kibosh him without even turning around to see who it is in a gravel parking lot."

The Old Man hummed in agreement. "Okay, I buy that it's a possible murder. But even if it is, there are a lot reasons for offing someone that have nothing to do with selling high-tech secrets."

"Agreed, but I'd still like to know what Lonny was doing just prior to the mugging and who he'd been with."

"I'll get the case file."

"Good. I'm going to get chummier with my fellow boarders. Perry was the man's friend and coworker, not to mention the person who found the body. Hank seems like he was more."

"Keep me apprised of developments."

"Always, sir."

Alan stared at the computer screen and realized he had not read it or updated to a new screen in over ten minutes. Damn. His thoughts were not where they were supposed to be: on the case.

Instead, he couldn't stop thinking about Jillian . . . and not as a potential suspect either.

No, his thoughts were focused on the soft translucence of her skin, the supreme kissability of her lips, the enticement to his hand of the indent of her waist, the perfect curve of her breasts that made him want to explore them without the covering of clothes, no matter how sexy or bright the outfit. And he could not get the image out of his head of her holding that dildo in her hand. Why had the women been holding the dildos? The prospect that they had been discussing the male penis was enough to make his cock sit up and take hard notice.

Damn . . . he'd be leaking in his shorts soon.

And he was supposed to be focusing on his investigation, not the prospect of sex with the most alluring woman he'd ever met.

Maybe he should just have sex with her and get the antici-pation and mystery out of his system. He didn't know if it worked that way. He'd never been in this situation before. Women did not preoccupy him. Not even Beth. When he was on a job, he had been able to put his former fiancée out of his mind so his focus would be absolute. Looking back, maybe that had been part of the problem with their relationship. He couldn't imagine her new husband and fellow agent Ethan being able to totally forget Beth for any length of time . . . even on the job.

Of course, Alan would have considered that risky, not to mention weak, behavior for an agent before he'd met Jillian. He wasn't in love with her or anything, but man, was he ob-sessed with her. It was a strange and highly uncomfortable feeling. One he had to get rid of at all costs. He was a profes-sional and there was no room for obsessions in an investiga-tion.

Trying to dismiss the obsession wasn't working, so he had to believe that giving in to it might be the only way to get rid of it.

Jillian had her rule about not getting involved with house-mates, but Alan had made a career of circumventing the rules of others.

Now that he had established his objective, Jillian didn't stand a chance.

He got an opportunity to start his campaign sooner than expected when a knock sounded on his door. He opened it to find Jillian on the other side.

She was smiling. "I just wanted to say thank you for last night."

"For what? I didn't do anything."

"Not only did you take charge and keep the situation under control, but you stopped me from making a real idiot of myself."

"What do you mean?"

"I thought something entirely different was going on . . . not that I could have anticipated what actually happened. I mean, I've never had a renter, or even a friend, discover a dead body. And I mean, what were the chances it was someone another of my renters was, um . . . intimate with? So it wasn't like my idea was completely off the wall, but if I'd expressed it, I would have sounded like a royal bitch, not to mention a real idiot." She blew a strand of hair away from her face. "I'm babbling, aren't I?"

Alan gently pulled her into the room before she realized what he was doing and then he closed the door. "You're cute when you babble."

"Cute?" she asked, sounding dazed.

"And alluring."

"Alluring?" Her eyes went impossibly wide.

"Yeah . . . but what was the idea that would have made you look so stupid?"

"I . . . um . . ." Jillian looked around as if trying to figure out how she'd come to be inside Alan's room with the door shut. "I . . . uh . . . thought Perry and Hank had gotten involved and were breaking up and that I was going to have to evict them both."

"Both?"

"Well, I couldn't play favorites, you know? Even if Perry has been a friend for a long time."

"You really thought the two of them had a thing?" Was she totally blind? "There's no chemistry between them at all."

"And you're the expert?"

"It's my job to read people."

"I usually pride myself on being able to do the same thing, but with enough motivation, people can hide who they are, what they are feeling, and what they are doing amazingly well."

He moved closer with subtle precision and she moved back without seeming to realize she was doing so until her back was to the door and he was firmly within her bubble of personal space. Her breath hitched.

He leaned infinitesimally closer. "Have a lot of experience with that?"

"Wh . . . what?"

"People hiding who they really are."

"Oh. Uh, it's not that uncommon."

"I still find it hard to believe that you thought Hank and Perry were a couple breaking up."

"Like I said, it's not as if I would have guessed what really happened."

"No, I suppose not."

"Um, well . . . I just wanted to say thanks."

"Any time."

She tried sidling to the side and he moved with her. She frowned. "Uh . . . I should probably go."

He didn't think so. Not yet anyway. "There's something I've been wondering about for a couple of days."

"Yes?"

"What were the dildos for?"

Her eyes widened and this time her breath seemed to still in her chest. Then she took a deep breath, her mouth parting in unconscious invitation. "Excuse me?"

"I just wondered why you all were holding dildos the other day."

"They, um . . . we were discussing penises, how they're all different."

"You think dildos make good substitutes?" He paused, brushing a finger along her jaw. "As visual aids, I mean."

She shivered. "Better than nothing, yeah?"

"I suppose."

"Some women are very uncomfortable touching a man's hard-on. Getting them used to handling a dildo helps defeat some of that sexual shyness."

"I can't see that being a problem for you." He let his breath caress her lips, but just kept his body from touching her.

Her beautiful green eyes went unfocused. "Uh . . . what?"

She took a deep breath. "I mean, no. It's not a problem for me."

"Good," he purred.

She swallowed. "Good?"

"Very good."

"I . . . uh . . . Alan . . . the rules."

"You know, for a supposedly free spirit, you've got a lot of rules, sweetheart."

"Sweetheart? I don't think—"

He pressed his finger to her lips. "That's right, baby, don't think. Touching is way better than thinking." He closed the final distance between them, and damn if his brain didn't short-circuit from the jolts of electric pleasure arcing between them.

He could tell Jillian felt the same because she made a broken sound and melted into him even as her gaze reflected confusion underlying unmistakable desire.

He couldn't hold back his own groan of lust. "Rules can really be overrated," he whispered against her ear before gently biting the lobe.

"Oh . . ." She shivered against him.

He smiled and stepped back, forcing his need down. "Are you making dinner tonight?"

"What? Dinner?" She was slumped against the door, staring at him like he was speaking in computer code.

"I'll help," he offered with a wink.

"You're going to help with dinner?" she asked, sounding like her mental faculties were returning.

"Yep."

He liked the look of confusion that had not entirely dissipated from her expression. It meant she was wondering why he'd stopped and maybe even why he'd started in the first place. He knew he could get her in his bed, but wasn't sure he could keep her there. Too much chance she would have an attack of landlordly conscience. When he made his final move to secure his objective, he wanted her body so primed, her desire so fully engaged that she would surrender without a single pesky thought.

He gently guided her from the room, very satisfied with the results of his first maneuver.

Jillian tried to concentrate on her breathing as she did her tai chi exercises in solitude in the basement workout room. But she was so familiar with this routine, so used to regulating her breathing for maximum effect, her mind had entirely too much freedom to dwell on things she'd rather ignore.

Things like the way Alan had been acting since she'd gone to his room the day before to thank him for his help with Perry and Hank. He had helped with dinner . . . and how. Unfortunately for her, they had been alone in the kitchen for the most part and he'd used every available opportunity and some he created himself to touch her. A brush here, a moment of full body contact there, speaking in her ear in a sexy whisper that sent pleasure pulsing between her legs.

She'd used her voice as a sexual tool with previous lovers, but no man had ever been as adept at it with her. And Alan wasn't even her lover. Yet.

Crap.

She wanted him and he made her feel like prey. With any other man, that would just piss her off. Hugely. But with Alan, it turned her on stronger than anything another man had ever done. No intimate touch, no sexual teasing, no adventuresome experimentation had affected her as strongly as Alan's subtle hunting.

Maybe because he was such a sexy animal himself. An alpha male who not only made her feel like he was strong enough to stand beside her and even protect her, but the underlying integrity she sensed in his character, the kindness he showed his fellow housemates, the way he didn't just stomp on Gavin even though it was obvious Alan wasn't even bi-curious, the way he handled the stuff with Perry and Hank, calming the men down, helping them both deal with the different kinds of grief they were going through. Alan might be a predator at the top of the food chain, but he was the alpha that knew gentleness, knew how to take care of those around him.

Wow.

She'd never met another man she respected as much, trusted as instinctively, and wanted as desperately. Okay, she totally respected and trusted Amanda's husband, Simon, but she didn't want him. The truth was, her reaction to Alan scared her silly. She needed to get a handle on herself and her feelings. She couldn't afford to start thinking about a future with a man. That was something she'd promised herself she was too smart to risk.

Men were good for friendship and sex. But if you loved them, they could hurt you. Love made a person vulnerable, and Jillian was completely and totally against the concept of vulnerability. The cost of being let down was too darn high.

She would never be her mother . . . and she would not return to her own younger self either. Not ever.

She needed to fit Alan into one of the slots that men fit in her life. She just wasn't sure which slot was the right one. Straight friendship wasn't going to work, not if he was going to stalk her sexually.

Maybe she should talk to him. She'd tried to last night, after dinner when he sat beside her on the sofa so close they touched. The whole group had been in the room, talking about Lonny's death and trying to deal with it. Again, Alan had instinctively known what to say to help each man through his pain, what to ask to get both Perry and Hank talking about the things they needed to say.

Regardless, after everyone else had left to go to their rooms, she had opened her mouth to chastise him for his sensual flirtation, only to feel her vocal cords literally freeze on the words. She couldn't do it. It had been so long since she'd really wanted a man, period. She remembered it was a week or so after Amanda and Simon's wedding. Jillian had been attracted to one of the background actors on her soap opera set. The man had been obviously flattered by her interest, but though the sex had been good—they'd both had multiple orgasms—she'd felt so empty afterward.

Jillian hadn't been able to forget the look in her best friend's eyes when she said her wedding vows. There was something so real between Simon and Amanda, something Jillian did not expect to find. Prior to seeing the two of them together, she had been convinced it was close enough to impossible to dismiss from the probable reality of life.

Jillian still didn't expect it to happen to her. Didn't really want it to. After all, what happened to Amanda if Simon—God forbid—died or something? But even so, having witnessed this kind of connection had done something to Jillian's sexual habits. It was almost laughable that she'd started the Sexual Suffragettes, considering how little sex she was getting, but the group was about attitudes, not practices. A woman didn't have to make a thousand sexual conquests to be comfortable with her own sexuality. Which was the goal of the group.

And Jillian was comfortable with her body and its natural desires. She just hadn't had as many of them the last three years. Maybe that was why Alan was affecting her so strongly. Maybe she'd been repressing needs she hadn't even recognized were there.

Something he had said in his room kept repeating in her mind. He'd said that for a supposedly free spirit, she had an awful lot of rules, or something to that effect. She didn't have that many rules, did she? The ones she did have were for self-protection. She was a smart woman, she learned from her mistakes or those of others. That's where her rules came from.

She'd discovered early in life that living with a man she had sex with made the inevitable parting so much worse. It just got messy. She hated messy.

So she'd created her rule about never living with a boy-friend or sex partner. When she'd bought this house, she'd extended the rule to her renters.

But if Alan was leaving in a few weeks anyway, the end of their relationship wouldn't have the complications inherent in living with a sex partner, a voice in her head whispered se-ductively.

Provided she wanted to spend the next few weeks sharing her body with him.

Did she? Apparently, her body needed the release of sexual tension she hadn't even realized was there. Would that ten-sion require multiple sessions with the sexy reporter? Something inside her said, "Heck yes!"

Okay . . . so what did she do? Did she wait for him to make his final move? She was sure he was building up to it, but if she waited for him, didn't that give him more control than she wanted him to have? She would maintain the upper hand on their sexual liaison and her own emotions if she was the one to initiate the final step.

Jillian was all about preemptive action. Hadn't she already instructed her agent to feel out casting directors before her soap opera producers had announced that her character was going to die to boost ratings? And when they'd made the an-nouncement, her agent had already approached her about auditioning for three other shows, including a rival daytime drama. Jillian hadn't felt powerless like she had the first time she'd been let go from an acting gig.

She didn't do powerless. Not anymore.

So, if she made the first major move with Alan, she would keep herself in a position of personal power.

Finishing her tai chi exercises, she nodded firmly to herself. Yes. If she was going to have sex with Alan, she was going to stay in control. She was also going to talk to her other board-ers. She was not the type to sneak around and she wasn't a hypocrite either. She needed to explain why her rule didn't apply to this particular situation. She hoped no one was too irritated with her.

It wasn't like relationships between her renters was all that big an issue. For one thing, the other three men were gay, so no chance of Sierra getting into something with any of them. As for their having relationships with each other, well . . . Gavin and Perry were just now becoming friends. No lover relationship there. And Hank had obviously been involved with the deceased Lonny.

Poor guy. But another good object lesson. Just look what happened when you let your heart get involved with sex. The man was in a lot of pain and all for a relationship that had given him mere months of pleasure, if that.

Jillian was definitely going to remember her other rules when she and Alan got together.

No emotional involvement.

No sleeping all night with a sex partner.

No using the L-word, in any form whatsoever.

She didn't tell her partners that she loved what they did to her, or how they felt, or how they looked, or how turned on they were, or anything else. Some words were too powerful to sprinkle around like sugar on a donut.

No penetrative sex.

She knew how to satisfy her partner without allowing him into her body. Going that far always carried complications. Men got possessive of women they copulated with. It was too easy to mistake the feelings from that kind of joining as emotions that weren't really there. That was one of the things she'd loved in the book about the White Tigresses. They didn't engage in penetrative sex except with their longtime lovers, which she didn't plan to have. There was a lot of pleasure to be had without that.

She'd never had a partner complain after an intimate session. She left most men gasping and insensate with pleasure. Of course she got her pleasure too. She knew how to pick her partners and to ask for what she needed.

She had a feeling that wasn't going to be all that necessary with Alan, though. When he arrived as she was just starting her toning exercises with the hand weights and immediately started the tease again, she was absolutely certain of it. Any man who knew how to move his body like that during a workout for sure knew how to use it in the bedroom.

Chapter 7

A lan studied the list the agency had compiled of potential technology to be auctioned in his case. Researchers who made it their job to predict stuff like this had gone over Prescott's known brokerages of high-tech information, cross-referenced that list with known sensitive developing or newly developed technology, and made their guess as to what might be at stake.

Pinching the bridge of his nose, Alan tried not to be too frustrated with the Old Man's instructions regarding studying the list. In his opinion, no matter how good these research agents were, trying to predict what he was looking for was like trying to predict the weather. Only a hell of a lot more risky if he bought into a prediction that turned out wrong and let himself get sidetracked looking for the wrong thing.

He still thought his approach to the case had the best chance of getting results. Investigating the production company, looking for the suspect rather than the technology.

He was damn good at ferreting out suspects.

A soft knock on his door had him closing the encrypted file.

"Come," he called, not moving from his seat at the desk.

Jillian stepped into the room. "Hey."

He stood up and moved across the room to her. "You need something, sweetheart?"

"After the last two days, I'd say you know perfectly well what I need."

She was making the first move? Well, day-am . . . this he had not expected. He should have considered the possibility of a preemptive strike, especially with a woman as assertive and confident as this one.

"That's a definite possibility."

"I don't mind flirting, Alan. In fact, I enjoy the chase, but I don't play games when it comes to sex."

"I'm glad to hear it."

"I think the time has come to deal with this attraction between us."

"What about your rules?"

"I'm only circumventing one, but the reason behind it doesn't apply in this situation."

Interesting. "Why is that?"

"You are leaving in a few weeks."

"And?"

"My issue with the whole living with a sex partner has to do with how messy and uncomfortable it can get when the relationship ends."

"And all intimate relationships end for you?"

"Yes. I'm not looking for the white-picket-fence fantasy. I never have been."

Damn. It was a good thing he was approaching this as just sex and hadn't let himself start feeling for her like he had Beth and Ivy. But still, he couldn't help pushing. "You don't want someone to grow old with?"

She shrugged. "That's a pipe dream, don't you think? Over fifty percent of marriages end in divorce."

"Which means that close to fifty percent last a lifetime." His grandparents were still married and more than a little affectionate after fifty years.

"How many of them are happy?"

"How many divorced partners regret their choice?"

"I don't know."

"Considering the percentage that end up remarried, the answer is a lot."

"What, did you write an article on divorce statistics in America or something?"

It was his turn to shrug. "I've got a weakness for trivia of all kinds."

"Some marriages should end."

"I agree. Some people don't belong together."

"Some people don't deserve to be with anyone." The depth of pain in her voice said she had a personal reason for believing that, and Alan couldn't help wanting to know what it was.

"I agree with that assessment too." Abuse statistics were something he was also more than passingly familiar with.

"So, are you?"

"Am I what?" Had she asked a question he hadn't heard?

"Are you looking for the white-picket fantasy?"

"I was at one time." Maybe he still was, but he wasn't sure anymore if he believed he could have it.

"What happened to change your mind?"

"My fiancée dumped me."

Jillian's beautiful green gaze widened. "You were engaged?"

"Yes."

"And she dumped you?"

"She thought she had cause."

"Did you cheat on her?"

"No way in hell."

That made Jillian smile. "So, what did you do?"

"You so sure I did something?"

"You said she thought she had cause."

"I got held up on an assignment and I missed our wedding."

Jillian stared at him and then burst out laughing. "Are you saying you don't think she had cause?"

"She knew the dangerous nature of some of my assign-ments." Most of them, but again he stuck to the truth as closely as possible while maintaining cover. "She should have realized that if I hadn't literally been tied up, I would have been there."

"You were kidnapped?"

"It happens."

"Were you in a political hot spot?"

"You could say that."

"So she decided she didn't want to live with the risks of your job?"

"So she said. She didn't want to live with the separations, the unpredictable schedule."

"Some people aren't cut out for that kind of life."

"She ended up married to a man who does exactly what I do."

"Oh."

"Yeah. Oh."

"Do you still love her?"

That was a question he'd been asking himself for a long time, but as he stood in front of the incredibly sexy red-headed actress, he realized he finally had an answer. "No."

"It's a good thing she didn't marry you, then, isn't it?"

"What do you mean?"

"I think it takes a love that doesn't know how to die to make a marriage work for a lifetime."

"So you do believe it can happen?"

"For other people? Yes. That kind of love requires a level of trust I'm not capable of."

Oh now, that was too damn intriguing. "Why?"

"Maybe I'll tell you sometime, but tonight I'm more inter-ested in exploring something besides my past with you."

He cupped her shoulders and pulled her unresisting body into his. "You mean something a little more physical."

She smiled and something inside him clenched tight. "I

mean something a lot more physical. One hundred percent in the here and now."

"That sounds damned good."

"Doesn't it?" She clasped her hands behind his neck and tilted her head until their lips were millimeters from touching. "Very, very good."

And then she pressed her lips to his. She didn't use her tongue, but the woman knew how to use her lips to draw forth an intense response from him.

But Alan wasn't used to giving up the lead to anyone. He tipped his head just slightly sideways for a better angle and proceeded with his best frontal assault on Jillian's soft lips. He cupped the curve of her waist with one hand and used the other to caress the outside of one hip and part of her perfectly formed backside. From the sound of her moan, she liked it.

He liked the fact that she was wearing a clingy T-shirt and low-rider jeans. The hand at her waist found bare skin with no trouble at all, and that skin was silky smooth and warm and everything that a woman's skin should be. Other than getting under the hem of her top, he didn't move either hand from their initial landing spots, though. A slow buildup led to some amazing explosions, and he wanted to blow away Jillian's expectations.

He also wanted to drive her crazy. More than any other woman he had been with, Jillian challenged him and the primitive masculinity that resided beneath the surface of every man like him.

Advocates of political correctness would have a fit if he voiced the truth that he did not merely see Jillian as a woman to make love to, but as a competitor he was determined to beat at her own game. Because he was certain deep in his gut that Jillian had come to him with the intention of seducing him with her superior sexual prowess. She was like the hunting tigress, set on making him her prey—taken down not with force but with finesse. She wanted to be in control, to best him at the maneuvers he had started the day before. To prove her superiority.

She'd miscalculated, though, underestimated her opponent.

Alan didn't want to master her, but he sure as hell wasn't going to let her get the upper hand either.

Jillian seemed familiar with the slow buildup as well, though. Her fingers played against his nape and the back of his head, sending pleasure zinging along his nerve endings.

Never had such a simple touch made him weak in the knees, but if they didn't get horizontal soon, he was going to reveal his weakness.

Not breaking the kiss, he swung her perfectly proportioned body into his arms and carried her into the alcove with his bed. He laid her down, lowering his body alongside hers.

She broke her lips from the still-dry kiss. "In a hurry?"

"Not at all. I like to be comfortable, and with the difference in our heights, this makes things easier." It was a damn good excuse considering the state of his libido, not to mention his scrambled brain.

Her smile said she wasn't buying it completely but wasn't going to call him on it.

He grasped her waist again and pulled her onto her side, facing him, making both her front and back accessible to his touch. It was a good thing they still had their clothes on because he wasn't entirely sure that if he had her nude body as accessible he wouldn't cream his jeans. And damn . . . he couldn't remember the last time he'd done that. Had he ever done that?

He slid the arm against the bed under her neck, pillowing her head on his bicep and letting his hand come down on her side at a level with her breasts. Grateful for the length of his fingers, he brushed against the side of her breast, bringing forth a sweet moan from her. He let his other hand travel down her body to cup her backside and pull her snug against his hard-on.

Okay, it wasn't subtle, but if he maintained his control, he could still go for the slow buildup.

Her body jerked against his as he squeezed her lower cheek and he had to fight a smile of triumph. She would have felt it in the kiss and he didn't want her to think he was getting smug, because holy hell, he sure didn't feel it. This woman challenged his vaunted control like no one had ever before.

He massaged her backside while taking their kiss to the next level, slipping his tongue out in a barely there caress along her top and then bottom lip.

Her lips parted and her tongue came out just to touch tip against tip. There was no stifling the growl of desire that elicited as arousal transmitted through his body with lightning bolts of pleasure at the small contact.

He rocked his pelvis against her, almost shouting in pleased satisfaction when her leg came up over his hip so their sexes were pressed into intimate contact. They were both straining against each other, trying to pleasure the other one. For his part, it was a double-edged sword. Every bit of pleasure he was hoping to give to this amazingly sensual woman was coming back on him and driving him toward a completion he was not ready for.

His body said otherwise, though.

He fought it while they writhed together on the bed, their kiss going carnal with full tongue play and heated meshing of lips. His only consolation as his plan to drive her crazy exploded around them was that she seemed as turned on and out of control as he was.

His climax took him by surprise, he'd been fighting it so hard. He shot pulse after pulse of ejaculate into his shorts for the first time in memory. Jillian's body went rigid against him, her pelvis moving in little jerky movements that said at least he had not gone over the edge alone. Craving her aftershocks like an addict craves his next fix, he thrust his sensitized but still hardened cock against the juncture of her thighs while stopping her from moving back with his hold on her sweet little ass.

Not that she was trying to move away. She was moaning and reveling in her pleasure, meeting his thrusts with her own. And her body jerked again and again in orgasmic aftershocks until he was rock hard again and ready to be naked.

He broke the kiss, gasping against her panting lips. "That was amazing."

"Yes."

"I can't believe we didn't even get our clothes off."

Jillian took a deep breath and sat up, giving him a brilliant smile. "Maybe we can do better next time."

Then she crawled off the bed faster than his stupefied brain could process the fact that she was leaving. She stopped halfway across the room and turned back to face him. "Good night, Alan."

He forced his trembling limbs into moving and reached her before she got her hand on the door. "We're done? Sweetheart, I'm definitely good for at least one more round."

She shook her head with apparent regret. "Sorry, no can do. I have to be at the studio before the birds are up tomorrow morning. I can't afford to show up looking like I need sleep."

Well, shit.

But he stepped back from her. "I wouldn't want to be the cause of you looking less than your best," he said with only an edge of sarcasm.

He was not going to be like a child who had his favorite new toy taken away. Even if maybe he did sort of feel that way.

Jillian's smile slipped a tiny bit, but she opened the door. "Well, I'll see you tomorrow. I think I might have an idea to help you with your research some more, but I've got to check some things with the powers that be."

"Thanks."

"No problem."

He leaned down and kissed her temple, then the corner of her mouth and then her lips in a gentle salute he had to force himself not to deepen or prolong. "Good night, Jillian."

She nodded and left.

Jillian stumbled to her room, her emotions in turmoil. What had just happened? Since when did she climax from dry humping? With hardly any foreplay!

And there at the end, when she'd felt his erection growing once again as her body shook with the prolonged pleasure that was usually impossible before multiple buildups without release—the desire to strip them both naked and ride his rigid dick until they both came so hard they passed out? Where had *that* come from?

She didn't remember the last man she'd wanted to do that with. Heck, had she ever wanted to do that? Certainly, it had been years since she'd wanted to take a man into her body. She'd already broken one rule for Alan—she wasn't going to throw the whole rule book out the window. Not even for the man who excited her more than any other had.

She hadn't even fantasized he was her longtime crush—the sexy Brazilian actor. In fact, the longer she knew Alan, the less the resemblance even registered.

She was so screwed.

She'd run on the pretext she needed her sleep, but the truth was, she had planned on at least two rounds tonight herself. For sure, spending longer in Alan's arms. But she just couldn't stay. If they had gotten naked like he'd wanted, Jillian's strict rule about the type of sex she shared with her partners was going to disintegrate. She could not afford to let that happen. Especially with Alan. He was a bigger risk to her emotions than anyone had been since she left home.

Well, okay . . . her love for her best friend made her vulnerable too, but it was within the acceptable risk category.

Amanda Brant was not the type of person to hurt others. She and Jillian had had something really important in common. They'd both been betrayed by their families. They'd both turned that betrayal into a determination to be emotionally honest themselves.

She needed to talk to Amanda.

Her pace to her room picked up and she grabbed her cell phone the second she shut and locked the door behind her.

Amanda answered on the second ring. "Hey, babe. What's up?"

"I think I'm losing my mind."

"What are the symptoms?" Amanda asked with a soft laugh.

"I'm breaking my rules . . . over a man."

"Oooh . . . he must be special."

"No. He's just a guy." But even as Jillian said the words, she knew she lied. And lying—even to herself—was something she avoided at all costs. "Okay, maybe a little special. He looks just like that Brazilian actor I've had the hots for the last year or so."

"Seriously?"

"As a heart attack."

"That's major hunk appeal. What about his body? Comparable?"

Before she could answer, Amanda screeched and then started laughing, the phone dropping with an audible thunk at Jillian's end to the floor. She heard, "Of course you're the sexiest man, Simon." Another laughing shriek. "No, really. I'm not lusting after the Brazilian. It's . . ." Soft giggles and the sound of kissing. "Jillian's crush. Not mine," she said in a breathy voice that Jillian knew only too well. Amanda got that way around Simon pretty consistently.

If there were parallels to her friend's reaction to her hunky husband and Jillian's reaction to Alan, she so did not want to examine them. Not even her policy of self-honesty was up to that task.

"Jillian . . . are you still there?" Amanda asked with a laugh.

"Of course."

"So, tell me more about the h-u-n-k."

"I can spell," Jillian heard Simon say in the background.

"Go away, we're having girl chat."

"Trying to get rid of me?" Simon asked in what was no doubt supposed to sound like injured tones, but only succeeded in sounding like a man absolutely smug with the certainty that his wife loved him above any other.

"Go see Dorrie. Your nephew gave her a set of toy construction vehicles he grew out of and she wants to go down to the beach with them. If you don't hurry, Jacob is going to beat you to it."

With another kissing sound, Simon was gone. Or Jillian assumed he was.

"Whew. It's just us now."

"Construction vehicles?"

"If her cousins have anything to say about it, that girl is going to grow up to be the ultimate tomboy. Not that I mind. She loves to dig in the sand with the remote-control bulldozer."

"Are you sure that's not Simon? Dorrie's a little young to be running remote controls."

"They're made with big toggles for toddlers, simple stuff . . . that's why her cousin grew out of them. But yeah, Simon loves them just as much. Only not nearly as much as the toddler-friendly computer he built exclusively for our daughter."

"You are kidding."

"Not even sort of. I understood starting her tae kwon do training when she turned two. He doesn't push too hard and it's something we all share, but the computer thing? Yikes!"

"You're just jealous she can't read investment reports yet."

Amanda laughed. "Give her another year."

Jillian shook her head, her conversation with Amanda grounding her like nothing else could have.

"So, tell me more about this guy."

"He's a reporter doing an article on the Vancouver film industry."

"Oh, that renter Bobby recommended?"

That's one of the things Jillian loved about her best friend—Amanda remembered the stuff Jillian told her as if it was really important. Even the trivial stuff. "That's the one."

"And he looks like your Brazilian crush?"

"Yep."

"Is that all?" Trust Amanda to know where to dig.

"Not exactly."

"So, spill."

"I like him."

"*Like him* like him, or just like him?"

That sentence might not have made sense to anyone else, but Jillian knew exactly what Amanda was asking. "Like him, like him. I want him."

"Whoa . . . you've been almost celibate for a while, haven't you?"

"Not on purpose . . . just, I've been focused too much on my career, I guess."

"Or you've grown past the point where casual liaisons do it for you."

"If that's the case, then how did I climax from a dry hump . . . a short dry hump? And practically nothing more than a kiss."

"Too long without release?"

"Right . . . I've got toys."

Amanda's silence was telling.

"You're blushing, aren't you?"

"Maybe."

"You're married and have a baby, hon."

"Yes, but we don't use toys. At least not the kind you're talking about."

"Oh, really. What kind of toys do you use?"

DEAL WITH THIS 99

"Never you mind. You did not call me to discuss my sex life with Simon."

"No, I called to get you to help me get my head back on straight."

"Maybe you're falling in love."

"Not happening," Jiliian said in a flat voice that brooked no argument.

"Even you aren't immune," Amanda said, ignoring Jillian's tone.

"Trust me, I am."

"Jillian, not every man is like your stepfather."

"No, some of them are like my dad ... or yours ... or your creep of an ex-husband, or wait a minute, some are only as slimy as your ex-boss."

"Then there's Simon."

"He's one of a kind. The mold got broken with him. Trust me."

"Well, I'm certainly not arguing that, but then you wouldn't be happy with a man like Simon. My guess is this reporter guy—"

"Alan."

"Alan. My guess is he's the kind of guy who challenges your sense of self. A man who is infinitely confident in himself and somewhat sexually aggressive. I bet he's got a great sense of humor and is kind to old ladies and dogs, passionate about his work, and works out at least three times a week."

Jillian sat in stunned silence for several seconds.

Chapter 8

"How could you know all that?" Jillian demanded.

"Listen, doll, I know what kind of man it would take to get you in such a tizzy."

"I'm not in a tizzy. How did you know about the working out? And it's pretty much every day as far as I can see."

"So, you two have that in common too, huh? And if he's got a body like that Brazilian guy? He so works out."

"It's gay guys and their harried landlady."

"Huh?"

"That he's kind to. I don't know about old ladies and dogs, though I can guess."

"So, you've met this amazing man who is perfect for you. Tell me again why you're all bothered about this?"

"First, I don't do perfect for me. Remember, I'm not looking for Mr. Right. I have always been content with Mr. Right Now."

"That's why you've been practically celibate for three years."

"I told you, I've been focusing a lot on my career."

"Yeah, and sex with Mr. Right Now left you feeling empty."

"Well, sex with Alan didn't, and he can't be Mr. Right because he's moving on in a few weeks."

"You've had sex?"

"The dry-humping thing, remember?"

"Sweetheart, I don't want to shock you, but that isn't sex."

"Yes, it is." She and Amanda had had this argument before. When Jillian had told her about her nonpenetration rule, they'd had a long discussion about what constituted a sexual encounter. Because Amanda had such amazing, whole-body, full-experience sex with Simon, she couldn't imagine anyone else being content with anything less.

"If you say so."

"He calls me that too."

"What?"

"Sweetheart."

"Sounds serious."

"Right. For all you know, he calls every woman he meets that."

"If he did, you wouldn't have mentioned it."

"He's only spoken to a few other women around me."

"And does he use endearments indiscriminately?"

"Not that I've noticed, no."

"I would have guessed that."

"Right."

"Right. Babe, you don't like fake people, and the whole using-endearments-for-perfect-strangers thing is so one of your unspoken pet peeves."

"If it's unspoken, how do you know it?"

"I'm your best friend. I can practically read your mind."

"So, what's going on in my mind right now?"

"You're scared spitless. The last thing you want is to get in a relationship with a man who could really hurt you, but what you've got to remember is that if you don't take the risk, you'll never know the joys either."

"Not all marriages are filled with joy."

"Not all of them suck either, and you know it."

"You and Simon notwithstanding—"

"What about Simon's brother and his wife? They are so totally in love still."

"Okay, so two examples."

"I could give you a lot more, but I know you. You're determined to focus on the negative side of relationships. It's how you protect yourself, but it's also what keeps you lonely."

"I'm not lonely."

"What about that famous Jillian self-honesty?"

"Okay . . . hardly ever lonely."

"I admit filling your house with boarders you could nurture was smart, but it's not enough."

"Says you."

"Says your heart, smart aleck, or you wouldn't be so nuts over Alan."

"I don't know what to do, Mandy. This hurts and he hasn't even done anything wrong yet."

"Love is like that."

"You're the expert now?"

"Yep."

"Oh, you are such a turkey sometimes."

"This from the woman who I had to physically restrain from talking the first time she met my future husband?"

"Well, you were being deliberately obtuse about the whole pregnancy thing."

"And you aren't trying to hide from the truth?"

"I don't know . . . am I?" Jillian asked in that voice only Amanda ever heard anymore. The one filled with vulnerability.

"I think you are, babe. Listen, bring Alan with you when you come down for our Christmas shopping extravaganza."

"You want me to bring him to meet you . . . and Simon?"

"Yes. He can stay with you in our house on the island. You can even share a room."

"I don't share rooms with my lovers."

Amanda snorted, but said nothing to that.

"It'll make Jacob jealous."

"He's in love with your profession, not you, goofball."

"Yes, well . . ."

"Are you going to bring him?"

"I'll think about it, but what I want to know is how to avoid breaking any more rules for this man."

"I don't know, Jillian. Maybe it's time you started breaking a few. Rules can protect us, but they can be barriers to our happiness too."

"Thanks, oh wise one."

Amanda laughed. "You really are a smart aleck. Don't teach that stuff to Dorrie."

"Like she'll need me to teach her."

"That's true . . . she's got Jacob as her surrogate grandpa."

Jillian laughed. "Whatever."

"See you soon?"

"Definitely. I can't Christmas shop alone."

"Not and have fun. Elaine's coming too this year."

"Oh, cool."

"Jillian?"

"Yeah?"

"Don't be too hard on yourself . . . or Alan either."

"I'll try."

"Love ya, hon."

"Love you too."

"I know."

And she knew Amanda did . . . but suddenly as she disconnected the call it struck Jillian that the only person she said those words to anymore was her best friend. She'd never even told little Dorrie her aunt Jillian loved her. She never said the words to her little brother either. She signed her e-mails and letters with love, but that wasn't the same as verbalizing it. Maybe it was time she called Darien . . . just to tell him she loved him.

But that didn't mean she was going to let herself fall in love with Alan. She definitely should not invite him to spend time with her and her chosen family. So why did the idea sound so unaccountably appealing?

*   *   *

The next day Jillian concentrated on trying to set Alan up for a more in-depth experience of the Vancouver film industry. And tried very hard to ignore everything else about her relationship with him. Which would have been more successful if her mind had not kept conjuring up images of what the guy looked like naked. She'd seen him in pretty skimpy workout clothes. She thought she had a good idea of what the reality might be like.

Particularly after feeling his hardness against her. He was big down there. Not horse hung, thank goodness, but bigger than average.

And that was exactly what she was not supposed to be thinking about.

She grabbed the phone and dialed a number to call in yet another favor to make this thing work out for Alan.

Alan was riding a piss-poor attitude with the tenacity of a champion bull rider. He'd had one of the best orgasms of his life the day before. Also the most embarrassing. He hadn't even gotten Jillian naked. And he'd been left wanting. His boner had lasted late into the night and he couldn't even try to take care of it on his own. No, his cock wanted to be buried in Jillian's silky, wet heat, not jacked off by a calloused hand.

He couldn't even decide if he was angrier with himself for coming so fast and easily, or Jillian for disappearing before he could redeem himself. And true to her word, she'd been gone from the house (no doubt at the studio) when he'd gotten up at six-thirty this morning. So not only was he horny, but he missed her.

Which only added to his piss-poor attitude. Missing a woman had no place in a wholly sexual relationship. And Jillian had made it clear that was all that was on offer. It was all he wanted, but damn it, did she have to be sure nothing could work between them? For the life of him, he couldn't figure out what he'd done this time to show a woman that he wasn't long-term-relationship material.

He wished his brother wasn't on assignment, deep cover somewhere in the Middle East. He could really use a friendly ear right now.

He didn't even consider calling his grandfather. The man had very set ideas of what a man did with a woman prior to marriage, and Alan knew his proposed sexual relationship with Jillian wasn't on that list.

Grandpa would tell him to either piss or get off the pot, but he'd be talking about asking Jillian to marry him. Which was so laughable, he could cramp a gut thinking about it.

"What did that poor painting do to you?" Hank asked from Alan's left.

Alan snapped out of his reverie and realized he'd been standing in the hall outside his room, glaring at a brightly colored abstract painting.

He forced a smile for Hank's benefit. "Not a damn thing."

"I'm glad to hear it. Jillian loves that thing. I'm sure you've noticed, but she's got a real jones for bright colors."

"Yeah, I noticed."

"Apparently, she's got a jones for you too."

"What?" Alan demanded.

Hank put his hands up in a placating gesture. "Don't worry, man. She rounded us all up this morning to explain why she was breaking her own rule."

"Are you serious?"

"Oh, yeah. That woman is almost painfully honest."

"How did everyone take it?" He could think of a couple boarders who might be frustrated by the double standard.

"Everyone was cool. I mean, we all know what a crush she had on the Brazilian actor who looks just like you."

"She's using me to live out a fantasy over some actor?" His already ugly attitude headed south.

Hank shrugged. "That's what Sierra and Gavin think. They're both jealous, by the way."

That startled a short if hard laugh out of him. "And you?"

"Personally, I think it's Jillian's house and she can do what she wants. How many landlords abide by the rules they set for their renters? She's too egalitarian for her own good."

"She doesn't want to be a hypocrite."

"You know her well."

"As well as I can for such a short time."

Hank nodded. "It happens that way sometimes." His face creased with grief. "Love can come quick and disappear just as fast."

Alan reached out and squeezed the other man's shoulder. "I'm sorry about Lonny, but trust me, whatever is going on between me and Jillian is not love."

Hank shook his head and actually laughed. It was a good sound to hear from the man who was hurting so much. "Don't tell me . . . you don't believe in love either? Oh, how the mighty fall. Mark my words, Mr. Reporter Man, you and Jillian are headed for the flames."

"Living out a fantasy is hardly the basis for a deep and meaningful relationship." The annoyed edge to Alan's voice surprised him. Okay, he was in a bad mood, but standing in for Jillian's crush should be no big deal. Right?

"I said that was what Sierra and Gavin believed. Me? I think Jill's met her Waterloo and you . . . Well, no straight man has got a chance resisting that woman."

"I'm not trying to resist her, but that doesn't mean we have a future. I'm going to be gone in a few weeks." Probably off on another assignment, meeting someone else like Jillian.

Right . . . like there was another woman in the world like his eccentric landlady.

"Perry and I have a bet about that. One I think I'll win."

"What's the bet?"

"I'll tell you when it's over."

"If I'm around to hear it."

"I've got a feeling you will be."

Well, hell.

"You're not at work?" Alan asked, not just to change the subject. He had an investigation to conduct, after all.

"Editing is caught up until today's shots are in the can. In fact, we probably won't be called in until shooting is finished for the season. That means we work a week later than the rest of the crew, but we'll still have Christmas off." This made Hank's face twist with grief again, but he pushed the pain away and Alan admired his ability to do so.

Hank was a quiet man, but clearly strong where it counted.

"So you have the rest of this week and next week off?"

"Not exactly. I work on other shows and have work to keep me busy most of next week, but I took a couple of days off to deal, you know?"

"I hear you."

"It's so hard to believe he's gone, you know? We only met a few months ago, but we just clicked."

Alan nodded.

"I'll tell you one thing, if they find the bastard who did it, they'd better keep me away from him. I've never been a violent man, but I've thought about buying a gun."

"Don't."

Hank nodded. "I know you're right. The last thing Lonny would have wanted would be for me to seek revenge."

"The perp will pay, trust me." If Alan's instincts were right and the murder was connected to his case, he'd make sure personally. He'd want to anyway, just to help Hank find closure. He'd seen too many families mourn loved ones lost or killed by undiscovered assailants. His years in the FBI had been far from all sweetness and light.

Jillian came bouncing into the house after six P.M. that night. As far as Alan could tell, she'd put in more than a twelve-hour day. What had her so excited?

When he asked, she grinned at him, pleasure sparkling in her eyes. "I've got a surprise for you."

"What kind of surprise?" Suddenly his rotten attitude

started dissipating. "Something personal?" he asked with a wink.

She laughed. "Well, that too . . . later. But get this! I managed to get you signed on as one of the background actors on call for the rest of this week's shooting."

"What do you mean?"

"You'll get an up-close and personal experience of the film industry, working from the inside. For a few days anyway."

"What? Don't you have to be union or something?"

"Actually, background actors can be union or not. Union actors get more perks and better pay, but studios can use walk-ons registered with an agency."

"But I'm not registered."

"You are as of today." She grinned.

The last thing an undercover federal agent needed was to be caught on film, but no way was he going to say anything to dim the light glowing from Jillian's eyes. Damn, she was beautiful when she was happy. She was gorgeous all the time, but she wore happiness well. And her idea for getting him behind the scenes wasn't a bad one.

"That's great, sweetheart." He noticed she blushed when he used the word. Interesting. She didn't seem like the kind of woman to blush.

He pulled her into a hug, burying his face in her neck and inhaling her scent. "Thank you."

"You're welcome, Alan."

"You smell good," he whispered against her neck.

She shivered. "Thank you. Must be my shower gel. I don't wear fragrances."

"I think it's you."

"Get a room . . . please, some of us don't need our noses rubbed in this little fantasy."

Alan lifted his head but didn't let go of Jillian at the sound of Gavin's voice. "So, you've got a crush on the Brazilian guy too?"

Jillian went rigid in his arms, but Gavin gave him a flirtatious smile. "Who wouldn't? The man is too beautiful for words."

"I'm glad to hear it."

"Why's that?"

"Well, it wouldn't be so good for my ego for me to be stand-in for some dog boy, now would it?"

Jillian made a choked sound.

Gavin cocked his head to the side and gave Alan an obvious once-over. "A man as sexy as you doesn't need his ego stroked. You ooze confidence, yeah?"

Alan shook his head and chuckled. "I need a lot of confidence to deal with the fact the woman who wants to play with me is thinking of some South American while we're kissing, don't you think?"

Now Gavin laughed. Hard. "Oh, Jill, darling, you've got feathers to soothe, I think."

"And you are flirting again," Perry said as he walked up.

Gavin gave a mock pout. "You make it sound like that's all I do."

"Well, if you need me to spell it outright . . ."

"Oh, you!" With that Gavin turned on his heel and flounced away amidst Perry and Alan's laughter.

Jillian was conspicuously silent.

Perry gently tapped the back of her head. "Wouldn't want to be you right now." And then he left too.

Alan just stood there and looked down at the woman in his arms, waiting for her head to come up and her eyes to meet his.

"Who told you?" she asked his chest.

She sounded so forlorn that he laughed out loud. "Does it matter?" He had no desire to get Hank in trouble with his landlady.

"I suppose not."

"It seems all your boarders knew about this crush . . . except me, of course."

Finally, her head came up and she tilted back to look him

in the eye. "Uh . . . there's this Brazilian actor, and um, you look amazingly like him."

"And you've been crushing on him for a while?"

"Yes," she said in a small voice he did not associate with her.

"So, I'm just the stand-in for a fantasy? You must have been really disappointed last night."

"No . . . on both counts."

He just looked at her, one brow raised.

"Really. Look, yes, I've had this silly crush—"

"I heard it was a serious jones."

He got to see Jillian blush again. "I guess you could describe it that way, but I'm not trying to live out a fantasy with you. I'm not. And last night wasn't disappointing. It was scary."

He looked around. "I think the other renters know enough about our personal business. How about if we move this discussion somewhere more private?"

"We could go to my room." As soon as the words left her mouth, Jillian looked stricken, biting her lip in agitation.

He'd be willing to bet she had a rule about allowing lovers into her room.

"Great, let's go," he said, perversely determined to take her up on her offer.

"We could talk in your room, if you'd rather."

"No."

Chapter 9

Looking resigned, Jillian led him to her room. It so clearly reflected the personality he saw inside her that he had to smile upon entering. Her sitting area was furnished with a beanbag love seat and two beanbag chairs, all of them in Day-Glo colors. Her bed had no head- or footboard and was covered in a bright patchwork quilt and lots of pillows. She had a desk, but it was the same shade of purple as her front door with a matching purple mesh office chair. In the center of the room, the hardwood floor was covered with a huge abstract throw rug. A much smaller purple throw rug was to the right of her bed, maybe so when she got up in the morning her bare feet didn't hit cold hardwood first thing. The walls were neon green with strategically placed artwork that reflected the style of the painting in the hall interspersed with promotional posters for old black-and-white movies.

A single floor-to-ceiling bookcase painted that purple that Jillian seemed to love had several shelves of books, but the two shelves eye level for her had pictures from what looked like the different acting jobs she'd had. He walked over to it. Dead center on the upper photo shelf was a family portrait of a beautiful brunette, a man who even Alan could admit women wouldn't find bad-looking, and a very happy-looking little girl who couldn't have been more than two.

"Who are they?" he asked.

"Amanda and her family."

Ah. His gaze shifted to a formal shot of a young man. "Who is this?"

"My little brother. That was his senior picture. He's not really little anymore. I mean, he's been taller than me since he was twelve. He's actually close to a foot taller than me. But he's still my baby brother."

"You babble when you're nervous."

"I don't get nervous."

He just laughed.

"Okay, maybe a little nervous, but it's impolite to point it out."

"Not honest?"

"Not the kind of honesty anybody needs."

That made him laugh again, but then he got serious. "Why scary?"

"I thought you wanted to talk about the crush thing."

"I do, but first I want to hear why last night scared you."

"It didn't scare me per se."

"You said it was scary."

"Well, that's different."

"If you say so, but talking around the question isn't going to make me withdraw it from the table."

"Your reporter interrogation technique is well developed."

If only she knew. "Yep. Now, why scary?"

She crossed her arms defensively. "It was intense, really intense for what it was. You know?"

"I noticed."

"So, it was intense for you too?"

"You couldn't tell? You really think I make it a habit of coming in my pants?"

"Um . . . I guess not."

"Oh, now I am offended."

"As opposed to how you felt when you learned I'd been crushing on your doppelganger for the last year or more?"

"I'm reserving judgment on the level of my offense over that one."

"So, now you want to talk about that?"

"Sure." He was having too much fun to just let it drop even if he didn't want to know for damn sure her response to him was not based on some misplaced fantasizing. The fact that the intensity the night before had scared her was pretty convincing evidence to the contrary, though.

"I wasn't thinking about him when we were kissing and stuff."

And stuff. He wouldn't mind doing some of that stuff right now, only naked. "So, I'm not just an attainable substitute?"

"No. Like I told Amanda last night, the longer I know you, the less I'm aware of the resemblance."

"You called Amanda about me . . . last night . . . when you needed to get your beauty sleep?" he asked carefully.

Oh, man, now she really looked chagrined. "I often call Amanda before I go to bed."

He just grinned. "What does she think of us?"

"We're not an us. We're . . ."

"Sex buddies."

Her lips twisted in a grimace, but she nodded vehemently. "Yes, exactly."

Fascinating conflicting body language.

"And what does Amanda think of that?" He wasn't sure why he was asking, but he wanted to know. He liked the idea she'd called her best friend after leaving his room. Though why he should, he damn well didn't know.

Jillian chewed on her bottom lip and then sighed as if coming to some decision. "She wants me to invite you to come with us when I go south for our yearly Christmas shopping trip."

"South?"

"We meet in Seattle to shop and then I spend a couple of days on the island with her and Simon. It's fun. They have an indoor pool . . . the house is something out of *Architectural Digest*. Amazing."

"When do you go?"

"The day after we finish filming. I, uh, usually go down that night and stay the night in a hotel so I can just crash and not have to drive hours early in the morning to meet up with her at the mall in plenty of time to shop."

"You must take the shopping seriously. Don't stores have Christmas hours this time of year?"

Jillian grinned. "Shopping is a serious endeavor. We spend hours at the mall."

"Do you break to eat?"

"Sure, lunch at one of the surrounding restaurants . . . they're all good, coffee at Starbucks at least twice. We know how to shop and keep our energy up."

"Maybe I can meet you for lunch. But man, hours in the mall? I'm thinking no." Besides, that would give him some time to meet up with a couple of contacts he had in Seattle. One of them might have heard some rumblings about the upcoming technology auction. He'd met one of them, a man, on one of his first operations for the FBI. The woman he'd met a few years later. Both had their fingers in more than one pie, but weren't the type to share information unless asked and preferably in person. He'd been considering making the trip on his own, even though it was a long shot.

"So, you want to come?"

"Are you inviting me?"

"Amanda will kill me if I don't."

Now, most men would probably take Jillian's lack of enthusiasm as a slam against them, but Alan? He considered it a challenge. This woman would not have told him about her friend's request she extend the invitation if she didn't want to. No matter how close she and Amanda were, Jillian was not a woman to be bullied by anyone into doing anything.

She was balking at letting him know she wanted him around . . . wanted him to meet her closest friend. Now, that didn't sound like she saw him as nothing more than a sex buddy. In fact, the whole concept of an "us" was sounding more like a reality than she cared to admit.

Again he didn't know why that pleased him. Was it his competitive nature? He didn't want to be the only one feeling stuff he didn't want to be feeling.

They'd both agreed this thing between them was just sex and he couldn't see how it could be anything more, not with either of their careers. A famous actress was the last type of woman an undercover agent could afford to have in his life on a permanent basis. Not that he should even be considering the whole concept of permanent. He'd learned his lesson on that score, hadn't he?

Even if he had and he damned sure meant to, he wasn't the least bit bothered that he was more than a simple sex buddy to Jillian. Their connection might be based on sex, but that didn't mean they couldn't be friends too.

Friends, yeah, that was it.

Jillian watched Alan look at her as if he was seeing through her or something. It was a weird feeling. She wasn't used to being invisible when she was with a lover. Not that she sensed she was invisible exactly, just he wasn't actually seeing her in the present. Yet something told her without a doubt she was the subject of whatever thoughts had put that faraway look in his eyes.

"Alan?"

He jolted as if shocked she was still there . . . or maybe he'd zoned off. "Yeah?"

"About the whole sex-buddies thing?"

"What about it?"

"Want to be buddies right now?"

Oh, those gray eyes just went to molten metal in a heartbeat. It was enough to make her feminine center pulse with anticipation.

"Tonight we get naked," he growled.

She grinned. "You don't want another mess in your pants?"

"Not going to happen."

She sauntered up to him and brushed the front of his pants where his erection was already showing itself. "It's not?" she practically purred.

He grabbed her wrist with an inexorable grip. "No, it's not. Get naked, sweetheart."

"You don't want to undress me?" she taunted.

He didn't even blink. "Not this time. I think I'll just watch."

"You going to return the favor?"

"Strip for you?"

"Yes."

"Count on it. I want both of us naked."

But he thought he would get less turned on watching her than taking her clothes off himself? Oh, poor man . . . he did have some things to learn.

Playing a sensuous Eastern song in her head, she started moving her body in an undulating pattern she'd learned for a stripper role she'd played early in her career. She'd aced the audition because she'd not only learned to dance like a stripper, but she'd learned to do it to music playing in her head so she could do it convincingly at the audition. It had worked. And considering the flare of his nostrils and narrowing of his eyes, it was going to work on the stud in front of her.

Slipping into the mental space where her body moved without her even having to think about it, she grabbed the hem of her thin, clingy sweater and started to slowly inch it up to the beat in her head, exposing skin to his hot gaze.

"You have a piercing in your belly button."

"Like it?"

"It's sexy as hell."

She smiled, concentrating on sending smoldering thoughts through her gaze. "Thank you."

She hesitated for a deliberate three seconds when her sweater hem reached level with the bottom of her bra.

Alan's jaw locked, his expression going feral. Wow . . . the more excited he got, the more primal . . . almost intimidating he was. Only it didn't frighten her. Far from it. It excited her, made her want to prove that she could match him in every way.

Then in an unexpected movement, she yanked her sweater off and tossed it aside. That earned her a low rumble from the man watching her with such primitive intensity.

Next, she unclasped her bra, letting the straps slide down her arms and the bra fall to the floor in one smooth movement. Reveling in the way her breasts felt those first few unfettered seconds, she lifted her hands to her head, burying them in her hair.

Alan groaned, his hands fisted at his sides as if he had to keep them curled in to stop himself from reaching out to touch her. Yes.

She loved the way the air felt against her breasts, but especially after she'd worn a bra all day long. The sensitive tips were already beaded, but they hardened and tingled at the different stimulation from the confines of her silk bra. This was one of the things the women in her group strove for, the ability to enjoy their own senses, the effects every little thing had on their bodies.

She'd been called a sensualist and she supposed that was exactly what she was, but she didn't think that was a bad thing. A woman should know her own body and the pleasure it was capable of feeling in and out of sexual situations.

When she'd saturated her consciousness with the freedom of being naked from the waist up, she dropped her hands to the button on her waistband. She undid it with a flick of one wrist, never ceasing the swirling movements of her body. Then she lowered the zipper one tooth at a time until it parted to show the top of her silk thong and the curls that peeked above the top.

"Natural redhead," he said in a husky voice.

"Was there any doubt?"

He smiled without diminishing the intensity of his look one little bit. "Not really, no."

She smiled back, feeling the smile somewhere deep inside her. This man did things to her. Really strange things.

She pushed her jeans down over her hips, toeing her shoes off as she did so. She turned, bent to take off first one sock and then the other, giving Alan a view of her naked bottom framed by the ultrathin straps of her thong.

Alan broke. She didn't hear him move, but she felt his hot, big hands on her hips as he hooked his thumbs in her thong and slid it down her legs until it fell to the floor.

She stepped out of it without moving away from that electric touch. Looking at him over her shoulder, she slowly straightened. "I thought I was supposed to undress myself."

"Jillian, has anyone ever told you that you are a freakin' tease?"

"I might be teasing you. I prefer to think of it as tantalizing, but as for being a tease? No way. I have every intention of seeing you satisfied tonight."

"Ditto, baby."

She let his hands caress her body as she turned in his hold. "Your turn." Some of the smug delight she was feeling in his reaction must have filtered into her tone because his eyes narrowed.

"You don't think I can match you?" he asked with a mocking look.

"I would be disappointed if you couldn't." And she would. Oh, she didn't expect him to undress like a male stripper, but she did expect him to challenge her in some way.

She went to step back, but he held her hips. "Stay there."

"If that's what you want."

"Oh, yeah."

He brushed his thumbs over her hip bones. "Tell me something, sweetheart."

"Yes?"

"Who do you think is more handsome feature for feature, your Brazilian actor or me?"

She looked at his face, studying it as he had meant for her to do, and found herself smiling. "He's not my actor, but in answer to your question . . . you."

"That's good to hear. What do you like better on me?"

"Your eyes. They're a darker gray . . . like molten silver right now. Your cheekbones are more defined . . . your jaw is just a little more square . . . more masculine."

He nodded and then lifted his black V-neck sweater over his head, revealing a perfect eight-pack underneath.

She seriously salivated at the sight, but it was the heat emanating from his naked skin, transmitting itself to her body that sent her pheromones blitzing. Darn . . . this man was hot.

"Like what you see?"

She realized her mouth was open on a gasp and she felt a flush climb up her cheeks, but whether it was embarrassment or arousal, she wasn't sure. "Impressive."

"I work at it."

"I've noticed."

"So, how do I compare to your crush?"

Oh, he was going to push this all the way to the end, wasn't he? "He has a beautifully defined six-pack."

"I have an eight-pack."

"And it's like cut glass."

"Nice of you to say so," he said in that sexy growl that sent her body into overdrive.

"You going to take off your pants?"

"Impatient much?"

She shrugged.

"You took your sweet time stripping."

"We didn't set a time limit."

He moved an inch closer. "No, we didn't."

Oh, the man was challenging her all right. Yum.

Finally . . . finally . . . he unbuttoned the top button on his fly. Of its own volition, her gaze slid down to watch with avid interest. He slid the zipper down slowly and she couldn't swallow back a moan. Who said women weren't turned on by the visual? Whoever it was had never had this man get naked in front of them. He was commando and his prick was hard. He'd adjusted himself while she was stripping, but she hadn't realized what he'd done. He'd made it so that as his fly opened the thick mushroom head of his prick poked out.

Oh my. What was that rule again? That . . . that could give a woman a lot of pleasure. Darn it.

She shook her head, trying to jostle loose the betraying thoughts. It didn't work, they just kept playing one different scenario after another in her head.

"What do you think? As good as what you fantasized about?"

"I never daydreamed about his cock."

"Right."

"Okay . . . maybe, but no . . . I never pictured quite that gorgeous."

"You think my dick is gorgeous?"

"Oh, please. I'm not the first woman to tell you so."

A strange expression crossed his features. "Actually, you are the first woman who has ever used that particular word to describe it. Other women concentrate on the size or maybe how hard it gets."

"Well, it's nice and big."

"Yeah."

"And it looks hard enough to drill through rock."

"It feels it."

"So, when do I get to see those amazing legs?"

"Amazing legs?"

"I saw them when you were lifting, remember? Very impressive."

"Oh, then I really need to let you see them now, don't I?" He moved closer again, though, making her have to tilt her head down farther to actually see his legs so close to hers.

Her forehead pressed against his hard pecs. A shiver of desire shook her body.

"You cold, baby?"

"No," she answered truthfully.

He chuckled, the sound low and sexy. "I didn't think so. I'm not the least bit cold either."

He was like a furnace, emanating heat from across the few inches that separated them. "No, I would definitely call you hot."

She could hear his smile. Don't ask how—she just knew it was there, pulling those sexy lips into a sensual curve.

He pushed his jeans down, revealing the muscular legs that had drawn her gaze down in the weight room. He flexed the muscles and she about choked on her own breath. Oh, this man? He knew how to turn a woman on.

He stepped out of his jeans and kicked them away, and it was then that she realized he was going barefoot. Sexy feet, perfectly formed . . . masculine. Big . . . but not too big.

Without the final confinement of his pants, his cock sprang toward her, pressing against her belly. Pre-cum moistened the tip and she wanted to taste so much, but that wasn't safe sex now, was it. Darn it.

"I've got to get a condom. I want that in my mouth," she said softly.

He cupped her cheeks and lifted her to meet his eyes. "I'm clean, Jillian."

"I can't take your word for it."

"I don't expect you to."

"You've got recent test results? With you?"

"Yep." He shrugged at her look of incredulity. "You never know when you're going to need them."

"Are you really that much of a horndog? I didn't peg you that way."

"No, but you will learn that I like to be prepared for any eventuality."

"You're serious?"

"Yes."

"What about me? My most recent test is four months old."

"Have you had unprotected sex in that time?"

"I haven't had any sex."

"I believe you."

"You're not supposed to."

He shrugged, as if it didn't matter.

"That should scare me . . . that attitude, only I get the feeling that you don't do this with other women, even if you do carry test results around with you."

"You're right."

"I don't want to take the time to get the paperwork right now."

"So, we use our hands for round one."

"Or a condom."

"You really want to suck latex?"

"No, but I can deal with it."

He just shook his head and pressed his lips to hers in a kiss so hot it singed her.

Chapter 10

The flavor of Jillian's mouth exploded across Alan's tongue and he closed his hands over her waist, lifting her body against his in an irresistible reflex. Without thought, he fit her mound against his hard cock and rotated his hips, rubbing his throbbing heat against her silken curls. It felt so damn good, he did it again.

She made a needy sound against his lips and this time he manipulated her body in a counterrotation as he moved his hips. Oh, yeah . . . that was good. Almost too good.

He was not coming again from a simple rub-off. Even if they had managed to get naked.

He wanted to touch this woman and he wanted to know the sensation of her fingertips against his skin.

Devouring her mouth, he moved toward the bed. The slide of his legs against hers as he walked added to the maelstrom of sensation buffeting him. Little sounds of want emanated in a steady stream from Jillian's throat and she brought her legs up to clasp around him, giving her the leverage to press her body even more intimately against his.

He tore her mouth from his and gritted his teeth against the orgasm trying to climb up his spine. "Damn, that's good, sweetheart."

This woman was lethal to his self-control.

She panted, her eyes half closed, her face flushed. "Oh, yes." She licked her lips as if trying to capture more of his taste from where his mouth had been pressed to hers. "Very, very good."

He'd reached the bed and he tipped her onto it, reaching around to unlock her legs from him.

She let him, but gave him a questioning look.

"Where is that dildo you were playing with the other day?"

Miss Sexual Suffragette herself blushed. "I wasn't playing with it."

"Whatever. Where is it?"

"Why, do you want to play with it?"

He just raised one eyebrow and waited for her to answer his question.

Looking more than a little intrigued and definitely turned on, she indicated the small nightstand with a tilt of her head. "In the top drawer."

He grinned. "Like to keep it close by, do you?"

She laughed, but she blushed again. "No comment."

He found the sex toy and returned to the sensual woman spread out on the bed in wanton abandon. He handed it to her. "Put both hands on it."

She obeyed with another curious look. "Like this?" She put both hands on the dildo in the same position she would use to give him a damn fine hand job.

He grinned. "Just like that. Now put your hands over your head."

Once again she obeyed without blinking.

"Love your uninhibited spirit," he purred his approval.

"I like to play."

"I do too." Though he instinctively knew that he could have the most intense, serious sex of his life with this woman as well.

He wasn't ready to go there yet; he might never be. But for now . . . they could have fun.

"Now, there are a couple of rules to this game."

"Oh, we're playing a game?" she breathed.

"Yes."

"What are the rules?" she asked with a look that said she could take whatever he could dish out.

Oh, man, Jillian was his ideal partner in making love.

"I'm going to touch you."

"Yum."

He laughed, the sound a little strangled by the desire riding him so hard. "If you let go of the dildo with either or both hands, I stop."

"Oh," she said in a husky, approving voice. "What else?"

"If I get you off in less than five minutes, I get to keep going."

"And if you don't?"

"You get a turn at touching me."

Pleasure sparkled in her green eyes. "Sounds good. Anything else?"

"You tell me if I do anything you don't like."

"I can do that."

He spread her legs, lifting her knees so she was completely open to him.

"Wait."

"What?" he asked, trying not to bark the word.

"I've got a stopwatch I use for exercise. It's in the top right drawer of my desk."

"I can see your alarm clock from here."

"Too easy to get sidetracked."

She had a point. He grabbed the stopwatch, set it for five minutes, but he didn't press the start button. He wanted to look at her. She was so damn beautiful. The freckles he'd noticed on her face were visible on her body as well, a light dusting over her milky white skin. Everything about her was perfectly proportioned . . . small, delicate hands grasping the naughty sex toy, toned limbs, a sexily indented waist, flat stomach he would expect of a television actor, but it was her sex that mesmerized him.

Flushed a reddish pink, lips full and swollen, glistening with the evidence of her excitement, the nub of her pleasure hardened and protruding just the tiniest bit.

"Are you just going to stare, or are you going to touch it?"

"Oh, I'm going to touch a hell of a lot more than between your legs."

"In five minutes?" she teased, but he could tell that his looking was having the effect he wanted.

It was exciting her. She was already on edge, just like him. Five minutes? More than enough time.

He leaned forward, huffing a breath of hot air over her clitoris without touching.

"Did you start the timer?" she asked on a moan.

"I'm not touching you yet."

"Cheating . . . oh . . ." Her words choked off as he blew a steady stream of air over her swollen pleasure button.

He clicked the timer on and dropped it as he snaked one hand up her side, skimming the soft skin with a barely there touch, leaving goose bumps in its wake. He fluttered the fingertips of his other hand against her inner thigh at the edge of her most intimate flesh. "You are so incredibly sexy, Jillian. I could touch you for hours. I want to feel you inside, to feel the clasp of your vagina when you come for me, the ripples of your pleasure squeezing me."

Those sweet needy sounds were back as Jillian's hips moved jerkily against the bed.

He cupped her breast, brushing the already hard nipple with his thumb while his other thumb trespassed into her heated wetness. "You are so tight. So wet. So damn silky."

She said something that came out a moan of jibberish.

He smiled to himself as his dick throbbed in sympathetic pleasure.

He slid his thumb out, only to replace it with two fingers.

She gasped. "Oh, darn . . . oh, yes . . . your fingers are so big."

She was going to strangle his cock when he finally got it inside her. He couldn't wait.

"Tighten around them," he ordered, wondering if she would comply and aid in reaching her own imminent orgasm.

She did a clasp and release that told him her outer muscles weren't the only ones she kept toned.

He rubbed back and forth, pressing upward until a strangled scream told him he'd found her G-spot. He continued to stimulate it while rhythmically caressing her breast, lightly pinching her nipple, then releasing it, over and over again. He let his thumb caress her labia just below her clitoris until she was writhing and moaning and biting back words that even only half formed sounded like begging.

Surging upward, he clamped his lips over her until-now-neglected nipple, pinched the one in his hand just a little harder than he had so far and pressed his thumb on her love button, swirling it while he pushed the two fingers inside her against her G-spot.

Jillian screamed and convulsed, her entire body going rigid and bowing up from the bed.

Alan moved his lips from her nipple to her mouth and kissed her through her aftershocks. He was lost in her taste when a continuous beeping infiltrated his consciousness. He reached blindly for the stopwatch, finding it near Jillian's foot. He pressed buttons until the beeping stopped, then cupped Jillian's face with both hands and deepened the already carnal kiss.

She made a mewling sound, her body restless beneath him. The temptation to bury his cock in her super-slick heat drummed against him. But talking about engaging in oral play without latex after seeing test results was a whole different thing from riding bareback.

He ground himself against the quilt, enjoying the friction but forcing himself not to press hard enough to get off.

When he finally managed to break the kiss, he moved to a kneeling position between her legs.

She looked dazed, satisfied, and just a little shocked. "I didn't think you could make me climax that quickly, no matter how turned on I was." She licked her lips, doing that postkissing tasting thing again. "At least not without a little direction from me. Which I was determined not to give you . . . until the five minutes was up."

He laughed, which made his prick bounce. "You underestimated your opponent."

"I don't know . . . I mean, according the game, you won, but I'm the one floating in postorgasmic bliss."

"You're too lucid for real bliss. I'll have to do better next time."

"Next time?"

"Remember the rules? If I win, I get to do it all over again."

Something passed through her eyes. "You're a very generous lover."

For some reason the praise made him uncomfortable, so he grinned and winked. "Maybe a competitive one."

But she didn't smile back and shook her head, a serious expression cast on her beautiful features.

He laughed. "You're really trying to deny my competitive nature?"

She did give him a small smile at that. "No, but I don't believe that's all it is. You really aren't as interested in finding your own pleasure as you are in seeing I have an excess of it."

He realized she was right. He'd never, not once, been accused of being selfish in the bedroom, but that was because he was a good lover. He went by the adage "She comes first." But never before had he actually not cared if he found completion or not. His dick was so hard it hurt, but he really wanted to see Jillian's face in ecstasy again.

Not knowing what to say, he just shrugged.

She nodded toward his throbbing cock. "It looks angry."

"Perturbed maybe, but not angry. He's having too much fun watching you."

She burst into laughter. "Okay, so you do have something in common with other men . . . talking about your penis like it's a separate entity. I don't know if you've noticed, but he doesn't have any eyes to watch me with."

He grinned. "Definitely too much sass for postorgasmic condition. And are you sure about the eye thing?" He gave his erection a nice long stroke before tipping it down so his "eye" winked at her.

She cracked up and then went all serious again. "I don't remember the last time I laughed so much during sex." She bit her bottom lip and looked at him through her lashes. "To be honest, I don't remember the last time I had so much fun with a man, period. Well, if you don't count Jacob. That man makes me laugh so hard, my sides hurt."

Alan dropped forward in a predatory rush and bracketed her head with his arms. "Jacob?" he asked, a low rumble sounding in his chest that he wasn't entirely sure he liked.

Her eyes widened. "Are you jealous?"

"Should I be?"

"No."

"Then I'm not. Now tell me who he is."

"Simon and Amanda's Man Friday and stand-in grandfather for their little girl."

"He makes you laugh?"

"Oh, yes. He'll make you laugh too. Trust me. Any man who enjoys pulling other people's chains as much as you do is going to appreciate that trait as refined as it is in Jacob."

"How old is this Jacob?" Alan asked, his tone only about half as humorous as he meant it to be.

"I don't know . . . fifty-ish, I guess. I would never dare to ask him."

"I see. I look forward to meeting him."

"Trust me . . . you two are kindred spirits in some ways. He was Secret Service before he went to work for Simon. He had unrequited fantasies of living out undercover roles which he has since found an outlet for in amateur theater and even doing a walk-on, single-line part for my show."

Alan and this Jacob guy had more in common than she knew.

He felt a small, feminine hand wrap around his hard-on. He sucked in a breath. "You let go of the dildo."

"We haven't started the second round of our game."

"We haven't?"

"We're talking."

"You mean you expect me to touch you in silence."

"Oh, no . . . your sexy talk is half the fun, I think."

He smiled, more pleased than he wanted to admit. "You don't get your turn to touch until I finish with mine."

"I get the feeling that if we stick with that, you'll send me into an orgasmic oblivion without ever coming once yourself."

"Would that be so bad?"

"No, but this . . ." She squeezed his aching cock and he groaned. "This feels like it could use just a tiny bit of attention."

Then, without further discussion, she changed the rules of the game with a single downward stroke. It only took a few caresses and he was bucking in her hand, spewing his hot ejaculate all over her stomach and breasts.

His mouth slammed down on hers and he plunged his tongue into her mouth like he wanted to do with his prick in her body. All too soon, he became extrasensitive and stopped all movement. Jillian sensed it and stopped moving her hand too, just letting it rest, fingers loosely wrapped around his still-hard member. Man. Would he ever go down around her?

His body shuddered and he had to concentrate on not collapsing on top of her. "I'd better get a towel."

"For what?"

"To clean you up."

"The White Tigresses teach their novitiates to rub a man's

come into their body as often as possible. They believe it keeps them looking young."

"Does it work?"

"According to them, yes. But a couple of scientific studies have shown that there are things in it that are actually really beneficial for the skin . . . even more effective than alpha-hydroxy lotion."

"You're kidding, right? No one actually did that kind of study."

"Oh, yes, they have. Don't you know researchers will experiment on pretty much any premise, especially when it comes to the male preoccupation with his sexuality?"

"Excuse me, but this sounds like women preoccupied with that very thing."

She laughed softly. "I may have to concede that point."

"So, you're, uh, not going to rub it into your skin, are you?" One the one hand, the idea of watching her do that was really hot, but he wanted to use his tongue on her body this next go-round and that was so not going to happen if his come was on her.

She giggled. "Not this time. I've discovered how talented your hands are; I think I want to see what you can do with your tongue."

"It's almost scary how alike we think."

"I know." But she didn't sound like she was joking at all.

Not ready for a serious discussion, not sure he ever would be, he pulled away from her and made a quick trip to her bathroom in search of a washcloth and hand towel. He found both and got the washcloth wet with hot water, then kept it clutched in a ball in his fist to keep as much heat in it as possible on the trip back to the bed.

He washed Jillian, using the washcloth not only to clean her, but to caress her and sensitize her skin.

"Mmmm . . . that feels good." She stretched like a sleek little cat.

"It's supposed to."

"Does that mean the second round has started?"

"Contrary to your assertion, the game never stopped."

"So, what are the rules for this round?"

"Multiple orgasms within two minutes of each other."

"And if you succeed?"

"I think you know the answer to that."

"You get to do it again?"

"Yes."

"I have an early call at the studio again tomorrow. I need to sleep sometime tonight. And eating wouldn't be out of the realm of desirable events either."

He looked at the clock. They'd been playing for about an hour and a half. She should probably go to sleep in about an hour. "I'll feed you now," he said as he headed toward his discarded jeans.

"I can come with you. We can make sandwiches or something together."

He shook his head decisively. "You need to conserve your energy. Believe me."

"I do." She winked. "But remember what goes around comes around, yeah?"

"I'll look forward to it."

"You do that."

He'd finished doing up his fly and headed for the door. "Be back in a sec."

"I'll be waiting."

"You do that," he said with just the smallest tinge of mockery.

Her laughter followed him out of the room.

The other boarders were drinking tea at the kitchen table when Alan entered.

Sierra gave a wolf whistle while Gavin pretended to faint and Perry caught him, taking his time righting the other man in his chair.

"Some women have all the luck," Sierra said with a chuckle.

"You should give some warning before flashing those abs," Hank said with surprising humor.

Gavin just sighed and Perry grinned, giving Alan a commiserating look.

"I didn't realize you all would be down here when I came in search of food."

Sierra got up and headed for the fridge. "We saved you two some dinner."

"Thanks." Alan looked at the others and got one of those feelings, the one that said he'd walked in on something a suspect didn't want him to see—or hear.

Considering the fact that he doubted his housemates were conspiring to sell pirated technology, much less aware of the fact that he was a spook, that left the probability they had been talking about him.

"So, what's got you all hanging out at the kitchen table?"

"You don't think a cuppa is a good enough excuse?" Perry asked with a half smile.

"You saying it is?"

"You're good at that," Sierra said as she started heating plates in the microwave.

"What might that be?"

"That . . . the whole reporter's interrogation without answering any questions yourself thing. I've noticed it before when we were talking."

"Jillian said the same thing." And damned if that wasn't something an agent did not want to hear.

Okay, so both Sierra and Jillian had put his interrogation technique down to his being a reporter, but was it really that noticeable? He'd never believed so before. Maybe it was the fact that they thought he was a reporter, so they were looking for it. Of course, just about any man could be private as hell and use his own questions as misdirection.

Gavin stirred sweetener into his tea. "I'm not surprised she

noticed. She notices pretty much everything about you. Has
from the first."

"That bother you?" Alan asked.

"Depends."

"On what?"

"On what you are going to do with her." For the first time
since Alan had met the man, there wasn't even a trace of
humor or obvious dramatization in his demeanor. Under his
hot pink spiked hair, his expression was intent, like he was
trying to see inside Alan's head.

"What we do together is between her and me, don't you
think?"

"Well, that's just it, we're not so sure." This time it was
Hank talking.

"How do you figure that?"

Perry spoke. "Jillian is important to us."

"She's our friend," Sierra added.

Gavin nodded. "She cares for us . . . we care about her."

Alan didn't get offended. He liked the fact that Jillian's
friends were looking out for her. He wasn't going to let
them dissuade him from enjoying a physical relationship
with her to the fullest, but he could appreciate the effort. "I
can't be the first man she's found interesting since you all
moved in."

"The fact is, as much as she might not like us telling you
this . . . you are." Sierra put the dinner plates on a tray and
added silverware, drinks, and napkins.

Stunned, Alan's body jerked in concert with his mind.
"No."

Perry sighed and ran his fingers through his hair. "Yes.
Look, for all her liberated ideas about women being comfortable with their own sexuality, she hasn't been indulging them
since I moved in."

"Maybe she doesn't bring men home, but that doesn't
mean she has been celibate."

Sierra leaned against the counter, crossing her arms and fixing Alan with a no-nonsense look. "Look, we work with Jillian . . . we live with Jillian . . . we socialize with Jillian. Unless she's having flings when she goes to visit her friend in Washington, you're a total anomaly in her life."

Chapter 11

"She's been really focused on her work, no doubt about it, but I still think the fact she's breaking her own rules for you means something here." Gavin copied Perry's earlier sigh. "Listen, normally we would never talk about her like this, but we don't want to see you hurt her."

"I can appreciate that." Alan let his gaze travel from one person to another until he'd met each of their gazes. "I do. But you have to let Jillian make her own choices."

"We know that," Hank said, not sounding particularly happy about it, though.

"I can't promise you that I won't hurt her, but then I can't promise she won't hurt me either. It's the risk we've both chosen to take."

Perry stood up and crossed to Alan, clasping his shoulder in a universal gesture of male understanding. "We know that. We only want to make sure you realize that despite Jillian's rhetoric, it's probable her emotions are more involved than she's willing to admit. Just keep that in mind, okay?"

Alan wasn't sure he agreed. Jillian had been adamant that their relationship was no more than sex, but he wasn't going to offend her friends by dismissing their concerns. "I will."

Perry nodded, letting his hand fall from Alan's shoulder. "Thank you."

"You don't have to thank me. I think Jillian is pretty special too."

Perry's smile was knowing. "I never doubted it."

"Uh . . . Alan," Gavin said from his seat at the table.

"Yeah?"

"We would appreciate it if you didn't mention this conversation to Jillian."

"She's got a pretty spectacular temper, and unlike most people with a temper, she doesn't just blow up and let it blow over. She gets even."

"I'll keep that in mind."

"You'd be smart to," Perry said in a tone of amusement.

"So, what you are telling me is that Jillian really can take care of herself?"

"Yep, but that doesn't mean she has to."

Alan found himself smiling. "That's good to know." He picked up the tray Sierra had prepared and winked at her. "Thank you." He let his look encompass the rest of them. "Don't worry. I won't tell her about you all warning me off."

Sierra gasped. "That's not what we meant."

He laughed. "I know." In fact, if he was reading these people right, they were hoping he would develop a serious relationship with Jillian.

How they all thought that was supposed to happen with him leaving in a few weeks, he wasn't sure, but it was clear they thought Jillian had more at stake than a mind-blowing orgasm, or ten.

Hank shook his head. "You've got a twisted sense of humor, Alan."

"I've been told that once or twice in my life."

Hank just shook his head again and Alan left the kitchen with the tray, glad the other man was looking a little less lost than he had been earlier. He figured his housemates didn't just look out for Jillian, but they looked out for each other too. They were good people.

He had to remind himself that people who sold other people's secrets weren't always as smarmy as Arthur Prescott. Truth was? Most of the bad guys had a little good in them, some even a lot of it. People had all sorts of motives for breaking the law and it wasn't always about self-interest. Alan had seen things in the Bureau that had taught him the criminal world was as diverse as every other cross section of society. There might be a predominance of certain character traits, but he couldn't afford to dismiss someone as a suspect because they exhibited different ones.

Jillian waited for Alan's return, her entire body tingling with the aftereffects of pleasure. When he'd said he would use his hands, she would never have guessed they were so talented. Most men didn't take the time to develop their ability to pleasure a woman with anything but their cocks and maybe their mouths, but there was so much more to sex than a little sucking and intercourse.

She'd never had a lover who fit her so perfectly. It was terrifying but incredibly wonderful too, and no way was she giving this ride up until it was officially over.

She figured pain waited for her at the end, but she'd had enough pain in her life to know when to appreciate the chance at pleasure to make up for it.

The door opened and Alan walked in carrying a tray with dinner on it.

He smiled. "Sierra had saved food for us and fixed us up when I wandered into the kitchen."

Jillian smiled. "Did they give you the don't-hurt-my-friend lecture?"

If she hadn't been looking for it, she wouldn't have seen the barely there flare of his eyes before his face returned to its former bland expression. "I didn't say anyone else was in the kitchen."

She snorted. "I know my friends, and if Sierra was there, chances are the others were too. And if they were all there, they were probably talking about us. It follows they wouldn't be able to refrain from saying something. They think they know me better than I know myself."

"Do they?" Alan asked quietly.

"That's always a possibility with close friends, but there are parts of my life that they know nothing about."

"Who does?"

"Amanda, and I imagine she's told Simon."

"No one else?"

"No."

"So you're saying they're handicapped in reading your motives by not having all the pieces?"

"Something like that."

"You know, I might agree with you if I hadn't spent my career assessing motives based on limited evidence and usually being right."

"Not everyone shares your perception. It must make you good at your job."

"It does." Then he gave her a strange look. "Usually."

"Well, we're all fallible."

"I never was before."

"What do you mean? Are you having a hard time writing the piece on the film industry because of our association? I would think it would give you a more intimate view."

"You would think that, wouldn't you?"

He brought the tray to the bed and set it down. "No more talking about me and my work. You aren't going to sidetrack me from my plans that easily."

"You're assuming I want to?" she asked with disbelief. What woman wouldn't want more of what he'd given her earlier?

"If I did my job before, no."

"Oh, you did your job, all right." She grinned and then started eating. She was starving and she could tell Gavin and Sierra had cooked tonight. The food was delicious. They were a good team in the kitchen despite how they snarked with each other.

Alan appeared content to let her eat and to finish his own dinner in silence, though his hot gaze played over her naked body between bites. She made no bones about preening for him, sitting with one foot dangling off the bed and her other knee raised, shielding her secrets from him temporarily while allowing him an unfettered view of her torso. Nipples that had softened while she waited for him to return went turgid under the heat of his perusal.

He noticed too, his nostrils flaring in arousal, but he continued to eat as if the sexual tension between them wasn't climbing faster than summer temperatures in the desert.

Darts of sensation zinged from place to place on her body, keeping her constantly aware of what was to come. Funny, but they followed the path of his eyes. How did he do that? Make his gaze as tactile as brushing fingertips?

She tried to return the favor, but looking at his studly body clad in nothing more than a pair of painted-on jeans only added to her own excitement. A shiver of awareness went through her, not just awareness of his sexy body before her, but the sense that maybe she had actually met her sexual match. She inhaled a short breath as shock coursed through her. It had just been too long since her last sex partner. That was all. He was only going to be here for a few weeks and by then, her libido would get satisfied and settle down.

It had to, because what would she do if it didn't?

Jillian didn't move as Alan took the food tray from the bed and put it on the desk. He came back and stood in front of her, saying nothing. At least with his mouth. His body spoke volumes. The way he stood there, his feet planted about a foot apart, his thumbs hooked in his pockets said, I'm ready to conquer new territory and I darn well know I can do it. His eyes said, I really liked what we did before, but now I'm ready to blow your mind. The loose curl of his fingers against his hip bones said, I know how to touch you. His heat reached across the distance between them to say, I can warm you up until you burn.

Her body shook with anticipation. She would be embarrassed by that reality except that she could tell he liked it . . . a lot.

After what felt like minutes, but could have been mere seconds, of this silent communication, he said, "Lie down, sweetheart."

"Aren't you going to take off your jeans?" Oh, man . . . talk about a husky tone. Her directors would love it if she could pull that tone off during a love-interest scene, but it was a timbre she'd never heard come out of her own mouth.

In answer he disposed of his jeans with unhurried, smooth movements.

She swallowed as his erection came into view. Didn't the man ever go soft? The same desire to taste she'd had earlier assailed her and she knew if she didn't do as he'd suggested and lie back, she was going to do something about that craving.

Positioning herself as she had been earlier, she took the dildo that was hidden in the pillows in a grip with both hands, stretching her arms above her head.

"Turn over. I want to start with your back."

"You know, you're really bossy."

"You like it."

Shocked by the truth of that statement, she flipped onto her stomach to avoid letting him see her reaction and simply said, "Just remember, what goes around, comes around."

"Like I said before . . . I can't wait."

She grinned against the bed. That was all right, then. She felt a lot better about liking his assertive lovemaking knowing that he was confident enough to let her return the favor.

Rational thought took flight just then as his tongue swiped right up her instep. "Oh!" she gasped against the bed.

"Like that?"

"Yes," she groaned as he did it again.

While his hands ran up and down her legs, he gave first one foot and then the other a tongue bath. It was incredible as his tongue touched spots that seem to have a direct link to her aching feminine center. She whimpered in a way she never would have done if it didn't feel so incredibly good. She couldn't help the sounds coming from her. If she tried to hold them in, she would explode and not in a good way.

His mouth moved up her legs, holding them together so he could flick back and forth between them with his tongue. Even his hold on her could not stop the tremors shaking her body as pleasure built inside her. When he reached the apex of her thighs, he pressed her boneless legs apart and took a single swipe of her wet labia with his tongue before moving right up to the small of her back. She'd been touched there before. Of course she had. And she knew it felt good, but she'd never been licked there . . . or nibbled . . . or sucked. He was going to leave a mark and instead of irritating her, the idea turned her excitement up another notch. He concentrated on that highly sensitive spot for a long time as if he was in no hurry to get anywhere else.

When he finally did move on, it was to touch the rest of her back. Not massage . . . every shimmering touch was intended to arouse, but when he reached her nape, she cried out. It felt so good.

He buried his nose in her neck. "You smell so good, have I told you that yet?"

He wanted her to talk? "Don't remember," she managed to mumble. Maybe he had—yes, she thought so, but thinking was a major challenge right then.

He nuzzled against her. "You do. It's unique to you. Turns me on."

"Uh . . ."

His teeth closed over her nape gently, not biting, but claiming.

"Oh . . ."

"I think I'm finally getting it right. You're not talking in whole sentences."

She just moaned as the whisper against her skin sent shivers all down her spine.

He was lying beside her, his hardness nestled against her backside. "I think it's time to roll you over. I'm about a second from making the tiny adjustment it would take for me to slip into your wet heat. But I didn't see any condoms in your bedside table."

Of course not. She never brought men to her room. Well . . . she never brought men anywhere for the last while, but he was right. Good thing he was thinking because she wasn't. Because she wanted to tell him to slide his hard cock right into her pulsing vagina.

She had to bite her lip to keep the invitation from coming out.

Completely unaware of her weakness, Alan gently turned her onto her back, whispering compliments and sexy promises against her skin as he did so.

Her legs fell open in unspoken invitation and he did that single swipe thing with his tongue again, only this time lingering a short while on her clitoris. Oh, wow . . . just . . . darn . . . so good. A couple more swirls of his tongue and she'd come, but he didn't stay down there.

This time he started with her head. Kissing her eyelids, licking along their seams with the very tip of his tongue before nibbling and kissing all over her face, her ears, the front of her neck. He did that same bite thing on the front of her neck as he'd done on her nape and it felt just as good and surprisingly right.

He lowered his body against her, letting his steel-like hardness rub right against her pleasure spot. How did he do that so unerringly? Was this man some kind of male geisha, or what?

Oh . . . her thoughts were getting really confused now, weren't they? He was a reporter. She remembered. He said so.

The tension inside her spiraled tighter and tighter, but just when she was about to come, he lifted his pelvis. She would have screamed her frustration, but his mouth was now mat-ing with hers, his tongue dominating and arousing at the same time. She tried to find the friction she needed again, but one of his hands went down and pinned her hips to the bed.

Oh, goodness, the man was strong. Very, very strong. One hand . . . she couldn't move even an inch.

He kept pillaging her mouth while his free hand began to caress the front of her torso. He didn't focus entirely on her fleshy mounds, but he didn't ignore them either. Every touch against one of her nipples made her try to gurgle out a demand for more. But he had his own agenda and she wasn't going to change it.

He brought her a hairsbreadth from climax twice more as she grew increasingly delirious with unsatisfied need. Sweat was running in rivulets down her body, soaking the quilt beneath her. But that was nothing compared to the slippery wetness she felt between her thighs. The wet spot was supposed to come from post–male climax when a condom wasn't used, not a woman's pleasure turned up so high she soaked the fabric beneath her. But Jillian could feel the warm wetness against her butt cheeks.

She whimpered and begged when Alan's mouth wasn't covering her own. Her head tossed back and forth, the hair around her temples soaked with sweat too.

"Please, Alan, please!" she cried, desperation giving her strength as she managed to lift her body against his.

He growled, that sexy, beautiful sound almost setting her off all on its own. Almost. But, darn it, not quite.

Then his mouth claimed hers with brutal intensity as his hips lowered again and his erection pressed against her ultra-sensitive, swollen clitoris. He humped against her, once, twice, three times and she exploded with the most amazing climax of her life. It went on and on and on and on, until she realized that one climax was rolling into another and her body's pleasure rigor was actually holding both her and Alan's bodies a few inches off the bed.

She could feel that familiar wetness pulse between them again and somewhere in her consciousness she realized he'd climaxed as well, but he didn't stop moving and her body continued to convulse until she was only vaguely aware of the world around her. She finally collapsed back on the bed, totally and completely melted, her brain shorted out so not even complete thoughts would form, much less words from her mouth.

"Your bed," she slurred, barely conscious.

"I'm comfortable here." He pulled her into his arms and she let him, her brain shutting down entirely.

Alan waited until Jillian was deeply asleep before sliding from the bed and going to the bathroom for another wet washcloth. He brought it back and cleaned the obvious streaks of his ejaculate from their bodies, but he didn't want to erase the scent of their lovemaking completely, so he didn't wash away her sweat or the copious wetness between her legs.

When he was done, he tucked them both under the quilt and pulled her back into his arms. He should probably return to his room. He had a feeling she would be way more comfortable with that situation in the morning, but a perverse part of him didn't want her comfortable. He wanted, no needed, to have an impact on her. He didn't wonder why he wanted to be different from her other sexual partners, merely accepted that he did.

Smiling at the success of his assault on her senses, he let himself fall asleep.

Jillian woke to the sound of her alarm. Disoriented, she tried to reach for it but there was a rocklike mountain in the way. Oh . . . a warm mountain. Smelled good. Like sex.

Oh, my gosh, her brain screamed as she sat straight up, the heavy arm around her waist completely freaking her out. Alan had slept in her bed last night. She'd let him.

She reached across him and pounded the alarm button to shut it off.

He smiled up at her, sexy as anything, first thing in the morning. "Good morning, beautiful."

"Um . . . hi. You're in my bed."

"Funny how that works. I went to sleep here last night and woke up this morning."

"I think I passed out from pleasure."

"Seemed like it, yes." Even in the filtered darkness, she could see the smugness of his expression.

"Last night was amazing. Thank you."

He reached up and brushed his thumb along her jaw. "Thank you, sweetheart. Your trust, your openness to everything I did . . . it was the single most beautiful response I have ever had."

Oh, man, did he have to be so perfect . . . even the morning after? Of course, the fact that he was in her bed was not exactly perfect. "I don't usually sleep with my—" She stopped herself just before she called him her lover. She'd done it in her mind on a few occasions, may even have used that word with Amanda, but no way was she going to use it with him.

"Men?" he prompted.

Heat climbed up her cheeks and she was grateful for the relative darkness. "So, you were too tired to go back to your own bed?" she asked, ignoring his comment.

She wasn't about to get into the fact that using men in the plural wasn't accurate . . . at least for the past three years.

"You felt too good in my arms to let go."

"Oh."

"Do you mind?"

She should say yes. It was a rule, after all, but she couldn't make the word come out of her mouth. She shook her head, but at least was able to prevent a verbal negative from slipping past her tightly closed lips.

"Maybe we can do it again." He didn't make it a question, so she didn't answer.

"I need to get ready for work. So do you, actually. You're scheduled to join the background actors today."

"Okay." He sat up, kissed her gently, and then climbed from the bed, his morning erection not a lot different from the ones he'd had the night before.

He grabbed his jeans, pulled them on, and left the room without doing up the fly. "I'll be ready in twenty minutes."

"Give me a half an hour." The stylists were going to freak because she was going to have to wash her hair this morning, which meant they were going to have to dry and straighten it before she could start filming. They'd asked her if she would consider having it permanently straightened and she'd refused. Her curls were her cover, but more than that . . . they were who she really was.

Chapter 12

Alan ran through possible scenarios of how to avoid actually ending up as a "meat prop" on Jillian's show. Maybe he could ask to be one of the aliens that required significant transformation, in the interests of experiencing another facet of filmmaking.

When he suggested the possibility, Jillian nodded. "Great idea. Only none of the aliens in today's filming are big transformations, but you can at least experience a minor make-up transformation."

As he sat in front of a mirror, being made up by a chatty young woman with more piercings than the owner of a tattoo parlor, he had to fight a grimace at the lack of success of his plan. Not only had he not managed to avoid being recognizable, but he was wearing make-up for the first time in his life and had pretty much guaranteed he would be used in the background on today's shoot.

He bit back an expletive, knowing the girl doing his make-up would not understand his need to vent and would most likely take it as a personal slight against her handiwork.

"I do some of Gavin's make-up too, you know? He's a regular on the show."

"That's, uh, quite the coup."

She nodded, sending her multiple dangling earrings tinkling against each other. "It really is. My mom couldn't believe it when I told her. He bats for the other team, you know?"

"Yeah."

"Hey, I heard you know one of the show's stars."

"Jillian Sinclair," he said, seeing no benefit in trying to deny it.

"She got you this gig, right?"

"Yes. I'm a reporter and I'm doing an article on the Vancouver film industry. She thought this would be a good chance to get a personal view."

"That sounds like her. She's really smart, you know?"

"I know." But his little witticism was lost on her.

The make-up artist simply nodded. "Gavin isn't a slouch either, you know?"

He just grunted agreement this time because she was doing something with his lips that he was fairly sure a guy was not supposed to have done. If he had pouty, kissy-face lips outlined in red when she was done, he was going to wash the whole damn thing off. He was.

"He's really nice too. Not stuck up like some can be."

Again, he was forced to make a sound of agreement without moving his head.

"He's been kinda weird lately, though, you know?"

"In what way?" he asked through barely parted lips.

"Oh, you're a natural. You did that really well. I hate working on someone who doesn't realize they need to try to keep still while make-up is being applied. Some actors are just so antsy, you know?"

What he wanted to know was what she meant by Gavin acting weird. "Gavin," he prompted.

"Oh, yeah. It's like he's sneaking around or something. I saw him coming out of the studio office and it wouldn't have even registered, you know? He's a regular, right? He could pretty much be anywhere."

"I know," he said before she could use her favorite phrase.

"Right. Well, like I said, I wouldn't have noticed except the way he looked around all sneaky like, trying to see if anyone noticed him. I did, but even nice actors don't really see me as a person of importance, you know?"

"Which office was he coming out of?"

"Well, that was the other strange thing. It's the empty one the execs use for visitors who need an office, or anyone who needs a place for a business meeting but doesn't have their own trailer or office, you know?"

Well, shit. He did not like the sound of this. He did not want Gavin to be his guy. The little flamer had grown on him. He'd even gotten used to and maybe even liked the pink hair and the eye color that changed daily from contacts.

"All done," the make-up artist announced. "What do you think?"

He looked in the mirror. Well, he resembled an alien all right, but his features were recognizable enough that they would register as familiar with most viewers' subconscious if not conscious mind. There were scenarios where that could lend credence to a cover, the sense of familiarity, but lots where it would work against him.

He would have to come up with Plan B, and before he ended up on film.

"You're amazing," he said as sincerely as he could.

She beamed and he figured he'd come off right.

Once he rejoined the background actors, he discovered what Gavin had meant about sitting around for hours waiting to work. He used the time to chat and encourage those who liked to gossip like his make-up artist to do so. He didn't hear anything valuable for the first hour and a half. He thought he was on to something when several of the background actors complained about the increased security on the lot, but none of them seemed to know why the producer had instituted the measures. Several were appalled that while the studio's security increased, the parking lot was not monitored and Lonny had been mugged and killed.

Some made noises about refusing to show up for a casting call for the show, but Alan easily recognized the comments for the hot air they were. Most of these actors were desperate to "get noticed" and maybe get upgraded to a regular actor on this show, or any other.

One man didn't sound particularly worried about his role as a background actor, though. A nice-looking blond, Taylor exuded a sense of peace that most of his fellow actors seemed to lack. He told a story about another background actor who had been so nervous that his stiff posture during filming caused the casting director to actually remove him from the set and replace him with someone else.

And Alan had Plan B.

Be a lousy background actor and get removed from the set. He told the others that this was his first time doing the background thing and got loads of advice. All of which he listened to closely and determined to do the opposite of.

It was just before lunch that he finally got some scuttlebutt on why the change in the security measures had been made. From Taylor. He was telling one of his stories when something he said started the other extras complaining again.

Taylor sighed. "Look, I know they're annoying, but you can't blame Frost Productions for wanting stronger safeguards after what happened."

Alan knew he wouldn't have to be the one to ask what the blonde meant. These people had proved that they loved their gossip. He had to wait less than two seconds before someone else asked the question he wanted the answer to.

"What happened?"

Taylor grimaced. "You don't know?"

"If I did, I wouldn't have asked." Oh, the snark was thick.

"Someone broke into the editing lab."

There were several gasps around him and Alan felt that tingle that told him this was something he wanted more information on. "Was anything taken?"

"I don't know," Taylor admitted. "Everything was kept pretty hush-hush. Though the bigger fear, I think, would be someone erasing the hard drives. Most television productions don't keep their imaging stored on film reels anymore, they use digitized storage."

"I didn't know that."

"Then you've got something for your article," Taylor said with a smile.

"So was anything erased?"

"Your guess is as good as mine, but they had to reshoot a scene for episode twenty. I know because I was in it. The directors said they weren't happy with the cuts, but maybe they didn't want to admit what had happened."

"That's serious, man," said another guy.

"Sure," Taylor agreed. "The studio could lose more than money with that kind of sabotage."

"So they think a competitor broke in and messed with the hard drive?" Alan asked.

"I don't know what they think, but that would be a conclusion a lot of people would draw."

Alan frowned. "Is it a conclusion *you* drew?"

The blond shrugged again. "If it was a competitor, why didn't he erase everything? Maybe he did . . . maybe episode twenty was the only one not backed up. But even with the old security measures, it's hard to believe a competitor made it into the studio and the editing room. The senior editor guards that room more rabidly than the prop master does his storage room."

"You think it was an inside job, someone disgruntled and wanting revenge?"

"More than one actor wasn't happy with the first take on that scene. It just wasn't working, but the director insisted on getting it in the can and what they got was shit, if you want the truth. Hell, anybody in the studio who wanted to see a better day's worth of takes on that scene had reason to erase it from the hard drive."

This was definitely something he needed to ask Jillian about. "Which of the regular actors were in that scene?"

"Both the male and female leads, that guy who plays the bald alien . . . Gavin, and the woman who plays his sister. But seriously? Producers would have as much motivation to delete that episode as the actors, or anyone else who didn't want to see a ratings drop. It's not all about art, is it? A really badly done scene can translate into financial losses and be the first step toward the end of a show."

"Anyway, I guess, it could be worse," the snarky actor said, referring to the security measure, Alan thought.

"Yes?" Alan asked.

"Definitely. There used to be this old guy working here. He started with Frost Productions when they first opened their doors. He was a total stickler for protocol. Worse than any of the other rent-a-cops."

"What happened to him?"

"He died in an accident."

"Lost control of his car on the freeway," a female actor added. "It was a real shame. He was only weeks from retirement."

The snarky actor looked knowing. "Planned to travel with his wife."

"How did you know that?"

"Taylor's not the only one who knows stuff," the man replied in a smug tone.

"It was about the same time as the break-in, I think," Taylor said, not sounding the least offended. "A real shame."

Alan agreed. An even bigger shame was the fact that this small piece of information hadn't shown up in any of his reports on the production company.

Damn it all to hell.

*   *   *

The heavily pierced make-up artist insisted on refreshing Alan's make-up after lunch. He listened to another litany of words interspersed with "you knows," but this time none of it blipped on his internal radar.

Ten minutes after she finished, Alan was one of the group of background actors brought in for the scene they were filming. They were given their instructions. Alan waited until "Action" was called before tripping on one of the many cables on the floor and causing a loud commotion. The next time "Action" was called, he stood stiff as a board, not moving at all as he'd been instructed. It took one more take before the casting director had him ushered off the set.

He stifled his sigh of relief and managed an appropriately disappointed expression.

Jillian teased him about it on the way home and the others joined in when they arrived at the house. Gavin was already there and he'd witnessed Alan's not-so-accidental faux pas. Alan just grinned over the gentle ribbing and nodded in agreement when Perry said he shouldn't quit his day job.

Despite what his housemates thought, Alan wouldn't call the experience a bust. Not after the info he got on why the increased security measures had been implemented, or receiving the tidbit about Gavin, no matter how unwelcome it was personally. Damn, he hated emotional connection with possible suspects and usually did a fine job of avoiding it. But this case was different for him in too many ways to count, most importantly the strange and overwhelming reaction he had to Jillian.

Alan called TGP headquarters while Jillian and Perry fixed dinner. He took his normal precautions to make sure he couldn't be overheard and was glad he had. The Old Man laughed so loud when he told him about his experiences as a background actor that Alan had to hold the phone from his ear.

"I just want to know one thing," Alan said after his boss's laughter died down.

"What's that, son?"

"Do I get hazard pay for having to wear make-up?"

That set the Old Man off again and Alan grinned. Life was too short to be serious all the time, even on the job. However, things got serious quick when he relayed what he'd heard about the probable cause for the increased security measures as well as the old security guard's death.

"I'm not happy we didn't know about the security guard's death."

"You said it was a car accident?"

"Yes, but it's too damn coincidental timing-wise. You know I don't believe in coincidences." And if he was right, his perps were responsible for not one, but two men's deaths.

"I don't either." The Old Man went silent for a few seconds, probably taking notes. "I'll find out if an official report was filed with the local authorities on the break-in and if there is any additional information on the security guard's death."

"From what was said, I'm betting no official report."

"Unfortunately, you're probably right. There are a lot of reasons for the execs wanting to keep details of the break-in out of circulation."

"Not the least of which is gossip. Everyone seems addicted to tittle-tattle around the studio, which makes my job easier in some ways."

"And harder in others."

"Right."

"Good thing you've got an instinct for weeding out the truth."

"Glad you think so, sir."

"You're a damn fine agent, Alan."

"Thank you."

"By the way, Frost's second background check came out as squeaky clean as the first. Hell, the man doesn't even have a parking ticket to his name. It's not natural."

"Makes you want to keep digging, doesn't it?"

"In a word . . . yes."

Alan nodded to himself. "Send me what you have and I'll do some research on my own."

"Will do. Learn anything else on your debut as a thespian?"

Alan told him what the make-up artist said about Gavin.

"That could be total imagination on her part or something incredibly significant."

"I'm a little worried because I'm hoping it's the former."

"Getting emotionally involved with your housemates?"

He didn't try to sugarcoat or downplay it. "Yes."

"It happens, Hyatt. To the best of us. The mark of a good agent is his ability to do his job in spite of complications like this."

"You don't want to send in backup?"

"Do you think you need it?"

"No. I can do my job, sir."

"You've never had this happen before, have you?"

"No."

"If you're an agent long enough, it's bound to happen sometime."

"Did it happen to you?"

"As a matter of fact, yes."

"What happened?"

"I ended up married to her. Ask your grandfather about it sometime. He's got his own story."

That was the second time the Old Man had suggested he do that. "Are you trying to get at something, sir?"

"What do you think of your landlady?"

"She's sexy as hell."

The Old Man chuckled. "Just checking."

"I'm not going to end up married to her."

"If you say so."

Before Alan had a chance to answer that impudence, his boss asked, "Anything else I need to know?"

"Jillian invited me to come with her when she visits her friend Amanda Brant."

"That will give you the opportunity to scope out the possibility she's attempting to sell Brant computer technology before it goes to market. Not everything Prescott brokered was a state secret, you know. He had his hands in some corporate technology wars too."

"Damn smarmy bastard."

"The more I learn about this guy, the more I want to see him serving a lifetime sentence in one of our undisclosed facilities for holding enemies of the state."

"Yeah, I think that DEA agent who lost her sister to his perversions would agree."

"I'm bringing her into TGP, by the way."

"Good. I think she needs a change of scenery to help get her life back in balance."

"It's hard to lose family."

"Yes, sir, it is." He still remembered the pain of his parents' deaths. He didn't want to imagine how he would react to the loss of his brother. The possibility in their line of work was all too real.

"I'm going to try to connect with a couple of old contacts when I'm in Seattle."

"You think they might have heard something?"

"It's hard to say. They both have diverse interests."

"It sounds like a productive trip, then."

"Yes, sir." No reason to mention the fact that he'd be hard-pressed to turn Jillian down even if he didn't have legitimate reasons related to the case.

Jillian seemed to be avoiding Alan after dinner. He didn't push it because he needed to establish some professional distance from her. So when she disappeared to her room right after she finished eating, he didn't follow.

He went to his own room and pulled up his secure connection to the agency's network. An hour of digging into Frost's background yielded no more than he already knew. Some people might think that a squeaky-clean background report removed suspicion, but Alan always had the opposite reaction. Very few people had nothing questionable in their pasts. Which usually meant that said clean background had been sanitized.

That took money and connections . . . did Frost have those? The money angle was something Alan could investigate. Provided he didn't have his holdings secured in secret, out-of-country accounts.

Fifteen minutes later and he discovered the man had more money than any single person needed in a lifetime. In fact, Alan wanted to know where all that money came from. And considering he had so much, why did he own such a small-time production company? With his resources, he could be part of something much bigger. He was executive producer on all the top shows for Frost Productions, but none of them were contenders for prime time and didn't look to become that way anytime soon, if ever.

Curiouser and curiouser.

Unfortunately, it was going to take deeper digging to find the source of the man's money. It wasn't inherited and he hadn't had such a big hit that he'd been set for life sometime earlier in his career either. Now, why hadn't the agency's researcher noticed this discrepancy and chased it down?

Alan shot off an e-mail to the Old Man with what he'd discovered and asked that the researchers focus on finding the source of the man's wealth.

Afterward, Alan went back over Gavin's file, trying to see a lead to follow. He was an openly gay man who had been disowned by his family when he came out of the closet at fifteen. Shit, what kind of parents threw a fifteen-year-old out of the house? Luckily for Gavin, he'd had an understanding aunt who had taken him in and encouraged his interest in acting.

He'd been arrested once at a party when a public disturbance call had been made. There had been dope at the party, but no evidence Gavin had been smoking it. He'd been let go

without charges filed. His aunt died the year Gavin had graduated from acting school. He'd had a DUI the week after,
paid his fine, done his community service, and never had another ticket for any reason.

The guy didn't have a lot of money, unless he was hiding it
somewhere. He didn't have questionable connections unless
you counted his fellow actors. Some of them were really out
there.

He'd never been in a long-term relationship, but he also
didn't date much. Now that surprised Alan. Gavin was the
consummate flirt.

But then after what he'd been through, it wasn't too
shocking that he avoided emotional commitments.

Alan reached down and idly adjusted himself, only then
realizing that he was half hard. What the hell was going on?
He was working . . . researching. There wasn't a single arousing thing about the information he was trying to see from a
fresh angle. He hadn't been thinking about Jillian. He was
working, damn it. He had better focus than that. But the moment he let himself acknowledge his semi-aroused state, he
became aware of the underlying buzz of sexual desire that
had been keeping his body on edge since Jillian had walked
out of the dining room two hours earlier.

This was ridiculous. She'd made it clear she wasn't inter-
ested in further exploring their sexual compatibility tonight
and he didn't blame her. She had to get up obscenely early to
be at the studio. At least they had today.

Alan preferred to work at optimum levels and certainly
understood her need to do so as well. She needed her sleep.

But his dick had a mind of its own, it seemed. As much as
he knew in his head that a night of establishing a better sense
of distance from his sexy landlady was a good idea, his body
craved the intensity of sensation it had known the night before. Hell, his arms felt empty without her in them, and that

was just not right. Jillian did not fit in his life any more than he fit in hers.

Even if he wanted to maintain a relationship with her after this case was over, it would be all but impossible. Jillian's career kept her on the West Coast. His kept him on the East Coast. Neither of their careers was conducive to an ongoing committed relationship.

Beth had taught him that, and he'd have to be blind and ignorant not to be aware of the difficulty actors had in maintaining relationships. It was his job to keep abreast of current events and that included skimming the human interest, make that read gossip-centered, stories in the news. Even if he thought they could make their incompatible lifestyles somehow merge, there was the simple fact that an undercover operative could not afford to be in a relationship with someone who would draw media attention to him.

A successful agent was invisible in his real life so he could fit into any scenario he needed to without risking exposure as a fraud.

And why he was even thinking this way was a mystery. Jillian had made it clear she had no desire to go beyond the parameter of weeks that defined their relationship's longevity. No matter what her friends thought, Jillian was not looking for Mr. Right. She was just itchy for a Mr. Right Now.

Which was exactly fine with him.

His dick pulsed in mockery of that thought.

That was just sexual tension and he could take care of it in the shower. Which is exactly what he did.

He was leaning against the wall, his fist around his now fully hard cock, leaking pre-cum as his mind played images from the night before like a sensual movie.

The sound of his door opening registered and Alan's dick went from pleasantly hard to practically exploding from his skin. The only person who had a key to his door besides him was Jillian, and he knew he'd locked the door.

Chapter 13

Rubbing his hand down the length of his cock, he turned his head and watched through the semitransparent shower curtain as Jillian came into the bathroom wearing nothing but a batiked silk robe in shades of green, the predominant one being the same emerald as her eyes.

She pushed the shower curtain aside. "Enjoying yourself, Mr. Johnson?" she asked, indicating his slowly moving hand still masturbating his rigid sex.

"Jacking off in the shower is a favorite male pastime." He let his fingers dance over his leaking head and moaned, making no effort to hide what he was feeling from her. The hot spray pelting his aroused body felt good and he tilted his pelvis forward to change the way the water stimulated him. "I thought you'd gone to bed."

Her gaze traveled from his eyes down to his prick and back up to his eyes again. "I was going to."

But she hadn't been able to resist coming to his room. "What changed your mind?"

Her eyelids dropped to half-mast and her expression turned carnal with need as she dropped her robe. "We've got a lot more ground to cover between us, and I don't like to leave a project unfinished."

"You think we can finish covering that ground?" He had

his doubts that even if they had a lifetime together he and Jillian would cover all the aspects of sensuality that fascinated them about each other.

She wrapped her smaller hand around his, and this time it was her fingers that played with the super-sensitive tip of his penis. "We can try."

He let his eyes slide closed and concentrated on the sensations going through his body. "Oh, yeah."

They worked in conjunction for three strokes before Jillian removed her hand.

He opened his eyes to see her contemplating her fingertips, wet with his essence. "I don't suppose your test results are someplace easy to find?"

He had to lock his knees so he didn't fall on his ass. She wanted to taste him. He thought quickly to determine if there was anything incriminating in the briefcase that the paper was in, but he decided there wasn't. It was his cover story briefcase and filled with notes on the supposed article he was writing, his passport with the false last name, and the test results.

Relief and anticipation shuddered through him. "My briefcase beside the desk. It's not locked."

Naked, she turned on her heel and went back into the room. He watched her walk away, the sight of her curves from the back inspiring thoughts of one of his favorite positions. He loved to take a woman from the back, pleasuring her silky wet heat with his cock while his hand was tucked under her front, stimulating her clitoris. He had to squeeze the base of his cock to stop from coming at the prospect of doing that with Jillian.

She was back a minute later, her smile nothing short of predatory. Damn, this woman was a good match for him.

"Find what you needed?" he asked.

"Yes." She reached for him again. "We're good to go. I want to taste you."

More blood surged into his already engorged cock. "Your sexual openness is a hell of a turn-on."

"It intimidates some men."

"Men too weak to match you."

She grinned. "Exactly."

"I'm not weak."

"No, Alan, you aren't." Her serious tone and the words themselves went through him, touching a place inside he didn't know was there.

Before he could respond, her hand was back on him, her fingertips sliding over his slit, bringing forth a groan from deep in his chest. His gaze was locked on her as she brought those fingertips to her mouth.

She delicately licked the shimmery viscous fluid from them. "Mmm. Sweet."

He groaned. With the way he reacted to this type of sex play with Jillian, he had no idea how he was going to survive actually getting inside her. All he knew was that he enjoyed the game so much, he had no desire to skip any markers on the board. And that in itself was enough to send a jolt of apprehension skittering through him. He couldn't remember a time he'd been so willing to take so long working up to the main event.

Jillian was special, no doubt about it, but he'd be a lot more comfortable if his every reaction to her wasn't so over the top.

She sucked her fingers into her mouth one after another as if savoring the taste of him. "Are you coming out, or am I coming in?"

"What do you want?"

"I want to watch you touch yourself until you shoot, but I also want to taste you."

"We can do both, but I have to warn you it will take you longer to get me off with your mouth if I finish jacking off in here."

"You sure about that?" she challenged.

Thinking about his explosive reaction to her touch, he had to pause before giving an automatic affirmative. "Only time will tell, sweetheart."

"Oooh . . . the man's tossed the gauntlet before me."

"Are you going to pick it up?"

"What do you think?"

He just smiled and went back to touching himself, figuring that would be answer enough. "Tell me something," he said as he spread his legs a little to give him more stability in remaining upright.

"What?" she asked, the aroused tone of her voice leaving no doubt how much she was enjoying her voyeuristic moment.

"Did other kids get you to do stupid stuff by daring you as a child?"

Her laughter washed over him and made his prick twitch in his hand. "Maybe once or twice."

"Me too," he admitted as he used both hands to caress his pulsing heat. It wasn't going to take any time for him to come now.

He watched her watching him and felt the familiar tingle in his balls and at the base of his spine. "I've never done this before," he panted.

"Masturbated?" she asked disbelievingly.

"In front of a woman."

"It's amazingly hot."

"From this side too."

She was licking her lips as if in anticipation of later. "I'm glad, because I really like watching."

"Have you done it a lot?"

"A couple of times. Most men I've known have been all about getting touched and can't see the sensual charge that comes from a situation like this."

"I never . . ." His breath caught and he knew he was close. "Never would have guessed myself, but it is damn sexy." He reached down and cupped his balls, squeezing just enough, and he erupted, his ejaculate spewing in ropy gushers as the intense pleasure consumed him.

He leaned against the wall, his breathing irregular, his body languid and yet still humming with unmistakable anticipation.

"That was beautiful," Jillian said huskily.

He just grunted, not sure how he was supposed to react to a comment like that. After several deep breaths that succeeded in calming his heart rate from supersonic speeds to merely pounding at the rate of a jackhammer, he asked, "You coming in, or am I coming out?"

"You'd better come out. The bottom of the tub is hard on a girl's knees."

Oh, damn. That image? Enough to bring his slowly deflating erection back to mission ready.

"Besides, the stylists at the studio will be happier if I can avoid washing my hair again between now and tomorrow's shoot."

"Sounds good." He could step out of the shower. He could.

He leaned forward and turned off the water before reaching for the towel Jillian held open between her hands. But she stepped back. "Come out and I'll dry you."

He did as she said, not even considering protesting. If she wanted to pamper him, who was he to argue?

She started with his hair, extending her arms to reach. He bent to make it easier and was glad he did when she used the towel to massage his scalp. "Mmmm . . . feels good."

"It's supposed to." She moved the towel down his neck and started drying his torso with careful movements, not rubbing vigorously like he did to dry himself, but using a light touch that sensitized his skin while removing the droplets of water from him.

"Oh, and speaking of?"

"Speaking of what?" he asked, confused.

She grinned, flashing mischief at him. "Going to the studio."

"Yeah?"

"The casting director begged me to keep you out of the background actors pool."

Alan's laugh turned into a groan as she moved below his waist with the fluffy towel. "Was I really that bad?" he asked, knowing the answer before she gave it.

He'd worked very hard to be that bad.

"The worst."

He laughed. "Don't hold back now."

She laughed too, but then cocked her head to one side and studied him. "I'm surprised."

"By what?"

"That it doesn't bother you more. You're a pretty competitive guy."

"Hey, part of being so good is knowing when to step back from something I'm hopeless at."

"I bet there have been very few things in your life you have admitted were hopeless. You're too much of a conqueror."

"Conqueror, huh?"

"It fits."

He shrugged, concealing his dismay at her perception. "You can't conquer everything. Even the Romans knew when to put up a wall rather than attempt to extend their borders."

She laughed. "I just hope you got what you needed today."

"It was very productive for my purposes even if I sucked at the actual acting part."

She tossed the towel in the hamper and smoothed her hands over his chest. "Time to concentrate on something more pleasant."

"I'm all for that."

She reached up and kissed him. Almost chastely . . . no tongue was involved and it wasn't a long kiss, but it still rocked his world.

He followed her out of the bathroom, but when he headed for the bed, Jillian stopped him.

"The chair," she said, pointing to the armchair in his "sitting area." "The angle is good."

"You're just trying to keep me out of the bed so you don't end up spending the night there."

She looked stricken, as if his recognizing her true motivation was tantamount to stripping her bare in a Starbucks at lunchtime. Or maybe it was the fact that he knew how tempted she would be to break her rule about sleeping with sex partners again. He got the sense sometimes that her rules were as much a security blanket as they were a wall she could hide behind.

Without further comment, he lowered himself into the cushy armchair.

"Scoot forward until your butt's on the edge."

"Your turn for being bossy tonight, huh?" he asked with a smile.

"Yes." She looked all too serious about it. "Now spread your legs."

He let his knees fall open, wide enough that she could easily kneel between them.

"Further."

He wondered what she was thinking of, but complied with the demand.

She grabbed a throw pillow from the sofa and dropped it on the floor between his feet, then knelt on it. Tracing his erection with her forefinger, she licked her lips. "I'm beginning to wonder if you've got an implant in this thing. I don't think I've ever seen you completely soft."

"You have that effect on me."

"Hmmm . . ." She seemed to study his dick, as if looking for its secrets, all the time tracing it with one gentle fingertip.

"Are you saying you aren't wet when you're around me?"

She brought both hands to his inner thighs and then slowly

traced the muscles from groin to knee. "Shh . . . no more talking."

"I like talking during sex."

"You can talk another time. Tonight I want you quiet." She met his eyes, her hands stilled on his legs. "Okay?"

He nodded and she smiled. "Good. Now lean back so your head is resting on the back of the chair."

He did as she instructed and found that it caused his cock to jut into the air while making his body more accessible to her. And she took advantage, caressing every inch of his exposed flesh, finding hot spots by listening to the cadence of his breathing and paying attention to any tiny sound he might make, then revisiting those spots over and over again. However, she studiously avoided one particular spot. His genitals.

He couldn't help tilting up his pelvis, trying to catch the brush of one of her hands. It didn't work.

It was the most intense buildup to a blow job he'd experienced. By the time she touched the area she had been avoiding, his body was shaking with fine tremors.

She didn't do the expected now either. Still avoiding his copiously leaking cock, she gently cupped his scrotal sac, causing a localized jolt of pleasure that had him moaning. She leaned forward and he could feel her warm breath on his balls, followed by her tongue.

His body tensed with desire and his ass came off the chair again. She pressed down on his inner thighs, rubbing them until he was more relaxed. Then she licked him again before very carefully taking one of his balls into her mouth and tracing it with her tongue. She did that for interminable seconds filled with incredible sensation before shifting just slightly so she was doing the same thing to its twin.

What had he said about his second climax taking a long time? He thought he might come before she ever touched his dick.

He wanted to warn her, to beg her, to give verbalization to his pleasure with more than grunts and groans, but she'd said no talking and he was going to prove he had enough self-control to follow through even if he shot all over his stomach instead of in her mouth.

His balls drew up, indicating that was more than a possibility.

But Jillian showed just how in tune with him she was because she took her mouth away right then, keeping up the massage on his inner thighs. It didn't bring him down, but somehow managed to push his climax from hair-trigger imminent to achingly almost there.

He made a sound of pure need.

"What do you want?" she purred.

"I get to talk now?" he asked with as much defiance as he could muster, considering he was one big throbbing puddle of need.

"Tell me what you want."

"You know."

"Do I?"

"I want you . . ." A moan . . . no more words . . . arching hips.

She grinned up at him, the light in her eyes both tender and diabolical. "*Say it.*"

"Suck me."

She did, taking the super-sensitive patch of skin near the base of his cock into her mouth and sucking hard enough to bring up a mark. He squirmed . . . and despite, or maybe because of, his super-heightened state of arousal, laughter exploded. He wasn't ticklish.

Until now.

Her laughter cascaded over him like a waterfall of music. Moving back up to suck his nipples, as if he hadn't just been a hairsbreadth from coming, she teased his hard tips with her tongue and her teeth. Again.

He groaned, the need so rich it was painful coursing through him. But he loved this moment of laughter . . . her teasing that was more than just sexual. She kept at his nipples, and then pressed more open-mouthed, biting kisses all over his chest until he was making so much noise, he could have been the soundtrack for an adult movie.

Her head came up and she looked at him with pleasure and satisfaction.

"What do you want?" she asked him again.

"Blow me," he growled.

"Gavin was right . . . that sound is pure sexual turn-on," she said with a small tilt of her lips.

Then the little imp bent down and blew . . . a puff of hot air right on the head of his prick. The feel of that air against the skin wet with pre-cum sent chills chasing up his spine. But he still laughed. Damn, she was special.

She laughed too.

But he couldn't take any more. He grasped both sides of her face and let her see the need radiating from his eyes. "Suck my dick . . ."

"Okay," she breathed.

And this time, he knew she meant it. No more games.

However, he was still expecting her to tease his hardness with her hands like she'd done the rest of him. And he didn't know if he could handle it.

He didn't have to. She closed her lips over him without warning. A primal yell was stripped from his throat as the heated wetness of her mouth singed him. Her tongue swirled around his corona and he thrust upward, seeking more but aware somewhere in his consciousness that he wasn't supposed to do that. It wasn't polite, but the primitive man she had unleashed fought the strictures of acceptable behavior.

He forced his pelvis to dip back toward the chair, his muscles shaking from the effort.

Jillian's head came up and she glared, her expression every bit as wild as he felt. "Give it to me. Let go, Alan. I won't accept anything less."

"I don't want to hurt you."

"I won't let you," she hissed.

"But . . ." Damn it, why was he arguing? It was what he wanted. Only he didn't want regrets on either of their parts tomorrow.

"Do you think I'm weak? You don't think I can handle you?"

"No!"

"Prove it! Let go." Then his cock was once again engulfed in sizzling wetness, only this time he went a lot deeper into her mouth and the suction was incredible.

He wanted it, but he had to make sure he didn't hurt her, no matter how strong she was. He forced his hands to release their hold on her face and grip the arms of the chair again. Confident she could pull back if she needed to, he let his pelvis surge upward. She moved with him, maintaining the amazing stimulation without letting him go too far. She massaged his balls while her other hand jacked the part of his prick not buried in her mouth.

He lost all sense of what was happening. He couldn't distinguish one sensation from another. He released his control completely and just rode the pleasure until the hot lava of his climax shot up through his dick into her mouth as he convulsed in the longest orgasm of his life.

He collapsed back into the chair, his muscles aching from the prolonged tension.

Jillian released him from her mouth, her expression one of unbridled desire. She climbed onto him, pressing her feminine center against his still-hard penis, and she rode him, pressing their sexes together without letting him enter her and making his body buck as even the slick softness of her inner labia was too much stimulation for his oversensitized organ. He couldn't make his mouth work to tell her, though.

But seconds later it didn't matter. She was coming against him, her body trembling in pleasure while she screamed his name, then slammed her lips onto his for a delirious kiss while she moved through the aftershocks, prolonging her ecstasy and his borderline agony.

Finally, she collapsed against him and their kiss turned tender, saying things about their lovemaking that neither of them would have spoken out loud.

Her head dropped to rest on his shoulder as they both panted in postcoital exhaustion.

"Can I talk now?"

"Yes."

"That was the most intense orgasm of my life. You're amazing, Jillian."

"The feeling is mutual."

She licked at the sweat from the dip made by his clavicle. "You taste good."

"I should have warned you I was ready to come."

"That would have been far too civilized. I didn't want refined. Or couldn't you tell?" He could feel the smile against his skin.

His own lips curved in a sated grin. "I got that."

"And I got what I wanted."

"I'm glad. Very." His arms closed around her and he just held her. He made no move to get up because he suspected that when he did, she would insist on returning to her room.

Alan woke the next morning, his hand seeking Jillian and finding nothing but cold sheets. Coming to full consciousness, he frowned. He'd been right the night before. She'd refused to sleep in his room. So why had he woken up reaching for her? His subconscious mind thought she should be there. Probably because of the astounding sex they'd shared. Wow. No one had done to him what she had with her mouth. And the way she demanded he let go of control. That had been so damn hot.

His cell phone rang, the tune that said it was the Old Man.

Alan grabbed it from where he'd left it on the nightstand and flipped it open. "Hyatt."

"Good morning, Alan."

"You got news for me?"

"We started tracing the money with Frost and hit a gusher. Whether it's what we're looking for or not is debatable, however."

"What did you find out?"

"It's hidden damn well, but Elle spent the entire night working on this—"

"Elle, what's she doing researching on my case? Not that I mind the help, but she's got her own job."

"She's at a standstill with her current case, thought taking a break to work on yours might loosen up something for her."

"Did it work?"

"I don't know, but do you want to hear what she found out or not?"

"Of course."

"It looks like the owner of Frost Productions has connections with organized crime."

"You're kidding, right?"

"No. If our suspicions are correct, he's using his company to filter money made in less aboveboard enterprises. A lot of money."

Frost Productions was a money-laundering venture? Hell. "That doesn't make any sense. If the production company is a legitimate front for other not-so-legal, but highly lucrative business ventures, why would he risk the setup for high-tech espionage? That's not the way these things usually work."

"Maybe he's not."

"Shit."

"Exactly."

"Well, that explains why the company renewed Jillian's show for another season despite the fact that it isn't burning up the ratings."

"Sure does. What happened to the old standby of setting up a restaurant as a front business?" He could almost hear Whit shaking his head.

"Maybe some of our organized crime buddies are looking for a little extra drama in their lives."

The Old Man groaned. "That was bad, Alan."

"What do you expect? The really good puns don't come until after breakfast. It's only six A.M. here."

"Time to be getting up anyway."

"Right. Look, tell Elle thanks for me, would you?"

"Send her a box of lemon drops and you two will be golden."

"Good idea." Alan wasn't sure he'd seen the female agent without one in her mouth. He'd asked her about them once and she'd said they were better than smoking.

He agreed. They were safer for an agent too. Smoking carried a scent it was damn hard to completely mask, which lent risk to any agent's discovery when they were in skulk mode.

Alan hung up and then immediately placed another call to a delivery service he'd used before and made his order for Elle. Lemon drops and the latest issue of her favorite specialty weapons magazine. He wasn't sure which she'd like most. The woman had a bigger jones for high-class weaponry than any trained assassin.

He wondered what she'd been before being recruited by TGP.

Chapter 14

Alan changed into sweats, figuring he could use a run to clear his head. He found Perry alone in the hall wearing nothing but a pair of jeans, an indecipherable expression on his face.

The other man looked at Alan and asked, "You going for a run?"

"Yes."

"Mind some company?"

"Not at all."

"Great. Give me a minute to change and I'll meet you outside."

"Perfect."

True to his word, Perry was outside within a few short minutes. "Do you want to run in the neighborhood or drive to a trail?"

"Let's stick with the neighborhood. I'm not looking for a total cardio workout." He'd gotten that last night with Jillian.

Perry smiled. "Sounds good. I'm on the late rotation today at the studio, but I didn't feel like hanging around the house."

"I hear you."

Perry eyed him sideways. "Jillian giving you fits already?"

They started running at an easy pace. "I'm not sure."

"That sounds familiar."

Alan laughed. "You think?"

"I've never had a relationship that didn't have some uncertainty."

"Have you had very many?"

"A girlfriend when I was a teenager, a couple of boyfriends."

"I thought you were gay."

"I didn't want to accept it, tried the being with a girl thing. It didn't work. I ended up with a crush on the captain of the hockey team my last year of high school."

"I'm surprised you weren't on the team."

"I was. The guy was my best friend."

"Complicated."

"Yep. He's straight too. Every gay boy's nightmare."

Alan smiled. "So what happened?"

"Nothing with my best friend. I never even told him, but the crush made me realize the lie I was living with my girlfriend. She deserved better, yeah?"

"You're probably right."

"She's happily married with a couple of kids now. We're still friends."

"A good decision, then."

"Definitely. For both of us."

"Well, I'm absolutely not gay."

Perry laughed and slapped his back. "After the sounds coming from Jillian's room the night before last and your room last night, I don't think anyone doubts that."

Alan groaned. "I thought the walls were thicker than that."

"It would have taken concrete a foot thick to completely muffle some of those noises. I was jealous."

Alan shook his head and laughed.

They ran in silence for a while and the longer they ran, the more Alan had a feeling that Perry wanted to say something.

"Something up, man?" he asked, trying to prompt the other man.

"You ever get in a situation that made you feel like a total ass?"

"I'm thinking that answer is yes for most men."

"I mean, something that makes you doubt your own sense of integrity?"

With the nature of his work? Oh, yeah. "Actually, yes."

Perry cast him another sideways glance, this one lasting a few seconds. "How did you handle it?"

"By being as honest as I could, both with myself and other people."

"And when honesty is not an option?"

"I said as honest as you can be. Sometimes, honesty isn't an option. However, I have certain standards I'm fanatical about maintaining."

"Me too. At least I did."

"Like what?"

"I don't know . . ." Though clearly, the man had spent a long time thinking about this. It was just a matter of his being willing to open up. "I suppose, never betray my country, my family, or my true friends."

Alan's gut clenched. "You in danger of doing one of those?"

Perry didn't answer.

"Perry?"

"I want to talk about it, but I can't. At least not right now."

"I'm here when you're ready. Sometimes, it's better to talk to a new friend rather than an old one. No history to get in the way."

"You're right, man. Thanks."

Alan didn't push any further. He knew when interrogation would be effective and right now was not one of those times. Perry's tone and body language made that clear. The fact that Perry had been the person to discover Lonny's dead body had a new and sufficiently sinister aspect that made Alan's insides twist in a way he did not like.

Damn, damn, damn this emotional involvement crap.

"Remember, if you want to talk, I'm here," he said as they slowed to a cooling walk about fifty yards from Jillian's house. And then felt like he was setting up to betray a good friend.

This was a case. He should not be feeling like that toward a potential suspect, but everything about this assignment was skewed. All because of one small redhead. It was like she'd destroyed the wall he kept between himself and others when he was working and because of that, the wall wasn't even sort of effective with the other housemates he'd gotten to know and like more than he should.

"Thanks," Perry said again as he stretched before going back inside.

Alan followed slowly, his thoughts and emotions at odds.

Jillian wrapped her straightened hair in the stretchy fabric the stylist had given her to sleep in. She didn't use it at night, but it worked to tuck her hair in before donning a shower cap for those days she didn't want to get to the studio early enough for the stylist to dry and straighten her hair. Mornings like today when she'd had to drag her butt out of bed after fitful sleep.

She'd exhausted both Alan and herself last night, so she should have slept like the dead. She hadn't. She kept rolling over, expecting him to be there and waking up when he wasn't. It made no sense. She didn't make a habit of sleeping with sex partners, so why was her body acting like it couldn't settle down without his next to it?

It had been hard enough to leave his room last night, especially when he asked her in that sexy, sated voice if she wanted to sleep with him. But she'd managed it, only to be betrayed by her body as it rejected her decision to sleep alone.

Oh, Amanda would get such a kick out of this situation. She maintained that Jillian was going to meet her Waterloo one day and then all bets were off . . . her rules were going to be dust.

Jillian finished her shower, feeling cranky and put upon even though she was fully responsible for the miasma of emotion tormenting her right now.

Well . . . her and a far too tantalizing reporter. She could legitimately blame him too, for all the good it did her.

"So, explain to me again why a long-term relationship is tantamount to rolling over and dying?"

Jillian glared, not that Amanda could see it since they were talking on the phone. "I don't do lifetime."

"Why again?"

"You know why!"

"I know that your dad is a self-involved artist who sucked at parenting and your stepdad sucks at being human, period, but why do their shortcomings mean you have to spend your life alone?"

"I'm not alone. I've got friends. I've even got a relationship with my family, such as it is."

"Yeah, you talk to your mom and stepdad so you can have a real relationship with your brother."

"He's worth it."

"You are too, Jillian."

"What do you mean?"

"You're worth sacrificing for. If Alan's the man you think he is, he'll look for a way to make a relationship between you two work."

"I didn't say I wanted a relationship."

"Yes, you did."

"I may be a year older than you, but I'm not senile. I said no such thing."

"Jillian, sweetie, your first question when I answered the phone was how did I know I was in love with Simon."

"So? I was curious."

"I think you're falling in love."

"Amanda," Jillian groaned.

"Did you realize you called him your lover the last time we talked on the phone?"

Crud. She knew she'd been using the word in her head, but she hadn't realized she'd verbalized it.

At her silence, Amanda sighed. "You never use the L-word. I think that's significant. I know it scares the crap out of you. Of anyone, I think I understand that fear the best, but I learned that love was worth taking a risk for."

"But Simon was so head over heels for you, it was sickening. Still is."

"Sickening?"

"No, you dope . . . he's still head over heels for you."

"And you're saying Alan doesn't feel that way about you?"

"He's totally cool with the uncommitted-sex thing."

"You sure about that?"

"He said so."

"You sure he wasn't saying what he thought you wanted to hear? You're kinda out there with your no-strings policy."

"Yes. He's . . . he's like me, Mandy. He doesn't do long term. I'm sure of it."

"Just because he's never done it before doesn't mean he won't want that with you."

"I don't want to be in love, Mandy."

"I know, sweetie. I know."

They confirmed their shopping and weekend plans and then Jillian disconnected the phone.

"Miss Sinclair, you're on deck in fifteen," one of the director's assistants called through the door.

"Thank you," Jillian replied.

Then, taking a deep breath, she picked up the phone and made a four-one-one connect call. When she hung up, exhilaration and fear warred for supremacy over her emotions. It was a good thing she had work to keep her mind occupied the rest of the afternoon.

Alan convinced Jillian to let him drive his rental for their trip to Seattle since it had a GPS and he would be driving around the city after dropping Jillian off at the mall to meet with Amanda and her sister-in-law. It was pure self-interest on his part. Sure, the GPS would come in handy, but even more important, he wasn't sure he could survive Jillian's erratic driving for that long a journey.

The wait at the border crossing was longer than he expected, but they were still in Seattle in time for a late dinner.

"You want to check into the hotel first or eat?" he asked her.

"The hotel first."

They programmed the hotel's address into the GPS and Alan managed to find it without having to backtrack once. Jillian had booked a hotel near the mall they planned to shop at. It was outside the city proper, so Alan didn't have to deal with a lot of one-way streets. He pulled up in front of the hotel and Jillian unbuckled her seat belt. "I'll check us in."

"I think I need to go in to get my room."

She shook her head. "I've got it covered. The reservations are under my name."

"Okay."

It took less than ten minutes before she was back outside telling him where to park. He pulled into a spot near the door and they got their bags out of the trunk. Jillian used a card key to open the outer door.

"Our room is on the third floor."

"Room? As in single?"

Jillian turned and led the way to the elevator. "Yes."

Miss I-don't-sleep-with-my-sex-partners wanted to share a room with him? Maybe she'd missed him last night too. He wasn't sure if that made him happy or worried him. But he made no further comment and the ride to the third floor was silent. Jillian let them into the room, turning on lights as she walked inside.

"Nice," he said.

"The beds are supposed to be super comfortable."

He grinned.

But she yawned and for the first time he noticed how tired she looked.

"Why don't we order room service for dinner rather than going out?"

"That sounds good." She sighed and just sort of deflated onto the bed. "Really good."

"You look like you could use a massage and a good night's sleep."

She looked up at him, her green eyes shadowed. "The last couple of nights have been really intense."

"Yeah."

"You offering the massage, or should I call and see if the hotel has a masseuse on call?"

"Sweetheart, you may be too wiped to make love, but that doesn't mean I have to give up all opportunities to have my hands on you."

"Who said I was too tired for sex?"

"The dark rings under your eyes. Tomorrow is going to take all the energy you've got, plus some. You need your rest tonight." Just the thought of shopping in a mall all day made him shudder and his feet ache in sympathy.

"I'm not that big a wuss."

"No one who would willingly spend more than a couple of hours shopping is weak. In fact, if it were me, I'd want combat pay to go."

She laughed and he smiled. "I'm going to run you a bath. You can soak until the food gets here and then I'll give you your massage."

"That sounds great, but I—"

"No buts."

She smiled, her green eyes soft. "Okay."

He ran the bath with hot, hot water, using the hotel shampoo to make bubbles. He was sure Jillian had brought her own toiletries, as had he. He was used to the smell of his shampoo. His brother called him anal because he refused to use any other kind.

Jillian came to the bathroom door naked. "I called room service. I got you steak."

"Sounds great."

"Where did you get the bubble bath?"

"I'm not telling. We all need our secrets." And he kept more than most.

He turned off the water, stood, and turned to face her. "Nice outfit."

"I remember you saying you liked it."

"I'll show you just how much . . . tomorrow night." He tugged her toward the tub, leaning down for a gentle kiss as she passed him. "But right now, relax in those nice bubbles."

"You don't have to tell me twice." And she stepped into the tub, giving a long sigh of enjoyment as she sank into the hot water. "This is perfect. The temperature is just right."

"Good." He left her soaking while he set up the bed for the massage.

He pulled back the down comforter and top sheet into a neat accordion fold at the end of the bed and pushed the pillows off to the sides, stacking the extras so there was a flat space in the center. He laid two hotel towels down and then rummaged in his bag for the massage oil he'd bought earlier that day when he'd taken a drive into downtown Vancouver. He'd bought some other things for the weekend as well, but he'd get to those tomorrow.

He pulled out the candles he'd bought, though. They were scented with vanilla spice and he took one into the bathroom, putting it on the counter and turning off the overhead light. Jillian's eyes were closed, but she smiled when the light went off. "That's nice."

He went back to the main part of the room and put the remaining four candles on the nightstands on either side of the bed. He didn't light them because he thought it would be better to wait until after dinner.

The food arrived thirty minutes later and Alan could hear Jillian splashing as she got out of the tub while he set the food up on the table in the corner.

"It smells good," Jillian said with a yawn as she wandered,

naked, out of the bathroom. "I like the way the candle smelled too."

He nodded. "Vanilla spice always relaxes me."

"You do the candle thing a lot?"

"No . . . it would get old if I did, but for special occasions . . ."

She looked at him curiously. "This is a special occasion?"

"Yep."

"Why?"

"Because you are a special woman."

Her eyes widened at that and then she shook her head. "I'd think you were just trying to get into my pants, but I'm already naked."

"So, I guess you'll have to accept the compliment in the manner in which it was intended, huh?"

"I guess so. Thank you." She grinned, mischief lighting her eyes. "Aren't you a little overdressed for dinner?"

"You think?"

"Well, I could always put some sweats and a T-shirt on."

"Not on my account." And he stripped.

She laughed, the sound musical. "That was fast."

"Never let it be said that I can't adapt quickly to a situation."

Dinner was good and so was the company. It shocked Alan that he could sit there naked, eating with a beautiful woman like Jillian, and be content to talk . . . about things besides sex. But he felt so comfortable with her and she seemed to feel the same way.

She pushed her plate away and he did the same. "Okay, massage time."

"You won't be offended if I fall asleep while you're working your magic, will you?"

"I'll think I've lost my touch if you don't. Now, go lie on the bed."

She did while he lit the candles and turned off most of the lights in the room. He went into the bathroom and took two extra towels and got them wet with hot water from the tap, almost too hot for him to wring out the extra moisture. Then he put the damp towels into the microwave in the small bar area and nuked them while he found a classical radio station on the cable television. Soft music filled the room and the microwave dinged. Alan pulled the now-steaming towels out and folded them in half before laying them in a double layer over Jillian's beautifully formed back. They covered her from neck to the top of her buttocks.

"Mmmm . . . that feels so good."

"It's supposed to."

"I love heat."

"I guessed."

"I think I'm part lizard," she said softly, a smile in her voice.

"You look all woman to me, sweetheart."

Chapter 15

He started the massage with her left hand, working his way up to her shoulder before moving to the other side of the bed and repeating the process on her right. She started making noises when he went to her feet. Grunts, groans, moans . . . it was extremely sexy, but despite his growing erection, he felt no urgency to find release, just a desire to relax Jillian and make sure she got a good night's rest.

He climbed onto the bed and then straddled her, his semi-erect cock brushing against her backside.

She laughed softly and then groaned as he started massaging the skin underneath the still-hot towels. "Doesn't that thing ever go soft?"

"I think we've had this conversation before. Around you, he's got amazing recuperative powers."

"We could—"

"Sleep. That's what we're going to do. Now, relax, my sweet little nympho."

"I'm not the one with the hard penis."

"And it's a good thing. Unlike Gavin, I wouldn't find that interesting at all."

Her laugh was muted as her body melted into the bed.

He kept working the muscles relaxed by the heated towels, refreshing the oil on his hands every time they started losing their slickness. When he was done, he wiped his hands on the top wet towel so he could massage her neck and scalp.

He was working her temples when her breathing evened out in unmistakable sleep. He finished and carefully lifted himself away from her. He got her tucked under the fluffy comforter and took the towels to the bathroom, making a mental note to request extra towels in the morning, so they could both shower. When he rejoined her in the bed, she rolled toward him, snuggling up to his body as if they'd been sleeping together in the same bed the last ten years instead of a single night.

And it felt good. Right.

Damn.

He was in deep trouble here.

Jillian woke the next morning to tender lips coaxing her toward consciousness. Her eyes fluttered open as she hummed against Alan's mouth. "Nice way to wake up."

"Yes, it is." He grinned down at her and it was then she realized he was fully dressed and his hair was still damp from a shower.

"No playing this morning?"

"If we played, you'd never make it to the mall."

"Good point."

He pulled away. "Time to get up. Breakfast should be here any minute and you've got thirty total minutes to get ready before we have to leave for the mall."

"A half an hour? You should have woken me up earlier."

"What for? You get ready faster than any woman I know."

"That's when I'm heading to the studio. They do my hair and make-up there."

"You don't wear make-up when you aren't working. As for your hair, I'm looking forward to seeing it all naturally curly again."

"You like the curls more than the put-together look?" she asked.

"I like it all, but yeah . . . the curls are the real you, so I like them a lot."

"That's nice." Then realizing how sappy she sounded, which was so not her, she jumped from the bed and headed for the bathroom. "I'll just take a military shower."

His laughter warmed her even as she shut the door to take care of her morning ablutions.

She was looking through a rack of men's sweaters when Amanda made a disgusted sound from beside her. "Okay, it's time to spill."

Jillian looked up. "What do you mean?"

"You're looking at sweaters," Elaine said, as if that explained Amanda's comment.

"So?"

"So, the day you buy a sweater as a Christmas gift for any of the important males in your life, I'm hanging up my shopping sneakers."

"You don't think Simon would like a sweater?"

"Sure, he'd like one," Amanda said with an exasperated expression, one hand on her hip. "But he'd keel over in a faint to receive something so normal from you."

"I got him a pet fish last year."

"You bought him a fifty-gallon aquarium and a school of piranhas. By the way, Dorrie loves to watch Jacob feed them."

"Simon doesn't feed them?" Jillian asked innocently.

Amanda laughed. "Right, like that's going to happen."

"The point here, ladies, is that Jillian doesn't buy sweaters," Elaine said pointedly and then she looked Jillian right in the eye. "So, what gives?"

"I guess I'm a little distracted."

"A little?" Amanda asked with a smirk.

"Hey, I wasn't this insufferable with Simon."

"So, you admit Alan is your Simon?" Amanda asked, shock filling her voice while Elaine just gasped in mock dismay.

Jillian glared at her friends, but then sighed, feeling extremely vulnerable. "He could be."

Amanda shook her head. "You know, I knew you'd fall in love one day, but I didn't think you'd ever admit it to yourself, much less anyone else."

"I didn't say I was in love, only that I could get there," Jillian said more acerbically than she felt.

"I think this discussion calls for decadent caffeine and brownies," Elaine said.

Amanda nodded. "I agree."

"Starbucks?" Jillian asked.

"Definitely," the other two said in unison.

It was early for their first break, but this was a unique situation.

They were seated at a table in the corner of the busy coffee shop, their drinks and brownies in front of them, before the inquisition started.

"So, what makes you think you might fall in love with this guy?" Amanda asked.

Jillian grimaced, not sure she was ready to talk now that the time had come. So, falling back on old habits, she misdirected. "Didn't you say you thought I was already there?"

Amanda wasn't buying it and her intense gaze said so. "I already know why I believe that; I want to hear why you do."

"I want to hear both . . . I've been almost completely out of the loop on this one," Elaine complained.

"Right. Like Amanda didn't call you about it," Jillian said with a grin, letting both women know she didn't mind. Other than Jillian herself, Elaine was the closest female friend Amanda had.

Jillian loved her best friend's sister-in-law too. Elaine was a really caring and honest person.

"She called, but she wouldn't give details. Said you'd have to if you wanted." Then Elaine grinned mischievously. "And that I could see for myself when you brought him to the island. Eric and I are coming for dinner tomorrow night."

Jillian just shook her head. "I should have seen that coming."

"Yes, you should have, which only highlights how distracted you are right now," Amanda said smugly.

Jillian took a sip of her peppermint mocha latte. "I haven't had any complaints at work."

"Good thing. If that happened, I'd be worried about a whole lot more than you being in love."

"Speaking of which . . ." Elaine said leadingly.

Sighing, Jillian gave in. "I only booked us one room for last night."

"And?" Amanda prompted.

"You know my rule about sleeping with men."

"Sure, but for a night of hot sex, even you are going to bend your rules. It wasn't like you invited him to your bed."

Jillian felt heat climb into her cheeks. "First . . . we didn't have sex last night."

"Why not?" Elaine asked, sounding scandalized.

Jillian couldn't suppress a laugh. "Because he wanted to take care of me. He wanted me to get a good night's rest for today. He gave me the most amazing massage."

Amanda nodded. "Sounds like something Simon would do."

Jillian broke off a piece of her brownie, but instead of eating it, just laid it on the napkin with the rest of the chocolate confection. "And, well, I let him sleep in my bed. Three nights ago," she hastily added as if that made it all better.

"Your bed . . . in your bedroom?" Amanda asked.

"Where else would my bed be?"

"Don't get snarky, missy. This is serious stuff here."

"You think?"

Elaine grinned, but remained silent.

Amanda was not so reticent. "So, what . . . you invited him to your room for sex? Seriously?"

"Yes." She wanted to roll her eyes at her best friend, but the truth was, the situation was every bit as unusual as her attitude implied. "And last night? I had a feeling we might not make love. The last couple of nights had been really intense and I think we both needed a breather."

"So you're saying you rented a single room between you just so he could hold you throughout the night?" Elaine asked. "That is so sweet."

Jillian frowned. "I'm not the sweet type."

"Definitely not," the other woman agreed immediately. "Which is what makes the situation all the more interesting."

"That's what I think," Jillian admitted.

"But you don't think you love him yet?" Amanda asked.

"I can't. I haven't known him long enough."

"Love doesn't come with a timetable," Elaine said with a gentle smile.

"How's the sex?" Amanda asked with another smirk.

Jillian just glared and Elaine laughed. "She already said it was intense."

"And that's all I'm going to say."

"Oh, come on. Intense is such a vague word."

"It's different," Jillian said.

"In what way?"

"Every way . . . the way I feel when we're together, the way I react to his touch, the way he reacts to mine, even the way my body responds to his proximity. And it's got to be mutual, because if the man is usually as hard as he is around me, I'd think it was a medical condition."

That made both of her friends burst out laughing and Jillian joined them.

"So, it's love," Amanda said with satisfaction.

"It could be," Jillian emphasized.

Amanda waved her hand in dismissal. "Semantics, dear one."

"What should I do?"

"Not to sound too old-fashioned, but what's wrong with simply waiting and seeing what develops between you two?" Elaine asked.

"That old standby?" Jillian asked with a smile that faded

quickly. "I'm not so good at waiting and seeing, you know? I want everything planned in advance."

"I'm sorry, hon, but love doesn't work that way."

"Tell me about it," Amanda said with a forced sigh that did nothing to disguise her underlying happiness. "Falling in love with Simon turned all my carefully made plans right on their ear."

"I don't want chaos in my life," Jillian said, feeling just a little desperate.

"Sometimes chaos is nice," Elaine mused.

"Not for me."

Amanda reached out and squeezed Jillian's hand. "Give it a chance, sweetie."

"The one certain conclusion I have drawn is that I don't have a choice about that one thing. I can't turn away from him, which means I have to give these emotions a chance to grow. I only wish I could sort them out."

"You'll get there," Amanda assured her.

Jillian hoped her best friend was right because she was not a fan of feeling so darn confused. In fact, she'd taken every precaution she could think of to make sure her life ran smoothly. But Alan was sending her rules tumbling out the window, and her heart was insisting on embracing the one emotion she had always been determined never to give in to.

What a mess.

Alan drove away from his first contact's office building. The man had certainly come a long way from selling knock-off merchandise from a table set up on the streets of New York. But he hadn't heard anything about a potential buy on any high-tech secrets. He *had* heard that the top producer for Jillian's production company had connections to organized crime, though. He'd even had a couple of names for Alan to plug into the computer, but the informant had agreed it would be really strange for the producer to risk his legitimate cover for pirated technology.

Unless it was something really huge.

That thought had Alan's neck itching all the way to his next meeting.

That meeting turned out to be productive in a similarly roundabout manner. The woman he met with had heard of an auction coming up on inside information on software used by more than one military application. But the timing for the auction was severely off for the information they already had on Alan's current assignment. As soon as he left the office, Alan made a call to his boss with the new heads-up and the other bits of information he'd managed to glean from his two meetings. He relayed everything his informant had told him, along with her certainty that she was unlikely to hear more, but if she did, she'd promised to call Alan.

Alan hung up with the Old Man and realized it was about lunchtime. He wondered if Jillian and her friends were ready for a short break from shopping. He called her cell phone to find out.

It turned out the women had not eaten and the other two insisted on meeting him for lunch over Jillian's objections. He would be offended, except he knew what it was like to be teased by friends. Hell, he was usually the one doing the teasing.

Lunch was going to be fun.

He picked the women up in front of one of the major department stores, feeling really grateful he hadn't had to park in the mall lot. It was insane.

Jillian slid into the passenger seat, while her two friends climbed into the backseat.

"Hi, Alan, I'm Amanda." The petite but curvaceous brunette reached between the front seats with her hand.

He shook it with his most winning smile. "Nice to meet you, Amanda. Jillian's told me a lot about you." He paused for a single beat and then said, "We might want to compare notes."

Amanda laughed and turned to Jillian. "You really have met your match, haven't you?"

"He's too wimpy to spend the day at the mall. I hardly call that my match," Jillian said with a sniff.

He looked at her with both brows raised. "Maybe I'll have to join you after lunch. I can't allow my masculinity to be impugned in this way."

The other woman, a sweet-looking woman with hair that color between light brown and blond, grinned. "Oh, good, we could use someone to carry our bags."

"Hey, I'll be doing my own shopping, thank you. I still have a cantankerous grandfather to buy for."

"You should ask Jillian for her advice. She's got a real knack for unique gifts." Amanda was grinning like there was a story or two behind that comment.

"You'll have to tell me all about that particular talent of hers over lunch."

"Hey, I'm not the conversation topic," Jillian protested.

"But, sweetheart, I can't imagine anything we'd enjoy talking about more."

"Yeah, sheesh . . . aren't actors supposed to like being the center of attention?" the other woman asked. "Oh, by the way, I'm Elaine, Amanda's sister-in-law and Jillian's other cohort in crime on these and other adventures."

"Nice to meet you, Elaine. Your husband is Eric Brant, president of Brant Computers, right?"

Elaine beamed with pride. "That's the one."

"Watch out, friend, this guy is a reporter. Anything you say is fodder for a future story."

"Maybe for a story idea," Alan said with a quick smile as he finally got out of the busy mall parking lot and onto a main road.

He headed to the restaurant Jillian had told him she and the other ladies would like to eat at. Usually they ate at one in the mall or the adjoining area, but they'd agreed a break from the bustle for some fantastic Thai food was in order.

"So, Alan, as an independent reporter, is your home base an absolutely set location?" Amanda asked with the subtlety of a Mack truck.

He couldn't help chuckling at her obvious fishing while Jillian looked over the seat to glare at her best friend. "Pushing, Mandy. Definitely pushing."

Amanda shrugged and he considered the question in relation to his real job. "Actually, I could live almost anywhere because I spend so little time at home."

"So most of your stories take you out of town?"

"Or country? Yes."

Jillian turned so she was looking out the window, giving him no idea what she thought of that. Amanda, however, was a cinch to read. She looked less than happy.

"It must be difficult to maintain long-term relationships that way," Elaine offered.

"I manage to keep my brother and grandfather speaking to me, not to mention a couple of good friends."

"But a personal relationship would require more, wouldn't it?" Elaine asked.

"I'd say my relationships are all pretty personal," he said with deliberate obtuseness.

Amanda made a sound of disgust that almost had him laughing, but he maintained his straight face. "Elaine is talking about a romantic relationship."

"Not that it is any of her business," Jillian said in a warning tone.

"I'm just making conversation," Elaine replied with her own rendition of the innocent routine.

"The truth is that my job has messed up more than one relationship with a woman. The problem is, it's a big part of who I am. I can't change that without changing me, and if I do that, I'm not the man the woman I care about learned to love." He wasn't sure why he was being so forthright. He'd started his usual teasing, but felt a need to explain the fact that there was almost no chance he and Jillian would have more than the few weeks he planned to spend in Vancouver.

"I used to think the same thing, but I learned that when you really love someone and know deep down where it counts that they love you too, you can find a compromise that works for both of you. It's part of the power of love."

Alan's lips twisted in a frown. "That aspect of love must have been sadly lacking in my past, then."

"What did you do this morning?" Jillian asked in an obvious bid to change the subject.

"I met with a couple of former contacts."

"It's important to keep those kinds of relationships up," Amanda said. "You never know when you'll need the connection."

Spoken like the business executive that Jillian had told him Amanda was.

Chapter 16

Alan found himself really enjoying lunch. He liked Jillian's friends and the way she interacted with them. She was more relaxed, less on her guard when she was around Amanda and Elaine. He wouldn't have suspected the difference in the way she related to her renters and these two women unless he had seen it.

"You going to see Darien for Christmas?" Elaine asked Jillian.

"Actually, he's coming to stay the week before New Year's."

"I bet your parents are thrilled," Amanda said with rampant sarcasm.

"Not." Jillian grinned. "But you know I kind of like pushing their buttons, so it's all good."

Alan laughed out loud. He loved this woman's attitude. "Darien is your younger brother, isn't he?"

"Yep." Jillian smiled. "He wants to look into finishing his degree at UBC."

"What is he getting his degree in?"

"Criminology. He wants to be a cop, or detective, or something."

Alan felt something inside him clench. Not in a bad way, but almost with anticipation. "He's not sure if he wants to go local, state, or federal?"

"Not yet, though he's said something about the FBI. Can you imagine?" Jillian shook her head.

"Sounds dangerous," Amanda said with a frown.

"So is being a soldier, but if no one was willing to join the armed forces we'd be in a world of hurt, wouldn't we?"

"Good point," Elaine said before dipping a piece of fried tofu in peanut sauce and popping it in her mouth.

"But it doesn't have to be my little brother, does it?"

"Do you really mean that?" Alan asked.

Jillian looked like she was thinking it over and then she sighed. "No. If he really wants to do it, then I'll support him completely. And be proud of him."

Alan felt himself grinning. "Good for you."

"It has the added benefit of being about the last thing our parents want him to pursue."

The whole table cracked up laughing at this.

It was late when they reached the marina where the Brants' yacht was docked, but earlier than Alan had expected, even after seeing Elaine home and transferring Amanda and her packages to Alan's rental car for the trip to the marina.

No doubt the women would have insisted on staying at the mall until the last store closed, but Amanda wanted to get to her island home that night. Apparently, for safety's sake, her husband had given the captain on his yacht instructions not to make the crossing if they could not set sail by a prearranged time. Amanda's adoration for her husband and baby was clear in her insistence they reach the marina before then.

Alan was impressed with the yacht. It was simplified luxury and damn fast. Amanda had explained that she and Simon kept two yachts for the crossing—the one they were on, which made the crossing in record time but only had one cabin and a small communal area, and another much bigger boat that was somewhat slower, but had enough space for a big group.

"Simon wanted us to use the bigger yacht." Amanda

rolled her eyes. "It's bigger, therefore safer—he thinks, but I wanted to minimize travel time."

"So, you let him win regarding the curfew for sailing and he acquiesced about which boat to take?" Jillian asked with a knowing grin.

Kicking off her shoes and putting her feet up, Amanda laughed. "Exactly."

Following her friend's example, Jillian took off her shoes and wiggled her toes. "Oh, that feels good."

Alan was sitting beside her and he patted his lap. Without hesitation, Jillian put her feet across his thighs and Alan started massaging them both, one in each hand.

She groaned and put her head back. "Oh, that's nice."

He smiled at her and then looked at Amanda, who was watching him with an unidentifiable expression. "So, how long will the crossing take?" he asked her.

"A little over an hour. Dorrie will already be asleep, but you'll be able to meet Simon tonight and if I don't miss my guess, Jacob will be there as well. He's nosy, but he grows on you."

Jillian laughed. "You sure you want to make that claim? You've been married to Simon for three years and you still call me at least once a week ready to clobber the man."

"He sounds like quite the character."

The women shared some of the Man Friday's escapades and Alan found himself sharing their amusement. He looked forward to meeting the former Secret Service agent. "He sounds like he'd get along just fine with my grandfather."

"Is he a cantankerous old man with suppressed thespian tendencies?"

"He's been accused of being cantankerous for sure. As for the other, I wouldn't say the tendencies ever got all that suppressed." Not with thirty years in the FBI, the majority of them as a field agent.

Amanda's dark eyes sparkled. "We'll have to get them together. I'd like to see Jacob get a run for his money with another patriarch type. He runs our house for sure, and our lives if we let him."

"That sounds like Sir."

"Jillian said your grandparents raised you?"

"After my parents died, yes."

"That must have been hard."

"My brother and I were blessed to have them. A lot of kids aren't so lucky when tragedy strikes."

Amanda nodded. "So, tell me . . . does your grandmother rule your grandfather? I've often wondered what Jacob would be like if he were married."

"Nana is a tiny little thing with a gentle voice and the sweetest smile. Not a man in her life wants to see that smile slip. I'd say she rules all of us," he admitted with a laugh. "Still does."

Though his and his brother's continuing bachelor status disappointed her, it was the only area of their lives she had a single complaint about. She understood their career choices and never suggested a change, not even when one or both of them had ended up back home to heal from wounds. "Nana is an amazing woman."

"Are you looking for someone like her to share your life?"

"Amanda," Jillian said in a warning tone.

Amanda merely blinked at them innocently and Alan had to stifle a grin, but he seriously considered her question.

He ended up shrugging. "In some ways, yes, any woman who shared my life would have to be like Nana, but I'm not looking for a carbon copy." He paused, something clicking in his head. "Actually, the two women I've gotten serious about seemed a lot like my grandmother on the surface. I never realized that before."

Both Beth and Ivy had Nana's gentle, quiet demeanor.

"But neither of those relationships worked?"

"No. Where it really counted, they didn't share Nana's strengths." Beth hadn't been able to deal with the demands of his job and Ivy hadn't been as perceptive as his grandmother, seeing the man he was below the surface of the role he'd played for his investigation.

Her future husband had seen Alan's true nature and that had brought out his possessive instincts, but Ivy had been totally clueless.

"What about Jillian?"

He didn't have a chance to answer because the redhead sitting so languorously beside him erupted into furious action, shouting her friend's name as she launched herself across the cabin and clamped her hand over her friend's mouth.

Knowing he was probably taking his life in his hands, Alan answered, humor lacing his voice. "I can say honestly, I've never seen my grandmother attack one of her friends and no one would accuse Jillian of being a restful person. She's totally high energy."

Both women were looking at him, no amusement evident in either of their gazes. Amanda looked—was it disappointed? And Jillian's expression bordered on hurt, maybe?

He shook his head and crossed the cabin, then lifted Jillian right away from Amanda and took her back to their couch.

He sat down with her still in his arms and winked at Amanda, causing her to blink at him in confusion. "But that's just the surface stuff. When it comes to standing up for what she believes in, or being there for the people she cares about, or going out of her way to help even a relative stranger, or being passionate about the things that matter to her, or keeping her commitments, I'd say Jillian and Nana have all that and more in common."

Jillian, who had been rigid in his arms, relaxed and tilted her head so their eyes met. Hers were soft and warm. "Thank you."

"You're a very special woman, sweetheart. Never doubt it." They might not have a future because their careers just did not mesh and he would no more expect her to give up hers than he could give up his. Both of them were defined in a big way by what they had chosen to do with their lives. But that did not change the fact that whoever did end up sharing her life was going to be one lucky man.

"I agree," Amanda said happily.

"You can just be quiet," Jillian replied grimly.

"Paybacks are a bitch." Amanda sounded very complacent.

"That was over three years ago!"

"Revenge is a dish best served cold."

"Stop talking in cliches," Jillian said with disgust.

Amanda just laughed.

A tall man with jet-black hair pulled back in a ponytail stood on the dock when they landed. His eyes were fixed on Amanda, the look on his face unmistakable. This man loved his wife. Completely. He came forward and rather than give her a hand to the dock, he picked her up with his hands on either side of her waist and swung her out of the boat.

"I missed you." He kissed her passionately, giving credence to his words.

"Sheesh, you'd think she was gone overnight or something." Jillian's tone belied the cynicism of her words. She clearly approved. Nevertheless, she added, "He's gone in his lab longer sometimes."

Simon's head came up and he grinned at Jillian. "I miss her then too."

"He just doesn't realize it until he comes out of his trance." Amanda wrapped an arm around Simon's waist, snuggling under his arm across her shoulders.

Alan tossed his and Jillian's bags to the dock, then clambered from the yacht and turned to lift Jillian out pretty much the same way Simon had Amanda. He didn't copy the passionate kiss, but he did put his arm around her.

Simon grabbed Jillian's bag and then started walking Amanda down the dock. Alan grabbed his duffel, his laptop case already over his shoulder, and guided Jillian with his arm around her waist to follow the other couple across the beach. They were headed toward an incredible house, of which almost the entire wall facing them was made of glass. Every room would have an amazing view.

"We'll bring the shopping loot up tomorrow," Simon was saying to Amanda. "Right now, it's time for bed."

Alan couldn't agree more. He ached to have Jillian's naked body pressed against his. Though he had a feeling that tonight it would be another platonic embrace. The first time he made love to her completely, he had no intention of being tired from a full day of shopping followed by a longish drive and boat ride.

When they reached the house, an older gentleman who had to be Jacob waited in the great room. He looked Alan over with keen eyes that Alan was sure missed very little. Just like his grandfather . . . or any other good agent. "I've prepared Miss Jillian's usual guest room."

"I told you we would need two guest rooms," Amanda said, sounding a little exasperated.

Jacob looked at Jillian. "And do we?"

If she said yes, Alan was going to find someplace private to discuss this little thing. Or simply wait until the rest of the house was in bed and go looking for her. He was not sleeping alone tonight and he was damn sure that no matter what she said, Jillian didn't want to either.

He looked down at her to find her frowning at Jacob.

He gave her a look that made Alan's lips twitch. "Well, missy?"

She sighed, her shoulders slumping slightly. "No. One room is all we require."

Jacob nodded. "As I surmised." The look he gave Amanda was nothing short of smug, and it was all Alan could do not to laugh.

He was definitely going to like Jacob.

Surprisingly, Amanda didn't look in the least put out. In fact, if Alan was reading her right, she looked pretty pleased with the outcome.

Jacob asked if anyone needed anything before he retired and they all declined. As Simon had said, it was time for bed.

Alan didn't pay much attention to the room once they got there. It was nice. Had its own bathroom, but all he cared about was the queen-size bed centered on the wall.

He dropped their bags on top of the long, low dresser. "You want to take a shower?"

"You know, that sounds good."

He nodded. It had been a long day and no matter how tired they were, they were both going to sleep better after some time under a hot spray of water.

Although neither of them made a production out of it, they watched each other undress. His heart rate increased and he had to fight to keep his breathing steady. If they did have a lifetime together, would he ever grow accustomed to seeing her enticing body revealed?

She laughed softly. "I see that junior is taking an interest in events yet again."

He didn't have to look down to know what she was talking about. His cock wasn't in the least tired and had started filling the second she tugged her shirt up and exposed her flat belly. He ran his fingertip down the slope of her breast and over a pebbled nipple. "My body's not the only one with a Pavlovian response to our mutual nudity."

"Touché . . . though I should mention that I get that reaction every time I take my bra off."

"So you're saying it's not necessarily me?"

She shrugged, giving him a flirtatious glance.

He crowded her toward the vanity until their bodies touched. "I know how to test it."

"What do you suggest?" she asked, just a little breathless.

He smiled. "I could always check the humidity level in a certain spot."

"You think?"

"Oh, yeah."

She shifted and he could feel her legs moving apart.

He ran his hand down her side, cupping her hip. "Do you have any idea what a total turn-on your openness about sex is?"

"Is that what makes this happen?" she asked as she gripped his rapidly hardening organ.

"Everything about you makes that happen." He brushed his hand over her thigh, headed toward the heart of her. "Now, it's time to test your reaction to me."

"Whatever you say. I'm a fan of scientific experimentation."

She opened her mouth to say something else, but all that came out was a gasp as his middle finger slid over her clitoris and down between her labia and into her vagina. He let it sink in up to his second knuckle, the path smooth with silken moisture. He wiggled it around a little. "Hmm . . . feels nice and wet to me."

"Yeah?" she whispered.

"Definitely." He brought his hand up to his mouth and tasted her essence. "Tastes like excitement too."

Her green eyes flared. "I suppose if it feels like it and tastes like it, that must mean you really do excite me."

"I never had any doubt."

"Arrogant."

"Confident."

Her arms wrapped around his neck and her head tilted up. "A rose by any other name . . ." Then she kissed him, effectively winning that particular verbal skirmish.

His lips were too damn busy meeting her passion to continue their lexical sparring.

Jillian didn't know how long they kissed, but they both pulled back as if by mutual agreement.

"Shower?" Alan asked.

She nodded. "Shower."

He stepped back and she had to grit her teeth to stop her body from following his. He turned and started the water while she wrapped her long hair in a towel, turban style. He stepped into the shower and pulled her with him, keeping her situated so the water didn't hit her towel-covered head.

"Are you always going to be so perfectly protective?" she couldn't help asking. She'd never had a lover who was so considerate and careful of her comfort and well-being.

He winked. "It's part of my charm."

She would have accused him of being arrogant again, but the fact was, it *was* part of his charm. She grabbed the shower gel and put some in her hand, then rubbed it between her hands and started washing his body.

He did the same thing, the tip of his hard-on brushing her stomach as he moved closer to wrap his arms around her and wash her back. "I like this showering together thing. It's a lot more fun washing you and vice versa than doing this all alone."

"I don't know, I kind of enjoyed watching you do it alone the other day."

That growly sound he made emanated from deep in his chest. "You are so hot, Miss Sinclair."

"I would say that in that particular situation, you were the hot one."

"You just go right on thinking that."

She laughed. "I will, thanks." She loved the way they interacted. "I don't intimidate you in the least, do I?"

His hands traveled down to her butt, washing her in sensual circular motions. "Not at all, sweetheart. I enjoy you."

"That makes me feel good," she admitted. "I intimidate a lot of men."

"Past sex partners?"

"Um . . . some." In fact, most. "I decided when I was seventeen that I would never again pretend to be something other than what I am, but I really like the way you don't make me feel like I should even consider doing so."

"You are perfect just the way you are, Jillian."

"Not even close, but we seem to fit."

A shadow passed over his features, but then he smiled. "Yes, we do." He leaned down and kissed the underside of her chin.

She tilted her head to give him better access and he pressed baby kisses all along her jaw. She was moaning with pleasure when he stopped.

His lack of movement and silence brought her eyes open. He was looking at her closely, as if trying to read her mind.

"Whatever it is, just ask. I'm pretty sure mental telepathy is not one of your many talents."

He didn't smile at her joke, but he did nod. "What did you pretend to be before you were seventeen?"

Jillian waited for the defensive shields she'd lived behind for more than ten years to come into place, but they didn't. All she felt was a desire, maybe even a need to share a pain in her childhood that shaped so much of the creed she lived by as an adult.

"It's kind of a long story."

"I'm betting Simon Brant is the kind of man to have a really huge water heater. Go for it."

She grinned. "I love how you can make me smile even when I'm thinking grim thoughts."

"Me too."

She took a deep breath. "It sort of started when my mom met my dad."

"Scorpio, right?"

"Right. He was the same larger-than-life, irresponsible egotist then, just not nearly as wealthy. He swept Mom right off her conservative middle-class feet. He was her big teen rebellion. She paid a bigger price than a lot of teens do for pushing the boundaries their parents set. At least according to her. Personally, I think the kids that end up dead or maimed because they or their friends drove high are worse off. In fact, I can think of a lot worse things than what happened to my mom, but the point is, she couldn't."

"What was her big price?"

"She got pregnant with me. She was only sixteen. He was twenty-two. My grandparents were appalled. They insisted on marriage."

"With less than happy results?"

Jillian's body filled with an old and familiar tension. "You could say that. Scorpio agreed to help out financially to the best of his ability, but he flat-out refused to marry my mom. My grandparents threatened to have him up on statutory rape charges, but the age of consent in Mom's home state is sixteen, and Scorpio was smart enough to have checked that out before messing with a teenager."

"What a prince."

She flinched, even though she agreed with Alan's sarcastic indictment.

He pressed their bodies together, derailing her depressing train of thought. "Let's finish this in bed, after our shower."

"Sounds good. We're about done, aren't we?"

He rotated them so he was on the other side of her. Then he turned her around so she was facing away from him. She felt him lean back against the wall, bending his legs until the head of his penis was lined up with the juncture of her thighs. He pulled her toward him and she squeaked as she felt his rigid manhood push between her thighs.

"Alan," she gasped.

He petted her, calming her, and then pressed her thighs close together so his hard flesh was trapped right below her apex. "Don't worry about it, sweetheart. This is all I'm going to do with junior."

He thrust and tipped back, rubbing his penis back and forth between her tightly closed legs. The water made him slide easily and it was a more erotic position than she ever would have expected. It felt so good, the stimulation subtle, but wonderful all the same.

Chapter 17

"That's nice, isn't it?"

"Yes."

"Feel free to tell me what you think of this." Then he started sliding his hands over her water-slick skin, touching every erogenous zone he had discovered that night he'd given her such explosive and mind-altering orgasms.

By the time his middle finger dipped down to circle her clitoris, she was shaking with pleasure. He kept up the steady thrusts from behind while using that single finger to caress her hot button one second and then dip between her lips the next before sliding up to touch her clit again. His other hand stayed busy touching every bit of her skin it could reach.

Her whole body suffused with the heat of preorgasmic ecstasy. "I'm going to come, lover ... please ... please ..." She didn't know what she was begging for, only that he could give it.

Then he did. Rearing up toward her, so his steel-hard shaft pressed against her labia, he pinched her pleasure nub and she screamed as her body convulsed. Harsh grunts sounded in her ear as she felt the large member between her thighs pulse with his climax.

Her knees buckled as the last spasm of pleasure shook her

body. "Oh, man, Alan, that was amazing," she said in a husky voice she barely recognized as her own.

"You are amazing."

"Let's see if we achieve the amazing feat of getting rinsed and dried off and into bed."

She wasn't sure how they did it, but they managed those feats as well as brushing their teeth and turning off the lights before snuggling down together in the bed.

He kissed the top of her head where it rested on his chest. "You up to finishing your story?"

"Funnily enough, I am. I feel good. Relaxed."

"Good."

She wondered if the lovemaking in the shower had been for her benefit. Oh, he'd gotten off, but he'd done it right when she'd started feeling depressed and all tense from her memories.

"So, Scorpio refused to marry Mom. It was devastating for her and my grandparents. They put great store by appearances. Mom was humiliated, not only to be pregnant at such a young age, but because she'd been dumb enough to get involved with such a louse. She admitted to me that she never believed he loved her. He was religious about not lying that way. The truth was, he was honest about pretty much everything from the beginning. He told her he didn't do commitment. The only promise he made was to give her a phenomenal initiation into sex."

"If he was your father, I'm going to go out on a limb and guess he kept that promise."

She smiled, feeling good rather than offended by the comparison. "I'm sure he did, but she never said."

Alan gave a low chuckle. "I bet she didn't."

"Mom had to drop out of school, but after I was born, my grandparents arranged for her to finish getting her diploma at a private school that overlooked her past indiscretion."

"What happened to you? I mean, it's obvious she kept you."

"Sort of. Mom went to boarding school in another state and one of her aunts took care of me in a nearby town so she could see me at least every couple of weeks. Not that anyone at the school knew she had a child, but my grandparents were adamant she not abdicate her responsibilities like Scorpio had. The funny thing was that he moved to a city in the same state so he could see me too. Mom refused to see him, so he visited me when she wasn't there. For the first few years of my life, that wasn't a problem. Shortly after she graduated from high school, Mom went into a two-year nursing program."

"Your mom was a nurse?"

"Yep. I guess the whole nurturing thing comes from her."

"And the brutal honesty from your dad."

"I don't know about brutal, but yes . . . the one thing I've never accused Scorpio of was dishonesty."

"So, how did your mother meet your stepfather?"

"It was so cliché. Really. She was his nurse in the hospital. He fell for her, courted her, and when I was seven years old, they married. Mom and I moved to his home in California. At first, it was classic happy families. Mom joined the bridge club and her husband's country club. He was the president of the local Rotary Club. They golfed together on the weekends with the movers and shakers of the city where we lived. His business is one of the bigger employers in the area and he makes an effort to rub elbows with influential politicians and the like."

"Sounds very *Leave It to Beaver*."

"Do you think Beaver's dad drank in the evenings and got ugly when he did?"

"He was a mean drunk?"

"And a smart one. He played the part of perfect husband and stepfather around others so well, my mom still buys into it, excusing what she calls his 'infrequent bouts of temper' as his response to all the pressures he is under being such a good business- and civic-minded all-around good guy." The sarcasm was dripping in her words, but she couldn't help herself. "Appearances were always more important than the reality to my mother. Do you know she denied being my mother in any public way until we moved to California to live with Stanley?"

"She doesn't have your personal strength."

Jillian let out a long breath and rubbed his stomach to comfort herself. "You're right. And I try not to expect too much out of her. She's got her own strengths, but her and Dan's weaknesses brought a lot of pain to both me and my little brother. Both emotional and physical."

"You said before you left when you were seventeen. What happened that pushed you that far?"

"Dan got elected Man of the Year by the Rotarians. In a city the size of the one they live in, with many chapters of the Rotary Club, that was a really big deal. And it was all so much utter bullshit."

Alan flinched. Jillian smiled against his warm chest. She rarely swore and even amidst the pain of her memories, she enjoyed this evidence that he knew her so well.

She snuggled into him, her body relaxing just that little bit as she drew strength from him in a way she had never done from another person except Amanda. "You know the real kicker?"

He combed his fingers through her hair, the casual affection warming that place inside she'd always protected so carefully in the past. "What's that, sweetheart?"

"When he went up to receive his award, I was wearing a long-sleeved blouse to cover the bruises on my arms he'd given me two nights before when we'd gotten into an argument. He had a tendency to make his point in a physical way when he'd been drinking, and he'd been drinking his favorite twenty-year-old Scotch that night." She laughed, the sound hollow. "He only drank the good stuff, as if that made his addiction less plebian."

Alan's body had gone rigid beneath her, and darned if that didn't comfort the old heartache. He would have cared. If he had known her then, this man would have cared because he was that kind of person.

He kissed the top of her head. "And your mother . . ."

"Blamed me. She said if I didn't push him so hard, didn't argue over every little thing, he wouldn't get so frustrated with me and lose his temper. According to her, it was my fault when he lost his cool with her too. After all, I was her daughter and hadn't he done right by me, insisting on raising me as if I were his own daughter? Only he never once smacked Darien. On the surface, we appeared to be the perfect family, but underneath, there was a fault that caused damaging quakes on a fairly regular basis. That night, my mom forced me to go to the awards ceremony. How would it look if his darling stepdaughter wasn't there? It was the final straw."

"But you left."

"A few months later, yes, I did. Unbeknownst to my mom and stepfather, I'd been keeping visual documentation of the abuse. Both my mom's and mine. Not that he hit her often, but I managed to get more than one picture of her bruises when she was still asleep. She used sleeping pills when they'd had an argument, and he slept like the dead after drinking."

"Taking pictures was pretty smart."

She warmed to his praise. Which was kind of pathetic, but nice too. "I was worried about Darien."

"You thought his dad might start hurting him?"

"No. I was worried he'd grow up thinking it was okay to be that way. I love my brother so much and I couldn't stand the idea he'd grow up to be a jerk like his dad."

"Do you have any idea what an amazing person you are?" he asked, his voice laced with disbelief.

Heat crawled into her cheeks. "You're being silly."

"Right." He snorted. "So, what did you do?"

"I showed Mom and Stanley my 'scrapbook' and told

them I would take it to the local paper along with my story if my stepfather didn't go into rehab and stop drinking completely."

"He never got violent when he was sober?"

"Never. In fact, sober, he was a pretty decent guy."

"Not decent enough to go into rehab on his own."

"Of course not. How would it look?"

Alan made a noise of disgust.

She nodded against his chest in agreement with the sentiment, hugging him a little tighter. "Exactly. But that was the first thing they said to me when I insisted on the course of action I had outlined. Mom tried to convince me that Stanley could simply quit drinking on his own. I told them if he was capable of that, he would already have done it. I didn't care how they covered up his stay in the program, but he had to go through it. And he had to stop drinking completely, even casually. I also said that my brother had to go to a counselor to help him see how wrong the type of behavior his dad had been exhibiting was."

"I imagine both of your parents were furious about that stipulation."

"That's an understatement. They were livid about both the rehab program and Darien's counseling. Remember, they still blamed me, not the alcohol, for my stepfather's behavior. I won't pretend I was easy to live with. I had a lot of pain to work out from the years my mom denied my role as her daughter and I hated the lifestyle we lived, but I refused to believe that it was okay for Stanley to hurt me physically, just because he could. They could have grounded me, darn it. Other parents did that. But if they had . . . well, then they'd have to admit to their friends and mine that I wasn't perfect. I mean if I couldn't use the phone, or go to a school dance, I'd have to tell people why."

"That's insane. Every child gets in trouble sometimes."

"Not in our house. Darien and I were perfect. We didn't talk back. We got good grades. We didn't fall in with the wrong crowds. Luckily for Darien, that was true."

"So did Stanley go to rehab?"

"Oh, yes. He and Mom tried to threaten me into backing down, but I wouldn't. The potential cost was too great. I would not let Darien grow up getting used to that kind of behavior. And maybe one day, Stanley would have lost it with his son."

"But you still left home."

"Well, Stanley got totally sober and stayed that way, but both he and my mom were furious with me for being so 'disloyal,' as they saw it. They treated me worse than they had before. If they had just ignored me, I could have handled it, but they both sniped at me constantly."

"So, you traded physical for verbal abuse."

"Exactly. I wasn't going to let Darien witness that, either. They were pretty careful to keep it under wraps around him, but eventually one or both of them was going to slip. And frankly, I was tired of it. Sick of the lies, sick of pretending to be a loving family around their friends when they treated me like they hated me in the privacy of our home. I moved out, went to Los Angeles, and never looked back."

"They just let you go?"

"I still had my 'scrapbook,' remember? In fact, I still do. I've used it to force them to let me see Darien, but as far as me moving away? I think they were relieved too. They made up a story about me being admitted into a prestigious acting school and how much they missed me, but didn't want to stand in the way of my dreams. They told that to all their friends and anyone else who would listen. No one was more vocal in their support of my acting career than my family. As far as the rest of the world is concerned, they still are."

"And you still hate the pretense."

"Yes, but because of it, I've gotten to see more of Darien than I would have just from the blackmail." She was silent for a moment. "You want to know something weird?"

"What?"

"A couple of years ago, when I was home for Christmas, Stanley took me aside and thanked me for making him get help. He said the drinking would have eventually destroyed his life. He'd seen it happen with more than one contemporary. He even apologized for hurting me all those times."

"What did you do?"

"I told him I'd forgiven him a long time ago. I had. I learned a lot about honesty fighting against the lack of it in my home. It made me a better person, I think. And you know, Mom and Stanley aren't all bad. They really love each other and Darien. I think, in some ways, they even really love me."

"No family is perfect."

"No. And I tell you, compared to Amanda's family, mine is borderline fabulous." She laughed, feeling better talking about this stuff than she had in a long time. "I joke about liking to drive them nuts, but really? It's been years since I did anything with the express purpose of annoying them."

"You love them too."

"Yes, I do, but we get along better living in different cities."

"Countries now."

"Yep . . . the distance is good, but I miss Darien."

"If he goes to school at UBC, you'll see a lot more of him."

"Yes. And the truth is, neither of our parents has put up huge objections to him doing so, though they are trying to get him to go to the University of Washington instead. He'd still be closer to me and they think he should get his degree from an American university."

"There's something to be said for that, considering the career path he wants to follow."

"He's going to like you. A lot." Jillian bit her lip. Darn it. She was talking like she assumed they had a long-term future and so far, they hadn't explored even a tendril of that possibility.

"If he's half the person you are, I'm going to enjoy meeting him too."

Oh. Alan planned to meet her brother. Jillian was going to stop while she was ahead. Which was so not like her, but her stepfather wasn't the only one who had learned a thing or two in the years since she was seventeen.

Alan woke early as he usually did, surprised that Jillian was still sleeping deeply. Her revelations of the night before had only increased his respect for her. She was unique, both in the way she saw life and how she responded to the challenges she faced because of it. His family would adore her.

Not that they'd ever meet, but if they did? His grandfather would take to her like he took to very few people. Nana loved everybody, but she would be impressed by Jillian. His brother would think she was . . . well, maybe introducing her to his brother wasn't such a good idea. The man had a way with women. He flirted with every female he met. He made Alan look shy and retiring when it came to women.

Not that Alan had ever wanted to conquer the female population like his brother, but he'd never had a problem getting his sexual needs filled or using his sexuality on the job to get him what he wanted. His brother still managed to make him feel like an amateur when it came to women. No, Jackson definitely didn't need to meet Jillian any time soon, if ever.

To avoid waking her, Alan carefully climbed from the bed. Jillian had told him that Simon had a martial arts studio and pool on the ground floor of this incredible house. He wondered if Simon had weights in his studio. Even if he didn't, Alan wouldn't mind a chance to work through some of his jujitsu forms. He usually kept up regardless of his cover, but he'd been sticking to running and weight training since moving into Jillian's house. He could feel the itch to put his body through the paces.

He found the martial arts studio with no trouble, seeing no one else on his journey through the house. It was barely six o'clock, so he wasn't surprised. He let himself in and began his workout.

He didn't know how long he'd been working out, only that he'd built up a sheen of sweat on his skin and pushed his muscles to stretch over and over in ways they hadn't in two weeks, when he sensed the presence of someone else on the mats with him.

He spun and landed in a classic attack pose.

"You're good, better than I would have expected a mere reporter to be," Simon drawled, his body held in a natural defense pose, his eyes focused on Alan with an unreadable expression.

Alan shrugged, not losing his form. "It's good exercise."

"What's your discipline?"

"Jujitsu."

Simon nodded. "I've just started studying that form."

"Jillian said you have a master black belt in tae kwon do."

"Yes."

Alan executed a kick that Simon blocked with almost lazy efficiency. "Have you been studying long?"

"All my life." It was Simon's turn to attack, but he chose to use his upper body.

Damn, the man was fast. Alan blocked the blows, but he had to spin away and step back to regain his space. "Same here. Though not jujitsu to start with."

"What discipline did you begin with?"

"A hybridized form of karate." Alan moved in with a combination his grandfather had taught him before he'd even learned to ride a bike.

This time, Simon took the step back after narrowly avoiding a solid kick. "So jujitsu, the classic hybrid, was a natural transition for you."

"Yes."

Neither man moved for several seconds. Then Simon came at him with a flurry of moves that Alan would have been hard-pressed to defend against if he wasn't so warmed up. The man didn't stop, though, and in a turn that startled the hell out of him, Alan found himself on his back on the mat, Simon above him. He swept his foot out and caught Simon's ankle, but the other man rolled and they both jumped to their feet, breath coming just a tad faster than normal.

Simon circled him, his expression intent. "You know, I have a policy of doing a background check on everyone who comes to my home. My family's safety is paramount to me, but I also have information in my lab I wouldn't want finding its way into the wrong hands."

His brain on instant alert, Alan met Simon move for move without giving ground, but without gaining any either. "Understandable."

Once again, they ended up on the mat together, this time in as close to a grapple as two men of their skill could do.

Simon attempted a submission hold that had little to do with martial arts, but was damn impressive regardless. "I'm glad you see it that way. Jacob did a background check on you."

Alan managed to duck out of the hold and knock Simon back. "Find anything interesting?"

Simon rolled up onto his feet, taking two steps back and dropping into a defense stance once again. "That's the thing . . . he didn't. According to Jacob, your background is just too clean."

"I believe the term I used was too canned, sir." Jacob spoke from near the door.

Alan didn't make the mistake of looking at the older man when he was sparring with Simon. They were too closely matched for him to give the computer genius that kind of edge.

"Canned?" he asked.

"As in created. Nicely done, but definitely not real."

"Funny, I sure feel real to me."

"No doubt you are real, but Alan Johnson, the reporter? I'm not so sure about him."

"If you did the investigation you said you did, you would have found my past, articles I'd published, proof of my reality."

"That's what's so interesting. The A. Johnson that published those articles could have been anyone. Johnson is the second most popular last name in America. Pretty generic and damn easy to use for a cover. It's the kind of background the spook agencies create as standby covers for their operatives."

"That's ridiculous." But Alan felt chills run down his spine.

Chapter 18

"I'm sure Jillian told you that Jacob used to be Secret Service?" Simon asked.

"Yes."

"He's damn good at this sort of thing."

"Thank you, sir."

Simon smiled, without breaking eye contact with Alan. "You're welcome, old friend."

"Watch who you're calling old."

Simon smiled and Alan laughed, but the sense that he was on a precipice he had not expected did not diminish.

"Alan, it's Jacob's professional opinion that you are just that. A professional. Now, the only question that needs answering is, are you working for the good guys or the bad guys, and then maybe, what the hell you are doing with Jillian."

"That's two questions."

Simon shrugged.

"If you're convinced of this, why did you let me come with Jillian to your home?" Alan asked, more than mildly curious.

"Two reasons." Simon switched to an offensive posture and moved in on Alan in an effort so smooth Alan was almost surprised by it. The man was really, really good. "One,

I have a better chance finding out what you are up to with you here."

"And two?"

"Jacob's instincts are telling him you're government sponsored, not an independent."

"Interesting conclusion to draw on zero evidence. Seeing as how I'm just a simple reporter."

"No. You are not."

Alan gritted his teeth at Jacob's confident tone.

"Though I would have been disappointed if you had admitted it too quickly. Fact is? Your cover starts fading fast two layers in. Depending on the type of job you're on, that isn't abnormal. You must not expect the people you are investigating to dig too deeply into your background, if at all." Jacob sounded absolutely sure of his conclusions.

"What if your wild theory was right? And I'm not saying it is. But if it was, you wouldn't expect me to divulge secrets, would you?"

Simon stepped back and dropped his sparring pose completely, fixing Alan with a serious look. "No, but if Jillian's involved I think you should."

"Why?"

"Because she's an innocent." Jacob came to stand close to them and spoke quietly. "We don't want her hurt."

"Jillian's a big girl. You need to let her look after herself."

"Not going to happen. She's family and that makes her our responsibility."

Alan had a choice. He could maintain his claim to innocence, but he knew that neither Simon nor Jacob was going to buy it. They were convinced he was not who he said he was and his gut told him that no amount of arguing on his part was going to make them believe otherwise.

So, that left him with the alternative of sticking to his cover for the sake of hiding the truth, making up a story to cover his alternate identity, or telling these men the truth. Alan wasn't in deep cover. He was on a case that by its very nature made his response to it necessarily organic and fluid. He had to utilize whatever sources he could if he hoped to identify the technology slated for pirating before the deadline. A deadline that was about the only information he had right now, not how it was going to be sold, who it was going to be sold to, or even what was going to be sold to begin with.

"Before I opt for Door Number Three, I need to make a phone call."

Simon nodded. "Make your phone call."

Neither he nor Jacob asked what Alan meant by his cryptic statement, which only reinforced his belief that they knew or guessed at least part of the truth. With Jacob's connections, it was possible they knew he was former FBI or quickly would now that his image had been recorded on Simon's home security system. Alan doubted they knew about TGP. Hell, he hadn't known about TGP before Beth's father had recruited him for the agency. But his status as a federal agent could be verified by someone with the right connections, and he had a feeling Jacob was one of those people.

For all Alan knew, Simon had the ability to access the information himself. The man was a computer genius and there was no reason to assume that genius was limited to hardware development.

Heck, Alan knew just how easy it was for someone who knew what he was doing to hack into supposedly secure information stored digitally.

It was one of his favorite parts of the job. His grandfather and brother called him a geek, but the truth was, he loved a puzzle and there was no puzzle more challenging than anti-spy software.

Alan went out to the beach to make his call.

"So, this guy Jacob has you pegged for a spook?"

"Yeah. They're making an assumption I'm on the right side, but I can't be sure what they'll do if I don't give them a reason to keep their suspicions to themselves."

"You don't have to do full disclosure, though, not if Jacob is former Secret Service. He knows the drill."

"No doubt Simon does too. He's developed computer technology used by the government."

"I'm hearing a 'but' in here somewhere."

"No one said your instincts had dulled with the desk job."

"Damn right."

"Look . . . I think Simon and maybe even that weird Man Friday of his could help with the case. It's a long shot, but right now—that's all we've got."

"You're up against the deadline on this case."

"We've been butting up against it since we discovered the connection of Frost Productions and Prescott."

"My agents work best under pressure."

Alan laughed. "Right." He flicked his gaze up to the windows facing the beach, automatically looking to see if he was being watched. He saw no one. "Any more information on Frost?"

"No."

"Are you going to pass on what's been discovered to the FBI?"

"There's nothing to say they don't already know and he is operating out of country. Technically, his activities aren't in their jurisdiction."

"They are if he's laundering money for a U.S.-based crime syndicate."

"We don't have any proof, and unless his probable connections show potential in regard to our case, we'll stop investigating them."

Alan bit back his initial argument that the information needed to be passed on definitively and immediately. He was no longer an FBI agent and his primary goal was his TGP directive. Besides, if his Seattle informant had inklings and his agency had found the connection as quickly as they had, chances were that information was in a database somewhere in Washington.

"Got it." Seeing movement in the great room, Alan decided he needed to wrap up his phone call. "So I have permission for full disclosure should I deem it necessary?"

"Use your best judgment."

Alan didn't get a chance to talk to Simon and Jacob alone again until after breakfast. Jillian, Amanda, and an adorable toddler named Dorrie were up eating breakfast when he returned from his walk on the beach. Alan had showered, dressed, and eaten his own breakfast when Simon suggested giving him a tour of his lab.

He was unsurprised when Jacob arrived seconds after Simon showed him into a room that would have looked at home as a set for a science fiction series.

"Are you sure it's a good idea to bring me in here? What if I'm not one of the good guys?" Alan couldn't resist mocking the other men's obvious complacency where he was concerned.

"We can always kill you and dump your body in the Sound," Jacob said deadpan.

"Good backup plan," Alan approved.

Simon shook his head. "Do all federal agents have such a twisted sense of humor, or is it just you and Jacob?"

"I don't see anything twisted about my sense of humor," Alan replied with a smirk.

"Of course not."

"You ever stop to think it's the rest of you that got a screwed-up view of life?" Jacob asked in a nicely done New Jersey accent.

"Your talents were wasted in the Secret Service."

"I thought that a time or two myself," the retired agent said.

Simon just sighed. "Can we focus here?"

Alan jerked his head once in acknowledgement. "I talked to my superior."

"Your editor at the paper?" Jacob asked mockingly.

Alan rolled his eyes. "Right."

"And he said?" Simon prompted, not allowing Alan and Jacob to continue with their bantering.

Spoilsport. "I have approval to disclose what I deem necessary to protect my cover."

"So disclose," Simon said, his eyes chillingly flat.

"You'd have made a good agent."

"I've said that a time or two, but everyone's got their roles in life, and this one . . . he's got his hands full influencing the future of technological development," Jacob said, his voice laced with fatherly type pride.

"I can restrain you both and test some theories I've got on electric shock aversion therapy," Simon said conversationally.

"Damn. You're almost as easy as Ethan."

"Ethan?"

"A friend."

"At the agency where you work?" Simon asked.

"As a matter of fact, yes."

"Speaking of the agency . . ." Simon let his voice trail off pointedly.

"I'm on a case, investigating technology piracy."

"How is Jillian involved?" Jacob asked.

"She's not, but someone at the production company for her show is."

"Who?"

"I don't know."

"What kind of technology is being pirated?"

"I don't know."

"What do you know?"

"That someone at Frost Productions arranged a sale of some sort of technology via an information broker named Prescott in less than two weeks' time."

"Prescott's not talking?"

"No, but that's not a big surprise. The kind of people he represents would make his life a hell of a lot worse than federal prison if he sold them out. I suspect we've kept him alive thus far only because we've kept him under wraps."

Jacob nodded knowingly. "You said Jillian's not involved. How are you so sure since you don't know who is involved?"

"The first time I met her, my gut told me she wasn't a suspect, and almost everything I've learned about her since has reinforced that belief."

"Almost everything?" Simon asked.

"She has dreams that require a lot of money to pursue."

"But . . ."

"But she's the type of person who would give up her dreams before she would give up her integrity to live them out."

"You've gotten to know her pretty well in a short time," Simon said.

"Yes."

"Your relationship with her part of your cover?" Jacob asked.

"No."

"But you aren't sure you're going to pursue it once your investigation is over," Simon said shrewdly.

"Our lifestyles aren't compatible."

Jacob snorted, but said nothing.

"Does she know you aren't looking at a long-term future with her?" Simon asked.

"You tell me," Alan said, feeling defensive though neither of the other men had accused him of anything. "You know Jillian better than I do. Do you think she would even get into a relationship if she thought I was looking for a future?"

Simon turned to something on the workbench closest to him and started jotting notes. "You're wrong."

"What?"

"I don't think I know her better than you do." Then he seemed to totally zone out on the notes he was taking.

Jacob made a tsking sound. "I assume you told us details on your case because you're hoping Simon has a clue what the technology is that is being sold?"

"Or you. Jacob, it's obvious you've got connections."

Jacob slid a blank notebook toward Simon as the other

man ran out of room on the sheet of paper he was taking notes on. He shook his head. "You'd think he'd take notes on a handheld or something, considering. But no . . . says he can't think the same without a pencil in his hand."

"Geniuses," Alan said sardonically.

Jacob smiled. "I like you, Agent. You've got a discerning sense of humor."

"According to Jillian, I like pulling other people's chains just like you do."

"Like I said, discerning."

"So, any thoughts, Jacob?"

"You know, of course, that guessing the technology is like taking a crap shoot and hoping the dice land just right?"

"That's what I told my boss when the agency came up with a list of potential technologies."

Jacob's expression was approving. "That's the guys in the white lab coats. They can't resist making their predictions, but if I told you the times the one scenario they never thought of happened when I was wearing the black suit, we'd be here until next month."

"I hear that."

"So, you want to know if I've heard anything that might be interpreted differently now that I've been given this new information?"

"Basically, yes."

"I figure you've already got the fact that Frost has distant connections to the mob?"

"We weren't sure how distant they were."

"You think I'd let Jillian be involved with the company if the connections were close enough to hurt her?"

Alan's respect for the older man rose a notch. "Good."

"But I don't think he's selling pirated technology. He's related to the Family, but keeps himself as clean as a man who doesn't disappear completely can. He would not risk his relatively normal life for something so trivial."

"Even if it was going to make him a killing?"

"No way in hell. The man has enough money—what he wants is legitimacy, but he's smart enough to realize that disappearing with his wife and children is more than just risky."

"So, he's got someone working for him that's putting his good life at risk?"

"That's about the size of it."

"That's what my instincts were telling me."

"Good instincts."

"So I've been told."

"Have you considered approaching Frost?"

"While he was still a suspect, no."

"But now . . ."

"It's something to consider."

Jacob nodded.

"Why a Canadian film company?" Simon didn't look up from his notes when he asked the question.

Alan sighed. "If I knew, I'd have a clue what we're looking at here."

"Maybe looking at that fact as a pertinent one would give you a clue to the technology."

"You're assuming the pirate is not just coincidentally working for the film company?"

"It's a hypothesis worth exploring."

Alan agreed. "Okay."

"The first, most obvious possibility is that the pirate intends to do a video demonstration of the product," Jacob said musingly.

"Or he's using the prop inventory as a cover for transporting the physical thing across the border."

"Or the pirate is aware of Frost's connections to the mob and hopes to use him as the fall guy if things go wrong." Again, Simon spoke as if he wasn't paying the least attention to their conversation, only it was obvious he was.

Something clenched in Alan's gut. "Or even if they don't."

Jacob nodded. "Maybe the film company's resources are of secondary interest to Frost's vulnerability."

"If the pirate is looking for a fall guy, he's either very careful or this piece of technology is big and comes with a significant enough risk that he feels the need to mitigate it."

"Shit . . . it's government, isn't it?"

"I'm guessing," Simon said as he drew an incomprehensible diagram on yet another blank sheet of paper.

"But it's still just a guess," Jacob warned.

"Right, only my gut says we're onto something."

"So does mine," Jacob agreed.

"I'm rarely wrong," Simon said, without the least sense of arrogance.

"His brain doesn't work like other people's, but when you get it working for you, you've got a secret weapon our enemies would trade military secrets for," Jacob said with obvious pride.

Simon didn't look like he heard, his mind apparently fully engaged in his notes again.

"Okay, so when we get back to Vancouver, I'll have Jillian set up a meeting with Frost."

"Good idea."

"Speaking of Jillian, what are you going to do about her?" Simon asked.

Damn, the man was a cagey bastard.

"What do you mean?"

"She's not just a lay."

"I know." But what good that knowledge would do him, Alan couldn't be sure. He couldn't get Simon's earlier words out of his mind. "Why did you say you think I know her better than you?"

"I didn't."

Alan just waited. As Jacob said, Simon's brain didn't work like a normal person's. Alan figured an explanation was coming.

Simon actually looked up from his strange-looking diagram. "I said I didn't know her better than you."

"Same thing."

"Not quite, though I'm not sure if it isn't the case. From what she's told Amanda, you understand Jill on a level no other man ever has."

"She doesn't believe in long-term commitment."

"That's not exactly true," Jacob said.

"For herself," Alan qualified.

"So change her mind."

"I don't know if that would be a good idea—for either of us."

Jacob shook his head and, surprisingly, glared at Simon. "Sounds like someone else I know. Damn smart in one area and dumb as a post in another." He turned his firm gaze to Alan. "You'll figure it out, boy, but I sure hope it's before you do something irreparably stupid."

"Well, thank you."

Alan's sarcasm rolled right off Jacob, who just shook his head again and turned to leave the lab, speaking over his shoulder as he went. "You going to remember you've got dinner with your cousin and his family tonight, boss?"

Simon didn't answer, his pencil scrabbling noisily on the paper.

"If you aren't down ten minutes before they arrive, I'll send in the troops, and you remember what she did the last time I let her into your lab and you were otherwise occupied."

Simon looked up at that, an expression of horror clearly on his face. "You agreed to keep Dorrie out of here."

Jacob didn't answer, just left.

Alan couldn't help laughing. "I take it your daughter is a good alarm clock."

"More like a miniature tornado with major destructive potential. Do me a favor and knock . . . uh, loudly . . . on my door at a quarter after six?"

"I could ask Amanda—"

"No." Simon shook his head emphatically. "She'll bring our daughter with her and then I'll have both of them in here and that can get really scary."

"Jillian said Amanda understood your disappearing act."

"She does, but she's curious and she's not shy about asking questions now. The thing is, she fiddles with my papers and even my experiments. She doesn't mean to, but . . ."

"And you don't want to hurt her feelings by saying no touching."

Burnished red skimmed across Simon's cheekbones. "Exactly."

"I'll pound on the door."

"Thanks."

Alan left the lab, considering the compromises both Amanda and Simon had made in order to keep their relationship strong. Was he capable of making similar sacrifices for a chance with Jillian? Did he even want to? And if he did . . . was it worth making the effort when she saw him as a sex partner, not a lover?

Chapter 19

True to his word, Alan pounded on the door to Simon's lab that evening and then didn't leave before reminding the other man of Jacob's threat. The computer whiz nodded and then went back to what he'd been doing. Taking pity on him, Alan gently tugged him by the arm until he had him out of the lab and the door shut. Only then did Simon's gaze focus on the room around him.

He grinned sheepishly at Alan. "Thanks."

"No problem."

Dinner with Elaine, her husband Eric, and their children was nice. The way the Brant family interacted reminded Alan of his own family. Alan was almost too comfortable with these people. The love and respect they all felt for each other was obvious and it was equally clear that both Jacob and Jillian were considered members of that family. Considering the strained relationship Jillian had with her own family, it was a good thing.

Alan liked the Brants even more for including Jillian so completely in their clan. He regretted the fact that moving on from his current assignment would mean leaving these new-found friends behind.

* * *

"So, you're certain now that Miss Sinclair is not a suspect?" the boss asked as Alan checked in with him via the phone while Simon, Amanda, and Jillian saw Elaine and her family off at the dock.

"Positive. She wouldn't betray these people." She wasn't the type to betray anyone. "She's one of the most personally honest people I have ever met. She's uncompromising with herself and others."

"Good."

"Uh . . . yeah. So, I've got your approval to talk to Frost?"

"I know your gut is telling you he's not involved, but that's a big risk to take."

"Are you saying you want me to hold off?"

"Until we can do some more background research, yes."

"You're the boss."

"But you think I'm wrong."

"Our timetable is tight. The longer I wait to pick the man's brains, the bigger the risk the perp is going to slip through our fingers period."

"You're assuming Frost is going to have something of value to add, but he's a long shot for information if he's not involved too."

"He's got a better picture of what goes on in his company than anyone else does."

"If he's not involved, whoever the pirate is will be careful to stay under his radar."

"That doesn't mean he's succeeded."

"Give it a couple of days."

Alan didn't argue further. The Old Man's tone had a finality to it that Alan had no problem interpreting. He said to hold off talking to Frost; Alan was going to have to hold off.

Simon and Amanda were absent when Alan came back inside from his walk on the beach.

Jillian was standing at the huge wall of windows in the darkened great room. She turned to face Alan when he came in. "I really enjoy Simon and Amanda, this view, and the peacefulness of this spot sometimes."

"But you couldn't do your job living on an island in Puget Sound."

"Dreams come with a cost."

"Tell me about it." His had cost him his hopes of a wife and children.

"Amanda changed her dreams when she met Simon."

"They both seem happy."

"They are, but not everyone can have that kind of happiness."

Alan crossed the room and put his hands on Jillian's waist, pulling her into his body. "You're right, which is why we should take advantage of the tastes of happiness we get."

She curled her hands over his shoulders. "Is this one of those tastes of happiness?"

"Making love with you is pure joy, sweetheart."

She melted into him, her head tilted up toward his, her lips a breath from his. "Give me a taste of that joy," she whispered.

He obliged, claiming her lips with a tenderness that he didn't stop to analyze. "You taste like spicy honey," he said against her lips.

"Sounds yummy."

"It is. You are delicious . . . all over."

She moaned and he swept her up into his arms and carried her to the bedroom.

Jillian lay on the bed, watching silently as Alan shut and locked the door, then turned toward her and started to undress. His storm gray eyes were fixed on her with an intensity that sent shivers snapping along her nerve endings. What was it about this man that touched her in places she hadn't even known she could be touched?

He made her wonder about things she'd long ago determined had no place in her life. He'd fit in so well with her chosen family. Both the Brants and her boarders. Tonight had been so much like any other time she'd been at a Brant family gathering. Alan's presence had in no way been jarring. It was as if he had always been there. Even everyone's assumption that he was her boyfriend, which implied a relationship without the time limit theirs was under, had not bothered her. She'd actually liked the implication that her relationship with Alan was something more than straight sex.

Which it was. No matter what they'd said at the beginning, the way they were with each other was too shattering to relegate to the merely physical.

The White Tigresses claimed there was a spiritual component to sexual intimacy, even the one-time encounters, but Jillian had never bought into that element of their teaching. Only she couldn't deny that when Alan caressed her body, he touched her soul as well.

"Are you going to undress?" he asked in a voice that was husky with a need that resonated with hers.

"I thought maybe you'd like to do it." She'd meant to sound teasing, but her voice barely made it above a whisper and the truth was, she felt paralyzed by the sexual energy emanating from him.

He didn't reply verbally, but he started removing her clothes. None of his actions were overtly sensual, but as each article of her clothing was removed, her arousal grew.

Maybe it was as simple as having a gorgeous, naked man doing the undressing, but she felt like it was more than that. Her sense of vulnerability grew as he systematically stripped her clothes from her body. And not just her physical vulnerability, but she felt her emotions were being stripped as well. Inexplicable tears burned the back of her eyes.

Alan finished removing her clothing and then came over her on all fours, straddling her hips, his hands on either side of her head, but not actually touching her anywhere. "I'm going to make love to you completely tonight, Jillian."

She opened her mouth . . . for clarification? To protest? To agree? She would never know what she would have said because his lips closed over hers in a kiss so intimate her body trembled in reaction.

Everything they had done before felt like a prelude to what was happening right now. They had teased each other. They had pleasured each other. But this was something beyond that.

Jillian had had many sex partners since becoming active, but Alan was her first true lover. She felt like they were making love, and that knowledge almost sent her over the precipice.

His kiss claimed her, body, soul, and heart.

Heat from his body enveloped her, his scent surrounded her, his solid muscles a barrier between her and the rest of the world. Nothing existed but his presence . . . but their presence together.

Her hands roamed his body restlessly, hungry for the feel of silken skin over taut muscle. She breathed as deeply as her labored lungs would let her, reveling in the fragrance that was unique to Alan. She'd never been so enthralled by a man, so ravenous to experience him in every way she could.

She tunneled her fingers into his hair, grabbing his head and pulling him closer for her own claim-staking kiss. She thrust her tongue into his mouth, instantly dueling with him for dominance as they fought a sensual battle.

One moment his tongue would take control of her mouth, the next she would be tasting his teeth, and all the while, their desire burned hotter until it was molten lava running through her blood.

He came down on top of her, bringing their bodies into total contact, and her brain short-circuited at the overwhelming sensation.

But he didn't stay like that. He tucked his arms under her back, closing his hands over her shoulders, and rolled them until she was on top. He arranged her legs so her knees were bent and close to his waist.

Then he broke the kiss and pressed her up until she was sitting on him. "I want to touch you."

"So touch me."

He did, his hands moving over her with the same blatant hunger that she felt. He touched every inch of her skin, stimulating the erogenous zones he'd discovered in their previous encounters, showing her that he had paid very close attention to what excited her.

She skimmed his hairy chest with her fingertips, tantalizing his nipples with light caresses and little pinches, loving every groan and erotic sound of approval he made.

She shifted until she was riding the length of his rock-hard erection, gliding her swollen flesh along the steel-like shaft but not taking it inside her. Each time her clitoris rubbed the ridge of his head, she jolted with electric sensation.

She leaned down until their lips almost touched. "I could come like this," she said with a groan against his mouth.

His hands clamped her hips and halted all movement. "No. The next time you climax, I'm going to be inside you."

Without giving her a chance to answer, he rolled them again, so he was on top of her. He reached for a condom from the bedside table.

Her hazy mind told her he must have put them there earlier, but then she stopped thinking in favor of watching him sheath himself. He draped her legs over his forearms and placed the tip of his erection at her entrance. "Ready?"

Was she? It had been so long since she'd let a man inside her. But this felt right.

"Yes."

He entered slowly, making her feel every centimeter of his penetration. "You are so tight."

"It's been a while."

"Good."

Ooh, possessive. And why wasn't that bothering her? But she liked knowing he felt all primitive about her because when it came to him, her own feelings were definitely on the primordial side. He started with a steady but deep and penetrative pace. Each strong thrust brought his pelvis in contact with her clitoris and his penis in contact with her G-spot. It was too much, but not. She cried out on every inward push and sucked in air on every withdrawal of his steel rod.

She had no traction in her current position, but still did what she could to meet his every thrust. "Alan . . . it's too much . . ." she gasped.

"No, baby . . . it's not."

And he was right. It was the most intense joining she'd ever known, but she craved more, not less, no matter what message her brain was giving her. On the next downward thrust, he leaned forward and started short thrusting, rotating his pelvis and maximizing her pleasure.

She had no idea how long the lovemaking lasted, but every time she got close to climax, he would change his pace or technique, or the position of her legs . . . though not once did he change the fact that he was on top. At one point, he rolled her onto her stomach and penetrated her from the back, once again hitting her G-spot, but this time with the tip of his big and stone-hard prick. He reached around and pressed his middle finger against her clitoris. "Come for me, sweetheart. Give me your pleasure," he whispered gutturally in her ear.

And just like that, she came.

So did he, his shout a sound so deep and animalistic it sent jolts of electricity snapping along her nerve endings. His body was rigid, poised above her as he growled through the longest orgasm she'd experienced from a man. Her body reacted to his pleasure, sending her spiraling into a second, intense climax almost immediately after the first. His finger remained pressed against her pleasure button, but he didn't move it, allowing her to take her joy without allowing it to get to a point of pleasure pain.

They collapsed at almost the exact same moment, his body going boneless above her.

"Too heavy?" he asked.

"No." She grabbed his hip with her hand. "Stay."

They lay there, panting in postcoital bliss for several minutes before he regretfully got up to take care of the condom.

Jillian woke the next morning with Alan's body wrapped around her. One of the reasons she never slept with her sex partners was to avoid this kind of intimacy, but it felt more than right with him. It felt necessary, and that was more than a little frightening. She had no urge to get out of bed and put distance between them. An absolute first for her.

But then she'd had a lot of firsts with this man. Not least of which was the inescapable sense that he belonged in her future, not just her present.

Jillian didn't do future speculations. Not just with men; she pretty much lived every relationship in the moment, the only exceptions being her family and the Brants.

Even her chicks in the rooming house were transitory. They would move on eventually, or she would. She simply dedicated herself to enjoying the friendships while she had them. Something deep in her soul told her that was not enough with Alan. She wanted to know he would be there tomorrow, next week . . . next year.

Crap.

This was so not good.

Panic pulsed through her as Jillian realized her feelings for Alan were deep enough to drown her.

Despite how much she enjoyed the feel of his arms around her, she had to get out of there. She needed to talk to Amanda. Careful not to wake Alan, she climbed from the bed. Then, barely taking the time to grab clothes to cover herself, she sneaked from the room. When she got into the hallway, she realized she'd grabbed her own T-shirt and Alan's boxers. Immediately after she tugged them on, they slipped to ride low on her hips.

Ignoring their precarious fit, she jogged silently through the house right up to Simon and Amanda's door.

247

She knocked quietly. "Amanda," she hissed through the door. "It's me. Are you awake?"

The door opened and Simon blinked blearily at her. "Jill, is something wrong?"

"I . . . uh . . . I need to talk to Amanda."

"Ah," he said, as if he understood. "Just a sec."

She heard him waking her friend up and then Amanda was there at the door, clad in a robe a couple of sizes too big for her. Jillian wasn't the only one who had poor aim when it came to picking out clothes in the wee hours of the morning.

"Jill, sweetie . . . what's up?"

"I think I love him."

Amanda's eyes widened. "What did you just say?"

"I know. I can't believe it either. I mean, I don't do love."

"Not that." Amanda started down the steps. "I knew you loved him; I'm just so shocked you admitted it."

Jillian's mouth opened, but nothing came out. She felt like a gasping fish all the way into the kitchen. Amanda started pulling things from cupboards.

"But, Mandy, I can't love him."

"Why not?" her friend asked as she made cocoa from scratch on the stove.

"He's leaving in a couple of weeks. He lives on the East Coast. I live in a whole other country."

"So?"

"Long-distance relationships just don't work."

"Ask him to move to Vancouver. He's a freelance reporter, right?"

"Well, yes."

"So, what says he has to have his home base a continent away from you?"

"But why would he want to change his life for me?"

"That's what people in love do."

"You think he loves me?"

"Definitely."

"How can you be so sure? You barely know him."

"He could be a perfect stranger and I would know. That look he gives you has universal interpretation."

"Oh, sure, right. He looks at me likes he loves me," Jillian said, her sense of panic not in the least abated.

"He does, missy." Jacob stepped around Amanda, taking over the cocoa making.

"You think so, Jacob?" Jillian asked, not in the least surprised the manservant knew she and Amanda had invaded his kitchen.

"Yep. Though I'm not sure he realizes it yet."

"Why wouldn't he realize it?"

"Coming from you, that is a pretty darn funny question," Amanda said with a snort. "You are the queen of denial when it comes to love and anything related to it. I'm still having a hard time processing the fact that you've accepted your feelings for him."

"Who said I accepted them?"

"What? You came to my room in the middle of the night to ask if I knew how to turn off your feelings?"

Jillian felt herself blushing when she realized she'd gone to her best friend for exactly that kind of advice. But all she said was, "It's early morning, not night."

Amanda made a derogatory sound. "It's barely after four A.M. That is not morning."

Jillian shrugged.

"It is my experience that deep affection cannot be turned off at will," Jacob said as he put mugs of hot cocoa in front of Amanda and Jillian, then joined them at the table.

"You have experience?" Amanda asked, obviously sidetracked by the idea her daughter's adopted grandpa had ever had a deep relationship.

Jacob's brows beetled. "You think I came to Simon without a past?"

"Without a personal one, yes."

Simon smiled at that instead of making a sarcastic rejoinder, which was weird enough that Jillian found herself intrigued enough to put her own terror on a back burner. "Spill, Jacob."

"There was a reason I took the Secret Service route rather than following my dream of undercover agent work."

"A woman?"

"My wife. We had twenty amazing years together. She died the year before I met Simon. Going to work for him was the change I needed to find a semblance of peace again in my life."

"See?" Jillian demanded belligerently. "That's exactly why this love thing sucks so bad."

"You think that the pain I went through when Candace died negated twenty years of joy?" Jacob asked in a more condescending voice than he'd ever used with her.

And it made her stop and think. "I don't know. Didn't it?"

"Not a chance. A single day with my beloved would have been worth all the pain."

"Oh, gosh, Jacob. That's so romantic," Amanda said as she leaned over and hugged him in commiseration.

"You don't think Simon feels the same way?"

Amanda's smile was misty when she nodded. "I'm sure he does. Just like I do."

Jillian eyed them both askance. "I think you're both nuts."

"Tell me something," Jacob insisted.

"What?" Jillian asked.

"If you could go back to the day you accepted your role on that daytime drama you were in, would you change it?"

"Of course not."

"But it ended."

"It took my career forward, and even if it hadn't, it was fun while it lasted."

"So, you think the only risks worth taking are professional?"

Chapter 20

Alan woke with the sense that something was wrong. He reached for Jillian, but she wasn't there, and the sheets where she had been were cool. His gaze flicked to the digital alarm clock beside the bed. It was five-thirty. Too early for Jillian to have left the bed long enough ago for the sheets to be cool. He knew she got up early for work, but this was ridiculous. They weren't planning to head back to the mainland until after lunch.

Which left only one conclusion to draw. The intimacy of the previous night had been too much for her. She didn't want a long-term relationship, no matter what her friends seemed to think. And because of it, she'd rejected the sense of oneness they had achieved the night before.

She'd already told him she didn't sleep with her sex partners and she'd broken that rule for him, but apparently it wasn't comfortable for her. Or maybe it had been the almost otherworldly pleasure of their joining the night before. Either way, she'd found it necessary to go.

He couldn't be angry with her. She'd made her position clear from the beginning. As had he. Just because he had begun to change his mind didn't mean she was obligated to change hers. They both had good reasons for being leery of relationships. Apparently she was even more impacted by hers than he was by his.

Or maybe she didn't feel the intense connection to him that he felt to her. That had been true of Beth. He'd loved her. Enough that he would have looked for a desk job if she'd asked him to. But she hadn't. She'd simply written him off and that was that. Her subsequent marriage to another agent was proof positive that the issue hadn't really been her need for personal stability, but that her love had been too shallow.

And Jillian had never even claimed to love him. In fact, she'd been very out there with her lack of belief in that particular emotion.

It wasn't as if he'd ever said he loved her, either. Not even to himself. So why did he feel like someone had carved his heart up with a rusty blade?

Despite the best efforts of both Jacob and Amanda to calm her down, Jillian spent the rest of the morning quietly freaking over her newfound revelations. Every time she would get a handle on her sense of panic, Jacob's question about whether professional risks were the only ones worth taking would pop back into her mind. She'd refused to answer the question when he asked it, but she'd given a dozen mental answers in her overwrought brain since then. The problem was, the reasoning behind all the negative ones was flawed in some way and she would find herself shredding each argument before she realized what she was doing.

At one point during the almost two-hour-long conversation in the kitchen, Amanda had asked Jillian if she wanted to spend the rest of her life without the special intimacy that came from two people belonging to each other. Even Jillian's answer to that had rung false as she said the same words she'd uttered so many times before about how her friends were enough. Jacob had chimed in again, saying that as much as he loved the Brants, he still missed his Candace. Which had put a speculative spark in Amanda's eyes. If Jillian had been less confused herself, she would have immediately dragged Amanda off for a walk on the beach to plot.

As it was, she took that walk alone, only coming back after the sun had risen.

Alan was up and swimming laps when she returned to the house. She did her best to avoid being alone with him because the man was too perceptive. She was sure he'd recognize her inner revelation if she gave him the chance, and she wasn't ready for that. She wasn't sure when she would be.

Jacob and the Brants joined Alan and Jillian for the trip back to the mainland, providing a buffer between the two of them. But even when they were alone together in the car, Jillian appeared content to maintain a sense of solitude. Alan didn't push her to communicate. At first, he was too wrapped up in his own private thoughts, but as the miles passed along with the minutes, the professional agent began to reassert himself. He was furious with himself for wasting his time wondering about a relationship that was obviously not going anywhere. The deadline on his current case was coming too damn close to let his personal life get in the way even for a few hours.

His gut told him to talk to Frost, but the Old Man had been adamant that would not happen until they could establish that Frost was not a suspect. Alan wasn't sure he could do that unequivocally, but he could try to eliminate reasonable doubt.

At least he had been enough of an agent to get Jacob aside and quiz him on what his background check on Frost had uncovered. Jacob had done him one better and given Alan a copy of the file he had on Frost and the other higher-ups at Frost Productions. Alan would spend that night comparing those files to the ones he'd gotten from TGP and his own findings. Hopefully, there would be something he could latch onto to substantiate his gut feeling.

He spent the rest of the drive mentally reviewing everything he knew about Frost and his colleagues in the production company. Nothing stood out any more than it had before. In light of both Perry's pseudorevelations and Gavin's questionable behavior, Alan mentally reviewed their files as well. It helped to have a mostly photographic memory, but even with it, he didn't have any lightbulb moments. He knew he was missing something. He could feel it . . . like he had a vital piece of information he just wasn't recognizing. He kept coming back to Lonny's murder, but nothing new was jumping out at him about that.

"Are you okay?" Jillian asked as he pulled in the long line for the border crossing. It made all the difference when you crossed the border how long the wait was, apparently.

He flicked her a glance. "Sure."

"You've been awfully quiet."

"Thinking about work. I'm sorry if I've ignored you."

"No. I wasn't talking either."

He nodded, not asking her why she'd been so quiet. If she wanted to tell him, she would. But the truth was, he'd prefer she didn't. She'd made it abundantly obvious that she was content with their original status quo. Sex with no strings. Meaningful conversation about feelings was only going to jeopardize the professional distance Alan was trying to reestablish.

There was too damn much at stake to do otherwise.

Jillian watched the line of cars move slower than a government agency as she realized that Alan had been withdrawn from her since the first time she'd seen him that morning over breakfast. She hadn't noticed before because she'd been too preoccupied with her own thoughts.

Weird.

They'd shared the most profound sexual encounter of her life the night before. She was almost positive it had been as soul shattering for him as it had been for her. So what was with the silent treatment?

Was he feeling as discomposed as she was? Had he discovered he was in love with her? *Was* he in love with her? Amanda and Jacob were certainly convinced, but Jillian wasn't so sure. It only seemed fair that if she had to deal with the emotional tumult of possible—okay, probable—love, that he did too.

Only if she didn't want to take a chance on that love, it would be a lot easier if he didn't share it. On the other hand, if she wanted to take the risk, she for sure wasn't going to take it alone!

"So, what's with the silent treatment today?" she asked.

She might be discombobulated, but that didn't mean she'd all of a sudden gone shy.

"Excuse me? Silent treatment?" He sounded genuinely surprised by the question, so whatever was making him ignore her—it wasn't on purpose.

Right?

"Yes. You've barely spoken a private word to me since we met over breakfast this morning."

He cast her a sideways glance. "We didn't have any *private* time."

"Well, you can't get much more private than two people in a car."

"Actually you can, but I get what you're trying to say."

"And . . ."

"And you've been just as quiet."

"I know why I haven't been talking. Tell me what's kept you from starting a conversation."

"I've been thinking about my current assignment."

"Do you think you'll have enough material for the article you want to write?"

"I hope so, but some things just aren't gelling right now."

"I'm sorry to hear that." She licked her lips and looked out the passenger window for a count of ten before turning to face him again. "So, um . . . there was nothing else of a more personal nature on your mind?"

A positively ferocious scowl went across his features, but was gone so quickly she had to wonder if she'd seen it. He also didn't answer.

After several seconds, she prompted. "Alan?"

"No. The answer is no."

Only as straightforward as his reply was, it sure seemed qualified in some way. "No?" she gently probed again.

"Not while we've been in the car."

"So you were thinking things of a personal nature earlier today?" No wonder women got frustrated discussing emotional stuff with men.

Forget the whole different planets theory. She could swear right now that when it came to this, she and Alan were coming from different universes.

"You could say that. Yes."

"You sound like someone being interrogated." Or interviewed by the media. Huh. Maybe being on the other side of the microphone made people as wary as did having their words twisted by one too many interviewers. "What I'm asking, Mr. Letter-of-the-law, is would *you* say that?"

"Yes."

"But you're not thinking those personal thoughts now?" Was that good, or bad?

"No point in dwelling on something that can only have one outcome."

"What do you mean?"

"Why don't you tell me what's kept you from talking privately *with me* before we continue this thread of interrogation?"

"I don't want to."

"Okay." That was it. Calm, matter-of-fact. He didn't fill the one word with a wealth of meaning that she would have been hard-pressed not to interpret correctly.

He didn't give her a look that said he wanted her to spill her guts. He didn't try to convince her with words to share her innermost thoughts.

And Jillian felt cheated.

Part of her really wanted to tell Alan what was going on inside her thoughts. But another part was scared to death. It came down to whether or not she was willing to take an emotional risk.

"Are you mad at me?" she asked.

"No."

"You sure?"

"As sure as you are that you aren't mad at me."

"How can you be sure I'm not?" She hadn't talked to him all day. She might have been mad. Though over what, she had no clue. But still.

"Verbal communication is only a portion of what humans use to reveal their emotional state."

"Yes, Dr. Johnson."

He chuckled. "I'm not a doctor . . . but I took more than one psych course in college. I figured they'd come in handy in my future work, and they did."

"That makes sense, but I'd still like to know why you're so convinced I'm not mad at you."

"Your body language. Your nonlingual sounds. You've been distant, but not angry. Preoccupied, but not focused on me—or anyone else—with negative thoughts."

"You're so confident of your conclusions."

"Tell me I'm wrong."

"You're not. Mostly."

"What part did I get wrong?" he asked as he pulled up to the customs booth and rolled down his window to answer the routine questions.

She waited until they were given their go-ahead by the customs agent before answering him.

"I was kind of annoyed with you at certain points today." Like just before they started talking when she considered the possibility that she was in a pool of emotional turmoil designed for one rather than two.

"You hid it well, then."

"Oh, for crying out loud . . . okay, it was really recent." Why did she have to be such a stickler for personal honesty again?

"Since we started this rather bizarre discussion?"

"No." Triumph at his having gotten it wrong filled her.

"Then when?"

"Right before," she admitted grudgingly.

"Why?"

"It's all part of what I was thinking about all day."

"Are you having a difficult time dealing with last night?"

"Why should I be?" Belligerence made a great conversation stopper. She'd learned that dealing with other reporters.

"Because it was more intense than probably either of us was prepared for."

Oh . . . dang his honesty too! "I'm not a wuss. I can handle anything you can dish out."

"Physically. Even sexually, on a strictly physical level, I believe that."

"But?"

"I didn't say *but*."

"Funny, I heard one."

"But I think the nonphysical connection we made last night scared you."

"Isn't it boring being right so often?" she asked huffily.

"Not really, no."

She gave a long-suffering sigh.

He grinned. "Oh, come on. You aren't saying you don't share that particular quirk."

"Are you saying I do?" she asked, doing her best to sound offended.

"I'll take the fifth on that one."

"Have you ever had to, for real?"

His head jerked like she'd surprised him with the question. Considering it had come from so far in left field it might be a foul, she could understand that.

"No."

"You've never had to protect a source?" Okay, it was a blatant change of topic, but his assertion that she had been scared by what had happened last night hit much too close to the most distressing part of the truth for her to deal with at the moment.

"Nope. I haven't written that kind of article."

"Hmm . . . maybe you should. I bet you're really good at ferreting out secrets and bad guys."

Alan made a noncommittal sound.

And Jillian slipped back into self-protective silence.

When they got to the house, everyone was home and happy to see them. Or at least she thought they were. Perry had been . . . bothered. Hank was still grieving. Sierra had been on two dates—in as many days—with the linebacker wannabe. And Gavin was simply himself. Teasing Jillian and flirting with Alan.

As much as Jillian loved Jacob and the Brants, it was nice to be home.

Well, right up until Alan made it clear that he expected to sleep alone that night.

Oh, he didn't say anything, but like he'd mentioned—a lot of communication went on without a word being spoken. Jillian could only be glad she hadn't blurted out her love in the car. Though, honestly? That hadn't been a real threat.

When it came to emotions, Jillian Sinclair was cautious. And it was a good thing too. She shuddered at the thought of what would have happened if she'd shared her feelings with Alan in the car.

She could hear him trying to let her down lightly. Or worse, giving her a disgusted look that said, "We had an agreement. What's your problem?"

Okay, so that wasn't a rational thought. But rational went out the window sometime after two A.M. when a woman had a caffeine buzz from too much peppermint mocha. Sierra was a whiz with the espresso machine. She'd said the coffee she used was decaf, but Jillian was sure Sierra had been mistaken.

She was so keyed up, she could barely rest in the same position for more than a minute. It had to be the coffee.

What if Alan's withdrawal stemmed from her inability to share her emotions, rather than a true lack of them on his part?

Sheesh. Like she needed more questions to torment her mind. She was still mulling over Jacob's question, and hadn't she about beaten that horse to death? This love stuff sucked. Hugely. She didn't understand why so many people wanted it when it brought so much pain and confusion.

And she hadn't even admitted it to Alan.

She'd barely admitted it to herself. Then she'd spent a good portion of the time she walked on the beach trying to convince herself she was mistaken. She'd tried that with Amanda and Jacob, but her rationalizations had been a total bust. Truth was, it had been easier to simply shut up about not loving Alan than deal with those two when they tag-teamed.

Man. Who would have ever thought Jacob and Amanda would make such good allies?

The older man doted on Dorrie for sure, but since first meeting Jillian, he'd had a soft spot for her. She sure hadn't seen it that morning. Jacob had been hard as nails and plenty irritated with her unwillingness to take a leap of faith when it came to loving Adam.

Jillian tossed and turned in her bed, sat up and punched her pillow. Hard. Twice. It didn't help.

She lay back down.

All right . . . so suppose Alan *was* feeling as shaken as she was. Suppose . . . just suppose he needed to hear her say she loved him. It was entirely possible he was feeling every bit as wary as she was. Hadn't Jacob said just that?

Only Jillian just couldn't see Alan vulnerable and confused and *scared* of his feelings.

But then before meeting him, she couldn't see herself that way either. Even with her family, she'd never felt this particular type of fear. It was more personal, and that really rocked her thinking. How could love have different levels of intimacy?

But it did. What she felt with her mom and stepdad was different from how deeply she cared for her brother. She sort of felt the same way about Amanda and her family as she did about Darien, though. She'd always assumed that was as deep as love could go.

After all, she would give her life and her own happiness for any one of them. Well, maybe not Simon. Or would she, to protect Amanda? Heavy thoughts.

Thoughts that were just a blinking distraction and she knew it because what they were tap-dancing around was the fact that what she felt for Alan was even more primal than all of that. It went deeper and connected to a part of her no one else had ever touched.

A part of her no one else *could* touch.

Oh, man . . . was she screwed.

Jillian looked like she hadn't slept, and Alan felt guilty. Which was ridiculous. There was nothing to indicate she'd had a hard time sleeping because he hadn't shared her bed.

Nothing except the fact that he hadn't slept either. Even when he'd fallen into bed mentally exhausted after spending hours working on the case.

Well, and her admission at the hotel in Seattle that she *wanted* him to share her bed. That had been a big step for her, but then why had she disappeared from their bed the night before last? After making love. Wild, passionate, devastatingly intense love. He couldn't even call it sex in his own head without cringing. It had been so much more.

And that "more" had sent her screaming.

But he still felt guilty.

Hank slid into a chair across from Alan, beside Jillian. He rubbed her shoulder. "You look like crud walking, Jill."

She grimaced. "Thanks. That's just what a girl wants to hear first thing in the morning."

"Girl? What happing to the raving feminist who insists on being called a woman, that *girl* is a term for females under the age of consent?"

Alan watched in fascination while Jillian blushed. Then frowned. "I think the coffee last night must have had caffeine in it."

"It did not. I checked," Sierra said as she joined them at the table.

"Maybe they made a mistake at the roasters when you bought it?"

"Nope. Not possible. You know how I am if I have caffeine after lunchtime. And I slept like a baby."

"It's all that sex you're getting with Mr. Atlas. It's exhausted you," Hank said with a smile that Jillian was frankly glad to see.

"If that's the case, Jillian should have slept like the dead considering her nocturnal activities with Alan."

For some reason, the comment only added to Alan's guilt. Maybe it was the look of confusion and tinge of sadness that flitted over Jillian's features.

The banter continued, but Alan only listened with half an ear until Hank said something that caught his complete attention. Though at first, the agent wasn't sure what was so significant about the words.

Jillian replied to Hank's initial complaint—the comment that had snagged Alan's interest.

Hank said, "Sometimes I wonder if the production staff isn't *trying* to keep the show in the lower ratings sphere."

"Why in the world would they do that?"

"Well, if my old granny were here, she'd say they were a front for the American mafia." Hank smirked.

"You're kidding," Jillian said while Alan quietly choked on his coffee.

"Not a bit. She's convinced every restaurant that doesn't

do a booming business, every furniture sales shop that goes out of business is exactly that."

Everyone laughed, even Alan, though it was an effort. If only Hank knew.

"Still, I don't think the upper brass are engaging in deliberate ploys to keep the ratings down."

"If you say so. But then if we have got access to higher-tech special effects, stuff with a real wow factor, we should utilize it. You know?"

Both Jillian and Sierra nodded, but it was Jillian who said, "Definitely."

"Then why aren't we? Maybe you can ask one of the big producers. I'm just a lowly editorial assistant and they're not about to listen to me."

"If you're really that concerned, why not take it to the film editor on credits?"

"I'm not supposed to have seen these rushes."

Alan's sixth sense tingled like he'd stuck his finger in a light socket. "What did you see that you weren't supposed to?"

Hank looked embarrassed for a second, but shrugged. "The film editor was showing some friends, or potential investors, some rushes. It was a private viewing, closed to the rest of the crew, but I snuck in. I wanted to see if he was going to show any of the scenes I'd edited. I've been pretty proud of some of my work lately and hoped he'd noticed the quality."

"Understandable," Jillian said with a commiserating smile.

"He only showed a couple of scenes from film in the can and then he showed some footage that we haven't used and probably won't. The special effects were out of this world but the cinematography sucked. Though it was pretty apparent someone had tried to improve it with digital enhancement."

"What was the footage of?"

Chapter 21

Hank frowned. "It was freaky . . . looked like pictures of the UFO supposedly found near Roswell."

The fine hairs on the back of Alan's neck stood on end. Rumors had been flying for the past year about a privately funded research company trying and maybe succeeding at reverse engineering from the Roswell saucer.

"Like I said, the cinematography was rough, but the saucer was killer. The way it looked in juxtaposition to the trees and things around it made it appear mammoth in size, but it maneuvered like a Maserati and damned if it didn't look like it accelerated to multimach speed. The special effects were just awesome."

If Hank was describing the fabled re-created saucer, he hadn't been able to see the most amazing aspects of it. They were invisible to the naked eye. By using a rotating, highly energized fluid core of mercury in powerful electromagnetic fields to virtually eliminate the saucer's weight, the multiton vehicle was in effect weightless. Not only was it supposedly able to accelerate to multimach speeds in seconds, it could stop on a dime with no g-forces, dingle balls and hula girl not even swaying on the dash.

The first word that came to Alan's mind was *shit*.

He realized he'd said it out loud and rather vehemently when the others at the table stopped talking to stare at him.

If this fabled technology actually existed, it was worth billions. And everyone would want it. No way would the auction be handled through a contact at a small film company . . . not even if he had connections to Prescott.

Something this big just didn't hit the market that way. Which meant whoever was trying to sell it from here had stolen it.

Damn. Finding out the name of the company that had created a working model would be as important as keeping it out of the wrong hands.

"Do you think you could find this footage on the hard drive, Hank?"

Jillian gave Alan a strange look, but she waited in silence for her friend to answer.

Hank thought for a second. "I think I may be able to do you even one better. Something has been bugging me about that footage ever since I saw it. And now I realize what it is. The technique used to enhance the cinematography was something I'd only recently taught Lonny how to do. He must have found the footage and started playing around with it. Now that I think about it, the edits have his signature all over them."

"So how can you do me one better?" Alan asked, not allowing himself to get sidetracked from his immediate purpose by the possible confirmation that Lonny had been killed because of the pirated technology.

"Lonny and I shared edited files back and forth all the time. He would send me stuff he was proud of. He gave me a file of his most recent work the morning he was killed." Hank's voice choked on the word *killed*, but he went on. "I couldn't look at it."

Sierra squeezed Hank's hand. "If you aren't ready to look at it now, I'm sure Alan will understand."

"Of course, but if you don't mind me looking, I would really appreciate it."

No one asked why, no doubt assuming it had something to do with his article, though the look of speculation had not left Jillian's beautiful green eyes.

"No . . . I'd like to look too. I guess it's my last part of him. You know?"

Pain shot through Alan on the other man's behalf. Losing someone you loved was one of the worst things that could happen. He'd accepted that his professional distance was shot on this job and this was just another example, but as he got up to put a comforting hand on Hank's shoulder, Alan couldn't regret that reality.

The grieving man needed all the friends he could get right now.

As eager as Alan was to see the video, he felt bad for Hank when the film editor's fingers shook just a little as he opened the small DVD case.

Jillian hugged his shoulder. "You don't have to do this, Hank."

"It's okay. I need to."

She nodded and stepped back to give her boarder space as he popped the DVD into the computer and brought up the menu.

"I think it's this one," he said as he clicked on one of the titles in the menu.

The video began to play and Alan's jaw clenched against a curse.

Double damn.

No question about it. The flying ship was the fabled reverse-engineered Roswell saucer. Or a very good simulation of one.

"Is there any way to tell if the original film was doctored?" he asked Hank.

"Not really. At least not from this video. Once the digitized changes are saved, there's no way to easily tell what was original to film or not. But this is special effects. No film company is going to build a ship that big and get it into the sky, even assuming they could. No doubt it's a model, but even so, the detail and special effects are awesome, don't you think?" Hank studied the video. "There are only a few modelers in the business that do work at this level. None of them on Frost Productions' payroll."

"You said one of the editors was showing this video to a group of investors?"

"Actually, it was one of the producers."

"Frost?"

"No. One of the small moneymen."

"Who?"

"Patrick Kirby."

Alan recognized the name. The producer's file had been short and clean. Not so squeaky clean it had raised alarms, but nothing so dirty that it had either. It was time to start looking deeper.

"If he showed the video in the studio, there should be a list of names for those he was showing it to in the security logs, right?"

"Yes," Jillian answered for Hank, giving Alan another one of those strange looks.

"Do you think you could get access to the original clip of this sequence?" Alan asked Hank.

"If it's still on the hard drive. Sure. But why?" Hank asked.

"I need to see it. As soon as possible."

Hank didn't ask why again, he just nodded. Alan didn't know if his grief muted his natural curiosity or if he simply didn't feel the need to know. Whatever the reason, Alan was glad. He wasn't ready to get into his real reason for being there. Wasn't sure he was going to tell his housemates at all. On another case, it wouldn't even be a possibility, but this assignment had gone south of normal a long time ago.

"We could go to the studio right now," Jillian said.

"Do you know what editor was originally responsible for that clip?" Alan asked Hank before responding to Jillian.

"No, but once we find the original clip, we'll know. It should be stored with the information on the date of its take as well and who was on the crew during the take."

Alan very much doubted that information would be available, especially if the clip was, as he suspected, either stolen from the developers or the result of a covert cam during a test flight. "I don't want anyone to realize what we are looking for."

"Then maybe I should find the clip and save it to a DVD and bring it back here."

Alan shook his head. "I don't want you going alone."

"Why not?" Jillian asked.

Maybe the time had come to share some information. "If that clip is what I believe it is, I think it's possible Lonny died because of the unauthorized editorial work he did on it. More precisely because he had seen it at all."

"You're saying you think the man I loved was murdered over this clip?"

"Yes. And it's possible a security guard was killed for the same reason."

"What? Who?"

Alan told them, and both Hank and Jillian gasped. "But it was a car accident," she said.

"That happened very close to, if not the same night, as a break-in at the studio."

"You mean when the hard drive got erased?" Hank asked. "The execs were plenty upset about that."

So that was what happened. "Yes."

"Still . . ." Jillian said, her voice just trailing off.

"I don't believe in coincidences," Alan replied. "We can't prove the accident was anything but that at this point, but my gut is telling me it was."

"And these same bastards killed Lonny?" Hank demanded.

"I believe so, yes."

"Why?"

"There have been rumors about the development of an antigravity technology using reverse engineering from the Roswell saucer that would completely transform air and even space travel. I think that clip is of a test flight."

"But that's impossible. The Roswell saucer itself is just a myth."

Alan shrugged, not willing to confirm or deny that supposition.

"What was the clip doing on our production company's hard drive?" Hank asked, budding fury swirling through his eyes.

"My best guess is that someone stole it and is trying to sell the information."

"But what good would the clip do without schematics?" Jillian asked.

"We can't be sure they don't have those too."

"So we know Patrick Kirby is involved, but we don't know if he has an editor working with him, or anyone else."

"True. What are the chances he stored the image on the hard drive himself?"

"Maybe he didn't," Hank said. "He may have simply put the DVD in an archive file believing no one would access it. But Lonny and I often took old raw footage, especially scenes not used and previously edited, to work on. It was easier to teach him technique when he didn't have an image already established in his mind for a scene."

"So, it's definitely possible Kirby is working alone?" Alan asked.

"Yep," Hank affirmed. "Even our minor producers have full access to every part of the studio."

Jillian drummed her fingernails on the table. "But we can't be sure he's working alone."

"In fact, it's unlikely . . . even if his cohorts don't work for the studio." Alan frowned. "Which is why I don't want you going to the studio and looking for the original clip alone."

"I'll go with him," Jillian said.

Alan smiled. "I know you're tough, sweetheart, but I was thinking more along the lines of waiting until the staff has gone for the day and me accompanying him."

"But what if the producer takes the DVD out of the archives today?" Jillian asked.

"If he was going to do that, he would have removed it immediately after discovering Lonny saw it. So a few hours today aren't going to make a difference one way or the other."

Hank said, "Maybe Lonny had the raw footage."

Alan nodded. "I'm guessing that's why his laptop got stolen."

"He might have it on DVD at his apartment. His family plans to clean it out the day after tomorrow, so if he had it, it should still be there."

"Do you have a key?" Alan asked.

Hank's eyes glistened for a second. "Yes. He gave it to me a couple of weeks ago." He took a shuddering breath. "He asked me to move in."

Without thought, Alan pulled the other man into a hug.

Hank clung to him for several seconds before stepping away. "Thanks."

For reasons of her own, Jillian insisted on accompanying Alan and Hank to Lonny's apartment. For reasons he did not want to examine, Alan let her.

Lonny's apartment was a small but airy one-bedroom. His dining area was set up as an office rather than for eating and it was here that Hank went to search for the DVD. Alan powered up the desktop while Hank was going through the stacks of DVDs and CDs on the desk.

The computer prompted for a log-in. Alan asked Hank, "Do you know the password?"

"If it's the same as he used on his laptop, yes."

Alan tried the sequence Hank gave him but got an error message. He grabbed the small black backpack he'd brought with him and took out a CD, which he popped into the computer before restarting it. The program on the CD ran, circumventing the original boot and allowing Alan to access the hard drive. "What am I looking for in terms of the name of the file?"

"I'm not sure if he used the original file name, but if he renamed it, it was probably something similar to his final title."

Alan did a search on the most likely keyword from the title and waited while the computer whirred.

"Bingo," he said quietly before double-clicking on the file to play it.

"Is this the raw footage?" he asked Hank as it began to play.

Hank looked over his shoulder. "Looks like it to me. It sure doesn't have any of Lonny's fixes on it and it hasn't been edited, unless the editor really truly sucked at his job."

Alan nodded and proceeded to burn the clip to a DVD he pulled from his pack. "Any luck finding the original DVD?" he asked.

Hank shook his head. "It's weird, but it seems like a lot of his DVDs are missing. And the ones here are out of order. Lonny was kind of anal . . . he had a system for storing everything from the dishes in the kitchen to his computer archives."

Alan wasn't surprised the DVD was missing. He was only surprised the computer had not been stolen, but maybe the perps thought burglarizing the man's apartment would be too conspicuous and draw too much attention to Lonny as a victim.

"At least we got the raw footage."

"Apparently the bad guys didn't have one of your handy programs for getting past the Windows password protection." Jillian was looking at Alan with a definite question in her eyes.

"What can I say? I like to be prepared."

Her perfectly shaped red brows rose mockingly. "No doubt."

"So what's next?" Hank asked.

"We go back to Jillian's and I call some people," Alan said.

"I want to help nail these bastards," Hank said. "They killed my future. I want to make sure they're brought to justice."

Alan understood the sentiment, but he didn't want Hank put at risk. "I'll make sure of it, but you need to keep a low profile right now. Both for the sake of my investigation and for your own safety."

"There's got to be more I can do."

Alan understood the desperation in Hank's voice and couldn't ignore it. "There is. You can examine this footage and try to determine if it's special effects or real."

Hank nodded.

"I can ask Ralph for the name of the investors from the security log," Jillian said.

"I don't want you at risk," Alan said.

"I'm not going to do it in front of anyone else."

"You can't be sure Ralph isn't involved. At this point we don't know who might be on Kirby's private payroll."

"Not Ralph," Jillian said with absolute conviction.

Alan was inclined to agree, but at that moment he understood the Old Man's stance on not talking to Frost. If there was the least chance they were wrong about the security guard, he didn't want her talking to him. "Are all the logs kept in the security booth?"

"As far as I know. For a while anyway."

"I'll go looking tonight."

Jillian crossed her arms and tapped her foot, glaring at him. "Pretty stealthy for a reporter who doesn't do risky exposes, aren't you?"

Alan just shrugged. "We've all got our skills."

"Yes, and I get the feeling yours aren't limited to or even inclusive of writing the odd article here and there."

Hank was watching them both with unconcealed interest. "Do we have to have this conversation right now?"

"No, but we are having it," Jillian said, her voice deadly serious.

"Agreed."

"One question."

"Only one?"

"For now."

"Go ahead."

"Could my brother come to you for advice on his chosen profession?"

"Any time."

"Good."

He didn't believe it was going to be that easy, but right now he couldn't focus on the upcoming confrontation with the woman he loved.

Oh, shit . . . yes, the woman he loved.

What else could it be?

He shook his head and threw his backpack over his shoulder. "Let's go."

When they got back to Jillian's house, Alan headed to his room to call his boss and start a deeper investigation into Kirby's background.

Jillian followed him. "I can help. Just consider me a resource."

Alan didn't even try to argue with her. He merely indicated she should take a seat while he pulled out his phone to update the Old Man.

"That's big, Hyatt. Just being able to confirm the rumors would be big, but selling the schematics to the highest bidder would be huge."

"We don't know for sure our perp has anything more than the video."

"Well, find out."

"I plan to, sir."

Alan flipped his phone shut and went to his computer,

pulling up the connection to a secure TGP server. He began the research on the producer with some basic searches.

"I think one of the grips is his cousin or something," Jillian said from behind him.

"I thought you were going to sit in the chair and watch."

"I couldn't see anything from there."

"So, what's the name of this grip?"

"I don't remember, maybe Perry knows."

Alan got up. "I'll go ask him." He pulled a file folder from the stack on the desk. "This is his file. Go over it and see if anything strikes you as odd."

"Aye, sir."

He shook his head. "I don't see you on a naval ship, submitting to an officer's orders."

"I'd probably cause a mutiny. I don't like other people's rules."

"I know."

"We are going to talk later, Alan. Your name is Alan, isn't it?"

"Yes to both."

She nodded.

He cupped her cheek and leaned down to kiss her. "We have a lot more to discuss than the nature of my job."

"Yes, we do."

"I didn't like sleeping alone last night."

"Me either."

"It was my fault."

"You'll have to make up for it."

"Count on it."

She hugged him, pressing her face into his neck. "This thing is bigger than both our fears, isn't it?"

"Yes, baby, it is."

She shuddered. "I'm so glad you think so too."

He kissed her temple and then stepped away without another word, leaving the room because he had to.

After striking out in the rest of the house, Alan stopped

short upon arriving at the workout room. Well, this would certainly explain Gavin and Perry's secretive behavior lately, and the comments Perry had made on their run the week before. The couple was locked in a kiss so scorching Alan had to fan himself. He'd suspected there was something going on between the two of them. There was just too much chemistry when they were together. He still found it hard to believe Jillian had ever thought Perry and Hank might be a couple.

Speaking of . . . "Uh . . . guys, if Jillian walked in right now, you'd be toast."

Gavin went to spring away from the kiss, but Perry kept him by his side with a firm arm around his waist. "We're going to tell her later today."

Alan nodded. "Good idea."

"As much as I'd hate to move out, I don't want to hide what I feel any longer," Gavin said, relaxing into Perry's side.

"You two weren't doing the best job of hiding it anyway."

"From you maybe," Perry said. "But there aren't a lot of people as observant as you."

Alan gave the other men his signature smirk. "Too true."

Gavin laughed. "You are so alpha, you should come with a warning label."

"Hey, I'm plenty alpha for you, babe, and don't you forget it." Perry laid a definite claim-staking kiss on Gavin.

When he lifted his head, Gavin was looking dazed, Perry looked smug, and Alan was biting back laughter. "Hey, Perry, Jillian said that one of the producers, Patrick Kirby, has a friend or cousin working as a grip. Do you remember the grip's name?"

"Sure," Perry said. "Rob Francis."

"I know who you're talking about," Gavin said, his tone leaving no doubt what he thought of Francis.

"You don't like him?" Perry asked.

"We've had our run-ins. When I was doing background work, mostly. Though when I first got promoted to a regular on the show, he gave me a hard time too, but I threatened to go straight to Mr. Frost with his attitude. It wouldn't matter who he was related to then. Rob Francis is a first-class homophobe and Mr. Frost is known for his intolerance of any type of overt bigotry."

"He's a good guy," Perry said with a squeeze to Gavin's shoulder. "I'm glad Rob isn't giving you any more trouble, but if he does—"

"You'll take care of it?" Gavin interrupted with a grin.

"Yes." Perry wasn't smiling. Not even a little. "I doubt Rob will keep his position much longer despite being union and related to Mr. Kirby. The guy spends way too much time jawing with his cousin and not enough doing his job. More than one of the bosses has noticed."

"Well, thanks for your help." Alan turned to go.

The sound of a playful smack on resilient flesh preceded Gavin's giggle and Perry's admonition to the other man to keep his eyes off Alan's backside.

Alan was still smiling when he entered his room.

Chapter 22

Jillian had moved to the bed with the file's contents spread around her. She looked up, her bottom lip caught between her teeth.

"Find anything?" he asked.

"I'm not sure, but I noticed a couple of things that are missing."

"What kind of things?"

"Mr. Kirby's mom was married three times, I think, and he's got some stepsiblings, you know?"

"I thought we had them listed."

"I think you've got the steps from one of the marriages, but I'm not sure about the others. I do know his stepbrother Eddie isn't on the list. They're pretty close. Eddie comes to visit Mr. Kirby every couple of months."

"What's Eddie's last name?"

"I don't know, but you should be able to find it, shouldn't you?"

"Yes." It should have been in the file to begin with.

"As far as I know, Eddie's from the U.S., like the rest of Mr. Kirby's family. He's also got a friend that comes to see him pretty frequently from the States. He's another small-time producer, but from L.A."

"I don't suppose you know his name?"

"Of course I do." Jillian batted her lashes. "He's in the business, after all."

"But Eddie's not?" Alan asked, amused.

"Nope. He's in security, I think."

Alan sat at his computer and started researching the names he'd gotten from Jillian and Perry. It took a phone call to get Eddie's last name, but once Alan had it, he was damn sure he'd hit pay dirt. The man worked security at a privately funded research facility that was so secretive TGP hadn't been able to get anything but the most surface information about what they were working on in the last five years.

It looked like it was time to get an operative placed on the inside. Especially if this was the company doing work on the antigravity saucer. Since Alan didn't believe in coincidences of this magnitude, he was pretty darn sure it was.

The friend was a small-time producer, like Jillian said, but he was also a known deal maker and Alan had to wonder if he was the one who had solicited the "investors" who had been in the viewing room when Hank noticed the clip of the saucer.

"I'd like to do a search of his house," Alan mused.

"Mr. Kirby's?" Jillian asked?

"Yes."

"He lives in a condo and I can help guarantee he's out when you go to do your search."

"How?" Alan wasn't sure he wanted Jillian involved, but he was willing to hear what she had to say.

"I can invite him to meet me for dinner someplace public and nice and safe," she said, showing she was onto his concerns. "I'll simply tell him I want to discuss some concerns I have about the show."

"Is it unusual for you to make that kind of request?" No way was Alan going to risk Kirby becoming suspicious of Jillian.

She grimaced. "Actually not. I sort of have a reputation for being particular. Not a bitch, but not easy either. I have meetings like this with directors and such pretty often. Or at least more often than the other actors on the show, except my costar. That man has the prima-donna role down to a science. He's a bigger princess than Gavin and he's not even gay."

She made the call and was able to get the dinner set for that night.

Jillian left Alan making phone calls while typing furiously on the computer. She couldn't explain the sensation that came over her that morning when Hank mentioned the special effects footage, except that Alan's interest just didn't ring true to that of a reporter. Which, when she thought back, didn't make a lot of sense. After all, why wouldn't a reporter be interested in that kind of thing?

Maybe it was the way he'd said "shit" with reverence, but also as if he was pissed off about something. There was no reason for a reporter to be angry about the content of the clip.

But now that she looked back, she realized it was more than that. There was something else that had been tugging at the back of her mind since she and Alan had been to Simon and Amanda's place. It was seeing Alan with Jacob that had triggered it. She'd noted the similarity in their humor from the first time she'd met Alan, but while they were staying at the Brants' she'd noticed something else.

How alike Alan and Jacob were in the way they reacted to the world. It became most noticeable when both Simon and his cousin were in the room. Seeing the difference between those two men and Jacob and Alan had started Jillian's subconscious mind down a path that had only found final fruition that morning at the breakfast table.

Alan was more aware of what went on around him than the average guy. She'd chalked that up to his being a reporter until she saw him with Jacob and realized how both men always seemed to be one step ahead of everyone around them in noticing things and realizing their implications. Maybe it was her own training that had led her to the realization, but if she had to define it, she would have said they both acted like men who had been in law enforcement.

Jacob had been Secret Service. Everyone knew that. What was Alan? Was he federal, state, local? She had no idea, but one thing she did know. Since that morning, he'd made no effort to hide from her the fact that he wasn't really a reporter. That had to mean something in terms of their relationship.

No matter where he'd slept last night, she didn't think he revealed his secrets to just anybody.

"Hey, Jill, you look like you've got some pretty serious stuff on your mind," Gavin said as he dropped onto a seat beside her on the sofa.

"Thinking about your new boyfriend?" Perry asked as he plopped down right next to Gavin.

Jillian had a moment of revelation similar to the one she'd experienced that morning, only this time it didn't have a thing to do with the man she loved. She groaned. "You two are a couple, aren't you?"

Perry slid his arm over Gavin's shoulder. "Yep."

She smacked her forehead. "How long and I didn't notice?"

"You can be forgiven for your ignorance, sweetie." Gavin smiled, looking really truly happy. "You've had other things, or should I say another man, on your mind."

"It hasn't been that long."

"It happened the night we went dancing with Alan."

"Wow. I can't believe I didn't suspect anything. I even thought you had a thing with Hank," Jillian said to Perry.

Perry's eyes widened in shock while Gavin frowned. "I don't think so. Hank is not his type."

"I don't have a type." Perry ruffled Gavin's pink hair. "You're in a class by yourself, princess."

Gavin preened and Jillian couldn't help laughing. Oh, Perry knew just how to handle the sometimes temperamental actor.

"So, what do you want us to do?" Gavin asked, looking more serious than she'd ever seen him outside the studio.

"No drama. If you two break up, you both move out because I'm not taking sides or playing favorites."

"We're not going to break up," Perry said with conviction.

Gavin looked at him, something warm and really pleased flashing in his eyes.

Jillian just stared at them until Gavin smiled and promised. "No drama. And if we break up . . ." He turned and kissed Perry right on the lips. "Not that we will, but *if* . . . we both move out. No questions, no arguments . . . no drama then either."

"Perry?" Jillian prompted.

"No drama . . . now or later."

She nodded. "Okay, then. We'll let the others know. We need to have a housemate meeting, I think."

"You mean a family meeting?" Gavin asked with a smile.

Jillian nodded. "Yes, a family meeting." One she hoped Alan would take part in.

Alan was waiting outside Kirby's condo when the producer left to meet with Jillian. Security on the building was pretty lax, so it was easier than Alan expected to get inside the man's home. Kirby's computer presented even less of a challenge since, like Lonny, he relied on the Windows password protection only.

What Alan found there surprised and disappointed him. A little. The man had schematics, but they were unfinished. Oh, they looked complete, but Alan was a major techno-geek and he'd spent a good part of the afternoon researching the rumored technology. He knew what had to be there. And key elements weren't.

His disappointment was due to the fact that it looked like the research company hadn't actually developed a fully working technology, but they were further along than any other researchers of this type TGP had files on.

There was no way to tell whether or not Kirby knew the plans were incomplete, but if his buyer had enough technical savvy, the man was going to be in trouble. Depending on who his buyers were, that could result in anything from a demand for the return of the buyer's money to death. Alan copied the schematics as well as the man's contact list to his flashdrive. Then he searched the rest of the apartment. He didn't find anything that would indicate when the sale was supposed to take place, but he had the most important piece of information as far as TGP was concerned.

He left and went directly to the studio and with a small pyrotechnic display was able to gain access to an empty guard house.

As Jillian had suspected, the logs from the previous week were still there and he found the list of "investors" that Kirby had checked in to watch the clips. Alan also noticed that Rob Francis had been on the lot at the same time. Since he'd signed in on the visitor sheet, he'd come outside of his scheduled work hours.

Alan was out of the guard house before security returned.

Jillian got home about the same time he did.

"Was the explosion at the studio your doing?"

"It was hardly an explosion . . . nothing more than kids playing with a few illegal fireworks."

"Right. Patrick Kirby went tearing out of the parking lot after getting the call on the disturbance."

Alan frowned. "Makes you wonder if he was stupid enough to leave a copy of the raw footage in the editing room even after Lonny found it."

"He's never struck me as the cookie with the most chocolate chips, if you know what I mean."

"That makes sense of what I found in his condo."

"What?"

"Partial schematics that could get him killed, slowly and with a lot of pain if he sold them as a working model to someone who knows what he's looking at."

"You're serious?"

"Oh, yes. The plans are further advanced than anything my agency was aware of to this point, but they're still missing key elements."

"So you think the test flight footage is faked?"

"I don't know. It could be that Kirby's cohort stole the wrong set of schematics, a prefinished product set." Alan was guessing the cohort in question was in fact the man's stepbrother, Eddie.

Jillian's eyes widened. "That's hard to believe."

"Not really. Crooks often think they know more than they do. These men may know a lot about smuggling information across borders, stealing, and even killing, but that doesn't mean they know jack squat about the technology they are trying to sell. They probably think they don't need to. Arrogance is the biggest stumbling block to many a perpetrator's success."

"So what are you going to do?"

"I'm not sure. I've got to talk to the Old Man and see how he wants to proceed."

"The Old Man?"

"My boss."

"At the magazine?" she asked with a hint of challenge.

"You know I'm not a reporter."

"And you've done nothing to hide that fact from me since Hank mentioned the footage this morning."

This was where things got tricky, Alan realized. Explaining who he was and what he did would be easy in comparison to explaining why he felt the need to come clean to her. Admitting a love that he had barely acknowledged to himself, but was nevertheless the deepest emotion he had ever experienced, was the true challenge.

Doing so would make him vulnerable in a way he'd promised himself he would not be again.

All his vaunted self-control and professional distance on the job went out the window when this woman was around.

Even his personal pep talk only yesterday had lasted less than twenty-four hours in effectiveness.

He grimaced. "About that."

She cocked her head and looked at him appraisingly. "Yes?"

"I'm a federal agent."

"Ah."

"I was sent here on assignment when it was discovered that someone at Frost Productions was slated to sell pirated technology."

"So why were you so shocked to see that footage of the saucer?"

"We didn't know what the stolen technology was, only that it was to be sold."

"I see. So you were working blind."

"Yes."

"Was I a suspect?"

"At first."

"When did I stop being one?"

"When we made love. I knew you couldn't be guilty of selling someone else's secrets, especially not those that could potentially damage your home country."

"You figured all that out from a little pleasure?"

"It was a lot more than a little pleasure, both figuratively and literally."

She said nothing.

"We connected on a level I don't think either of us was prepared for. And as much as I might have wanted to, I couldn't deny it."

"Why did you want to? Your ex-fiancée who dumped you because of your job? Which makes a little more sense now that I know what it really is."

"That was a big part of it, yes. But your own determination to remain unattached played its part as well."

Jillian climbed into his lap, resting one hand over his heart while looking into his eyes. "I didn't think I would ever meet a man like you."

"And now that you have?"

"I'm scared."

"You're not the type to run out of fear."

"I didn't say I was running, just that letting myself love you scares the bejeebees out of me."

"Ditto."

"Ditto you love me, or ditto you're scared?"

"Both, sweetheart. As much as I loved Beth, what I felt for her wasn't one tenth as intense as what I feel for you. If you had been the one waiting at the altar, I think I would have refused the assignment so close to my wedding date. Which says that she was right to break off our relationship. Neither of us was committed deeply enough to making it work."

"Are you committed now?" Jillian asked, sounding and looking a little worried.

"Yes."

"But how can an undercover agent be married to an actress? I keep a low profile, but I still get publicity. And you better believe my wedding and husband are going to rouse the paparazzis' interest."

"Are you proposing, baby?"

She grinned. "Maybe. Who says a woman has to wait for a man to do it?"

"Not me."

"I'm not getting on one knee and you're not getting an engagement ring."

"I'd settle for an engagement kiss."

"Are we engaged?"

"You're not getting rid of me. Ever. We might as well make it official." He didn't wait for her to kiss him but sealed their mouths together, for once letting his emotions surface without subterfuge.

The way she kissed him back told him she was doing the

same thing. He could feel her love and he only hoped she felt his as surely.

He would have loved to take her straight to bed, but he and the Old Man had too many logistics on the case to work out that night. Jillian stayed with him, though, sleeping in his bed while Alan spent hours on the phone and computer sending and receiving information from various federal officials.

It was decided that Canadian law enforcement would get first crack at Patrick Kirby and Rob Francis since their crimes had occurred on Canadian soil. Eddie had already been fired, though the company he worked for refused to confirm the plans had been stolen from their labs—or that anything had been stolen at all. Charges could not be filed against him for a crime the company refused to admit happened, which left nothing that could be done to Eddie for his involvement.

Through normal channels.

An anonymous informant tipped off Frost's less-than-upstanding relatives about the trio's obvious plans to make Frost their fall guy in both a murder charge and the sale of pirated information. There was no evidence linking Kirby's producer friend from LA to the crime, so he was left alone. Not only had a family member been threatened, but unwanted attention had been brought to the financial holdings of Frost Productions.

Frost's relatives were less than happy with this circumstance and no doubt planned to act accordingly.

"So, it's all over without you actually arresting anyone?" Jillian asked groggily when Alan finally joined her in bed in the early hours of the morning.

"Right. I work for an agency that is so secretive I didn't even know it existed while I was with the FBI. We often move in under the aegis of another agency when the final denouement takes place, or leave it entirely up to the other agency to clean up."

"Wow."

"That's what I thought the first time the Old Man told me about it."

"So, again . . . how is that going to work with you and me?" she asked, not sounding nearly as tired as she had a moment before.

"You mean the whole celebrity thing?"

She gave him a wary nod, and bit her lip in obvious concern. "Yes."

He pulled her tightly to him. "It would be an almost insurmountable problem if I stayed an undercover operative, but that's not the plan." For once, he had no desire to tease or drag out the revelations.

He wanted to wipe the look of worry from Jillian's features immediately. He didn't want her hurting for even a minute.

"What do you mean?" she asked, sounding no more certain of the outcome of this discussion.

He had to convince her that his plans were what he wanted and that their being together was the foundation of both their happiness. "One of my favorite parts of the job is research. I proposed a new position in the department to my boss and he went for it. Lack of internal manpower for research has been a problem with the agency for a while. I suggested he have an agent in charge of exactly that, one who could be available as reliable backup for other agents in the field and someone who could compile a better dossier than the ones we were getting from external sources. The Old Man went for it and you are looking at the new agent in charge of background and ongoing research for my agency."

Jillian's eyes filled with wonder. "You changed your life for me."

"I may have redefined one of my goals, but I didn't give it up. I'm a federal agent and probably always will be, but I'm your man and that means no more undercover work."

"I was going to tell you I would quit the show if you

thought it would help." Sincerity rang in her tone and his heart swelled with love for the amazing woman in his arms.

He grinned and dipped his head toward hers for a long, sweet kiss. "That proves how well we are suited, but I think my solution is better. And did I mention I can work remotely? Sometimes research has to be done on-site, but it's not the same as actually being the agent in charge of a case. And I won't travel nearly as much as I did as an operative."

"That's good." Happiness glowed around her like a halo. "I don't like the idea of being away from you, which is pretty funny given that I've never even let myself consider allowing a lover to sleep over before you."

"Sex partner. You didn't have lovers before me."

"No, I didn't. I love you, Alan Hyatt—oh, and I think that last name really suits you. Much better than your fake reporter last name."

He laughed softly, kissing her again, feeling his desire rise sharp and urgent as he knew it always would when she was in his arms. "I love you, Jillian Sinclair. Today, tomorrow, and always."

"Amanda was right . . . you are perfect for me."

Epilogue

Amanda helped Jillian get ready to walk down the aisle. "So, explain one thing to me," she said as she adjusted the surprisingly traditional veil over Jillian's vibrant red hair.

"What's that?"

"With your issues regarding honesty, why didn't you rip Alan a new one when he admitted he'd been lying to you all along?"

"But he hadn't been lying. Not about the stuff that really matters. And, Amanda, I of all people understand playing a role for the job."

Amanda shook her head and laughed. "Simon said it would be something like that, but he didn't get off as easily when I found out he knew Alan was a federal agent and *he* hadn't told *me*."

"Was that the explosion I heard clear up in Vancouver? And here I thought they were early fireworks or maybe a minor earthquake."

"Very funny. Let's just say that spies aren't the only ones who know how to torture a man."

Jillian laughed, no doubt in her mind that Simon had both enjoyed the torture and been suitably chastised.

"So, did you invite Elspeth?"

"I would have even if I didn't think she and Jacob would

be perfect for each other." Elspeth had been one of Jillian's first mentors.

A true grande dame in their world, but one who lived for the art rather than notoriety, she'd "retired" to teach in Seattle. She was also involved with amateur theater there. Jillian had often thought of hooking Elspeth and Jacob up, if only so he could find a more local outlet for his desire to play different roles.

But when Amanda had Dorrie, Jacob had gotten even busier, adding adopted grandfather to his list of duties.

However, ever since their talk in the kitchen that fateful morning when Jillian had realized she loved Alan, she and Amanda had been toying with the idea of fixing the two older people up. And what better venue than a wedding?

"Then she's coming?" Amanda asked, making no effort to disguise her glee at the prospect.

"Oh, yes . . . and I told her all about Jacob. You know, his past makes him sound really intriguing, and his interest in acting only added gilt to his edges."

"I hope they hit it off."

Jillian gave Amanda a knowing look. "Simon's not going to be happy with you if Jacob gets married and brings a wife to live on the island."

Amanda dismissed the thought with a wave of her hand. "He's gotten better about his privacy, but even if he hadn't, he'd simply have to adjust. It's time Jacob found some personal happiness."

"I hope it works."

"Spoken like a true convert to love."

Jillian laughed, joy giving her an incandescent radiance that made more than one eye tear up as she walked down the aisle toward the man who held her future in his heart.

Later at the reception Jacob and Elspeth *did* meet and did in fact hit it off. So beautifully that the Brant household had a new member in less than a month and she fit in beautifully with the other eccentrics living in the island home.

She also got Jacob involved with the amateur theater as well as doing guest appearances in the classes she taught.

Amanda and Jillian were very proud of their matchmaking efforts.

As was another consummate matchmaker . . . Whit Whitney, referred to as the Old Man. He attended his agent's wedding, and while the vows were being spoken let his mind flip through a mental file of his other still single agents, wondering which one of them needed the next helping hand.

Patrick Kirby and Rob Francis were found guilty of murder and accessory to that murder. Eddie had disappeared soon after Frost's family found out his and the other men's plans to make the executive producer a scapegoat for their crimes. Alan could only wonder how long the other two men would survive in the Canadian prison they had been sent to.

But he didn't let it take up too much of his thoughts as he and Jillian boarded a plane for their honeymoon.

He'd finally found what his father and grandfather and the generations of Hyatt men had found before him: the life he wanted as a federal agent and the perfect woman to share it with.